Praise for Ken Scholes and for
Diving Mimes, Weeping Czars and Other Unusual Suspects

"A mysterious voice, an alien songstress, a postapocalyptic Santa Claus, and a host of other bizarre creatures come together in Scholes's lively, arresting and gleefully offbeat second short story collection (after 2009's *Long Walks, Last Flights*), which equally startles with profound emotion and revels in absurd humor. In the brilliant 'A Weeping Czar Beholds the Fallen Moon,' a tearful ruler encounters a strange object and a young woman that bring both doom and renewal. 'Invisible Empire of Ascending Light' concerns a violent contest to take the place of a dying god. 'Four Clowns of the Apocalypse and the Mecca of Mirth' is a wide-eyed, bizarro-style caper involving the misadventures of four clowns in a wasted, radioactive America. By turns baroque, off-kilter, and haunting, Scholes's writing will delight lovers of the unusual and wildly imaginative."
—*Publisher's Weekly*

"The new collection is all clowns and suspicious deaths and naked soldiers and musical aliens, lost and found loves, and so much more. Slinky Boy! Ken Scholes knows how to suck us into a story, chew us up, and spit us out smiling. You get to a point reading Ken where you think okay okay so this is the ultimate depth, but then the story surprises you, and you go a little deeper!"
— Ray Vukcevich, author of *Boarding Instructions*

"These stories are rambunctious. Sometimes loud, relentlessly lively, occasionally defiant of expectations — they refuse to sit still. Once in a while they retreat into a dark mood, making you pay closer attention to the pain behind such tales as 'Grief Stepping To The Widower's Waltz.' But mostly they are a hell of a lot of fun. Ken calls them his 'paper children.' No wonder!"
— Jack Skillingstead, author of *Harbinger*

"*Diving Mimes, Weeping Czars and Other Unusual Suspects* is filled with wondrous stories of love, faith, sacrifice, salvation and redemption played out across lush worlds both recognizable and wildly different from our own. Ken Scholes writes stories that resonate with depth and thrum, holding the reader rapt with his own brand of magic. Excellent."
— Devon Monk, author of *A Cup of Normal*

Everything Ken Scholes writes packs an emotional punch. These stories are quick-witted, gonzo, heartbreaking, beautiful gems. Just pick one and start reading. You can't go wrong.
— Josh Rountree, author of *Can't Buy Me Faded Love*

Also by Ken Scholes

Last Flight of the Goddess
Long Walks, Last Flights & Other Strange Journeys
Lamentation
Canticle
Antiphon
Requiem (forthcoming)
Hymn (forthcoming)

DIVING MIMES, WEEPING CZARS AND OTHER UNUSUAL SUSPECTS

DIVING MIMES, WEEPING CZARS AND OTHER UNUSUAL SUSPECTS

KEN SCHOLES

FAIRWOOD PRESS
Bonney Lake, WA

DIVING MIMES, WEEPING CZARS & OTHER UNSUAL SUSPECTS
A Fairwood Press Book
October 2010
Copyright © 2010 by Kenneth G. Scholes

All Rights Reserved

Fairwood Press
21528 104th Street Court East
Bonney Lake, WA   98391
www.fairwoodpress.com

Cover illustration & design by Paul Swenson
Book Design by Patrick Swenson

ISBN13: 978-0-9820730-8-7
First Fairwood Press Edition: October 2010
Printed in the United States of America

For Patrick Swenson —
Editor, Teacher, Friend, and Literary Dad.

COPYRIGHTS

CONTENTS

INTRODUCTION
JOHN A. PITTS

Who am I, you might ask, to write an introduction to this lovely collection by Ken Scholes? Damn good question. I've known Ken for over a decade. We met just after my daughter was born, and we became fast friends. Ken frequently recounts that I'm his first writing buddy. We met at a writers workshop where we both learned we were better suited to critiquing each other's work, and leaving the rest of the crew to their own devices.

Over the next twelve years, we grew together, each of us maturing our writing craft until we began to sell. We wrote our first novels at the same time, racing each other to the finish line. He beat me by less than twelve hours.

I've read every single word Ken has written over the last twelve years, and each story is a gem. If you run into him in a bar at some convention, ask him about "Blakely in his Heart." That's the first of his stories I read, and I may be the only other person on the planet who has seen its many incarnations.

Ken is a tinker, a crafter of words. He enjoys the juxtaposition of odd ideas and exposing the deep emotional resonance of the varied characters that populate his worlds. It's a gift he has, seeing the world around us in story and metaphor. He has played guitar for a couple of decades, even going so far as busking on the streets in Germany in his army days. He loves to sing and write his own songs. I've seen him work a room with music and wit, keeping the crowd entertained by his presence and his will. This, I believe, is what makes his writing so strong.

Ken is a strong introvert who bleeds energy in a crowd, but he loves people so much, that he finds it difficult to avoid the parties and the group gatherings that expose him to so many good people.

I think you'll begin to get a glimmer of just who Ken Scholes is when you read this collection — this is his second gathering of paper children. You are in for a treat. The stories inside here will catch you by surprise.

If you're a fan of his *Psalms of Isaac* series, you'll love the opening story, "A Weeping Czar Beholds the Fallen Moon." It's set in the same world, only much, much earlier in history. This is a good example of what makes Ken's stories work so well — stunning language and deep emotional resonance. You will be lifted up with the elegance of his prose.

Ken's a master story teller. I've watched his natural talent blossom over the last dozen years through hard work and persistence to make him one of the most eclectic and enjoyable storytellers I've ever read.

And I'm not just saying that because we are friends. Take a gander at "Grail-Diving in Shangrilla with the World's Last Mime," which wraps the collection, and tell me he doesn't have a wicked sense of humor and strong story muscles. Post-apocalyptic, cross-dressing Baptist minister and his roving band of cohorts searching for the holy grail in a ravaged world, while fending off attacks from all quarters. How can you not stop reading this introduction and turn to the story immediately? I'll understand. Go ahead. I'll wait.

And the titles — oy — don't get me started. Every one is evocative and demands you read further just to see what story could be worth such an elaborate moniker.

Every tale here is chock full of parable and wit. He can turn a phrase with the best of them and take you places you never imagined existed. We all know that there are no new stories — not since man first learned to rub two sticks together. But if you pick up this collection, take the time to peruse the words, you will find that Ken has an uncanny ability to drive to the heart of story, and leave you sated in a way that may embarrass the good company.

There isn't a weak story in the lot. I'm equally fascinated with the story behind the story. I can pinpoint the event that spurred every story in this collection. He'll fill you in at the end.

Now, we've had our differences, and even got into a significant fight once. I'd just returned from a two week workshop with Kris Rusch and Dean Wesley Smith. I was full of energy and new found enthusiasm. I tried to convince Ken that he should be writing novels. This was back when he thought novels were beyond his skill. It was a pretty quiet fight, as far as they go, but it really put him off.

He thought maybe I'd lost my mind, and we'd stop being friends. He even wrote a story about the way he felt at the time—a touching piece called "The Night the Stars Sang Out My Name." It's telling in the detail just how much he and I have become the best of friends. Luckily, I calmed down a bit — mellowed — and he found his long legs.

Too be completely open here, you might notice that "There Once Was a Girl From Nantucket (A Fortean Love Story)" was co-written by yours truly. I think it's one of the more poignant stories in the collection, and not for the rhyming scheme. It was the second time we came to loggerheads. Collaborating is hard work, and teaches writers as much about themselves as about their writing partners. I know I am better for the experience, and the story is pretty fine. I look forward to sharing more worlds with Mr. Scholes.

But right now, that's what you need to do. Go share Ken's worlds. Immerse yourself in his psyche and enjoy.

A WEEPING CZAR
BEHOLDS THE FALLEN MOON

Frederico leaned close to smell the poison on his thirteenth wife's cold, dead lips. It tickled his nose and he resisted the strong desire to kiss her that suddenly overcame him.

That you might lose yourself from sadness by my lips, my husband and Czar, her open, glassy eyes promised him. He looked away, uncomfortable with her empty, inviting stare.

Behind him, the Minister of the Interior cleared his voice and spoke. "The cabinet feels it would be more stabilizing to consider this an assassination. Jazrel was a most popular wife."

Frederico nodded. She had quite a following among the young girls in Espira, the region she represented, and this was a dance he knew. He'd been in this very room three years ago to watch them cut his ninth wife's body down.

When Sasha had hung herself with a rope of knotted silk, six thousand young women in Borut had done the same to declare sisterhood with their region's wife.

"Assassination," he agreed. For a moment, he felt a stab of guilt when he thought about the young girls who spent their childhoods emulating his wives in the hopes that one day they would be chosen. *I've robbed them of an ending*, he thought.

He turned now to his Minister of Intelligence. "I assume you concur, Pyrus?"

"Yes, Lord Czar," he answered. Pyrus was a large man, his beard and hair close cropped. He held the Czar and his tears in quiet disdain but Frederico did not fault him for this. Pyrus had climbed the ranks from private to general during the fifty year war with their bloated southern neighbor, a nation of leftovers from the declined Engmark Republic. He'd retired into his intelligence role, bringing an edge to it that only a soldier could bring. He was a hard man from hard times. He ran a hand through his hair. "We implicate the Lunar Resurgence," he said.

Frederico's eyes wandered back to his dead wife and he sighed. "And then host a Purging?" He looked up now, forcing himself to meet Pyrus's eyes.

Pyrus nodded. "The black-coats are already lacquering their guns. We could put the Resurgence away quickly enough and be done with their idle mysticism."

The Czar contemplated this. He glanced back to his dead wife, Jazrel, and sighed again. "I suppose it would be timely," he finally said.

But not even the thought of a Purging could lift his downcast spirit.

Frederico took his midmorning chai on the observation deck of his winter garden dome but could not find peace in the bright colors and warm scents that surrounded him.

Jazrel's eyes and mouth haunted both his waking and his sleeping hours, though he knew this particular grief would pass soon enough.

Six days ago, the black-coats had begun their work under Pyrus's watchful eye, moving out through the cities and rounding up the Resurgence. They'd sent birds throughout the districts, leveling their charges and decrying Jazrel's assassination. And the people had responded much as they'd hoped. Outrage in the streets. Young Espiran girls attacking rumored Lunarists with hate in their eyes, curses on their lips and stones in their fists. Wagon-loads of prisoners deposited in the healing care of the Ministry of Social Behavior. Other wagon-loads winding their way to quiet forests where servants could dig quiet graves by moonlight.

Tomorrow, I eulogize, he thought as he sipped the cinnamon-bittered chai. A canary flitted past and he felt the brief wind of its wings move over his unkempt hair.

The softest chiming of a bell reached him and he lifted his own bell, ringing it twice to signal that he could be approached. A black-coat captain, his pale and nervous face starkly contrasting the deep velvet of his officer's jacket, materialized behind one of a dozen crimson-clad house servants that waited at the garden's edge. He carried something wrapped in burlap.

The captain bowed deeply. "I beg forgiveness and indulgence, Excellency, but Minister Pyrus is unable to attend you in person. He sent me in his place with apologies." The officer risked looking up and Frederico let their eyes meet. There was fear there and something else.

He sees your tears without disdain, a voice whispered in the back corners of his mind. Was it compassion? Perhaps pity? Frederico raised his silk napkin to dab beneath each eye. "You have my grace, Captain." Replacing the napkin in his lap, he raised the chai-cup and paused before it touched his lips. "What news of the Purging?"

"We've finished sweeping the capitol and outlying cities. The district outposts report similar progress." He shifted, his leather boots creaking as he did. "We've found the local Temple and set torch to it. Their priestess is in custody."

Frederico nodded. They'd made good progress in short order. The Lunarists had never completely resurfaced after the last Purging three years earlier. They'd remained quiet this time despite a thousand years of dying and coming back to life, a stubborn weed of mysticism that would not forego his family's garden. "I am grateful for the news. I hope they can eventually become productive, rational citizens again."

"Yes, Lord Czar," the captain said. "And we've found something hidden in the temple. The priestess is being questioned about it now but Minister Pyrus wanted you to examine the object and bid me bring it to you immediately." He started to step forward, then remembered himself and bowed again. "May I approach, Lord?"

Frederico lowered the cup and gestured for the man to step forward. The captain walked quickly to the small table and laid the object upon it. Then, with his white-gloved fingers he picked at the corners of the cloth until it fell away to reveal the metal horn beneath.

No, Frederico realized, not a horn. A crescent. And of such brilliant silver that it stung his watery eyes. Sunlight, already sharp and slicing through the crystal domes high above, struck the metal and burst into whiteness. He squinted at it until it took focus for him. There were markings on it — etched lines that were familiar to him. The line of a continent here, a mountain range there. He suddenly remembered summer nights spent staring up through the glass ceiling of his bedchambers. "It is the moon at first sliver," he said.

The captain nodded. "It was hidden beneath the altar. The priestess would have given her life to protect it if we'd not overpowered her."

Frederico stretched out a tentative finger, placing it on the surface. It was warm to the touch. "What metal is this? It's unfamiliar to me."

"We are uncertain, Lord Czar. Minister Pyrus has brought in scholars from the Triumvirate Universities as well as the Chief Journeymen of the Smithing and Alchemy Guilds. It's unlike anything we have ever seen."

It's beautiful, Frederico thought and didn't realize he'd whispered it aloud until the captain agreed.

"Yes, Lord Czar. But there is more, if I may?" At Frederico's impatient gesture, he lifted the crescent and came around the table. Careful not to touch his Czar, the captain held the silver object up to Frederico's ear.

At first, he was uncertain of what he heard and imagined it was merely the noise of his own garden, somehow bent around the sliver of moon much like the light had been. But as Frederico leaned his ear closer, he realized that the sounds he heard lay over the top of the noise surrounding him. His breath caught in his throat and something washed through him that felt akin to fear or perhaps wonder.

He leaned even closer, feeling the warm metal of the moon press against his ear before the surprised captain could pull way. His eyes darted up and he saw terror on the officer's face. "Hold," Frederico said in a quiet voice. "Your Czar bids you hold."

The crescent trembled in the young man's hands but he held it in place as Frederico brought all of his concentration to bear upon the sounds whispering out from this strange and wonderful object.

Water burbling, muffled and metallic. And above that, the distinct but muted music of summer frogs.

All that day, deep into the night, and all the following morning, he could not escape that incessant whispering. It hunted him even while servants curled and perfumed his hair and dressed him in golden robes. It pursued him through the black-laced motions and trappings of funereal statecraft as he pressed hands with the Lords and Ladies of his empire and those of the outlying lands. Even as he rode through the pomp and splendor of Jazrel's last procession, he found his memory returning to those sounds like a tongue to an empty socket. When they reached the Garden of the Fading Rose where she was to be buried, and when he stood and gave eulogy to her life — a simple girl chosen as the bride of a god — he found the sound of that running water and those croaking frogs always nearby.

When all was finished and when she lay at her final rest, Frederico returned to his private study in the western tower that housed his quarters, stripped off his feline gloves, and rang for Pyrus.

The old general, still in his black-coat and ministerial cloak from the occasion, came quickly enough. Frederico saw the lines in his face and the firm set of his jaw. *He is angry at the interruption.* But of course, he'd say nothing.

Frederico gestured to the chair before his wide, walnut desk and waited for Pyrus to sit. The Minister of Intelligence sat slowly, leaning forward slightly with both boots planted firmly on the carpeted floor. "What have you learned about the silver crescent?"

Surprise registered on Pyrus's face. "Nothing of real certainty. We continue to study it."

"What does the priestess say of it?"

Pyrus looked uncomfortable. "Mysticism and nonsense," he said. "My men broke her early this morning — it took some doing — and I fear they took her too close to the edge."

Frederico's eyes narrowed. "What did she say?"

"She says it is the whispering of the moon. Proof of life there."

Frederico looked up and out beyond the high glass ceiling of his office. It was too early yet, but soon it would rise, blue and green. "We know better than that. Did she say where it came from?"

"From Carnelyin," Pyrus answered. "She claims he brought it back with him."

Of course. Lord Felip Carnelyin's One Hundred Tales. The hundredth being his fanciful flight to the moon under the supposed auspices of an earlier Czar in the earliest days of empire, before the weeping bred itself into the great families. Before the world lost hope and meaning. The first of the Lunarists had emerged from those early times though there was no evidence whatsoever of a Czarist Lunar Expedition in the meticulous archives Frederico's forebears had maintained.

"We know of a certainty," Frederico said, "that it can not be so." Once maybe, he thought, before the plagues ravaged its blue green surface and killed the last of the Younger Gods who hid there away from a ravaged world below that hated and feared them.

"I suspect it is simply a harmless curiosity of Elder Times," Pyrus said. "Something dug out of the Runemarch that they've bent into holy relic."

A harmless curiosity. Frederico nodded. "I suspect so. What more do you think you will learn of it?"

Pyrus shrugged. "I doubt we'll learn more. The priestess is broken — I have no doubt she believes it is lunar in origin." Here, he smiled but it was a weak smile. "One can be sincere and still be sincerely mistaken."

He thought for a moment. "Or misguided," Frederico finally said.

"Yes."

Frederico felt a smile pulling at his own mouth and it surprised him. Judging by the look on Pyrus's face, the slightest hint of his good humor was also surprising to the Minister of Intelligence though the old soldier tried to conceal it. "If you believe there is nothing more to learn, I would like to have it."

Now Pyrus's surprise could not be concealed. "I'm not certain that would be advisable, Lord Czar."

"It is a harmless curiosity," Frederico said, his voice taking on an intentional edge.

Pyrus's eyes betrayed uncertainty at how best to proceed. "Aye, Lord, but it is also an invaluable artifact that —"

Frederico's smile widened as he interrupted. "That will be kept safest with the best-guarded man in the empire. At all hours, a hundred of my Red Legion are at watch over me." He sat back in his chair and watched his Minister of Intelligence. "And certainly," he added, "I will not interfere with its continued study should there be anything to gain from it."

Pyrus looked at him and Frederico saw resolve forming now in the line of his jaw. His tensed shoulders relaxed and the slightest sigh escaped his lips. "I will have it sent it over tomorrow morning once the current shift of scholars have concluded their study," he said.

Frederico inclined his head towards Pyrus — a gesture he rarely offered. "Thank you, Minister Pyrus."

The minister returned the nod, but his eyes betrayed a buried rage. "You are most welcome, Lord Czar." He stood and smoothed the crimson trousers of his rank. "If that will be all, I will return to my work."

He wanted it for himself, Frederico realized. But he put that knowledge aside. "Yes, Minister," he said. "That is all."

And after Pyrus had gone, after the servants had brought his liquored and foaming chocolate and collected the empty mug once he'd drained it, and after the sun had set and the moon had risen, Frederico still could not purge the sound of that running water and those singing frogs from his ears.

He lay awake and alone in his silk-sheeted bed, beneath his crystal viewing dome, and watched the blue green sliver where it hung haphazard in the star speckled sky.

Frederico gazed out over the crowded room from his private balcony. The men and women, dressed in their finest, warbled across the inside of his privacy screen as they moved about the ballroom twenty cubits below. They were a rainbow of colors bathed in light from the gem-lamps that spun and scintillated above, hung by fine strands of silver cable.

He sipped his chilled peach wine. "It is a good party," he said. But even he could hear the lack of enthusiasm in his voice. It had been seven weeks since Jazrel's suicide — six since the silver crescent had come into his possession — and the only comfort he'd taken had come from the unexplainable sounds from that artifact leftover from the Younger Gods. He'd not visited any of his wives in all that time though that was surprising to no one. He'd favored Jazrel and she was gone.

Tonight, down below, twenty of Espira's favored young women waited in hopes that the Lord Czar Frederico XIII would ask them to dance and initiate a conversation that might result in courtship. Over two hundred others waited at the palace gates, dressed in their finest and hoping one of the twenty would fail even though they knew they had no chance of being invited in. Back in Espira, another two or three thousand sat at home and hoped for notification that they would be considered if tonight's ball did not bear fruit. Publicizing Jazrel's death as an assassination had created both an anger bent towards vengeance and a compassion bent towards comfort — especially in the young women who hoped to replace her as his thirteenth wife and represent their corner of his empire.

Beside him, the Espiran senator shifted in his plush armchair. "They are a lively lot. Twenty of our very best. We've already received proposals from a dozen houses in the event that your Lordship does not find them suited to his taste and need."

Taste and need. A sudden memory of Jazrel took him by ambush. She was naked and upon him, her hips rocking slowly, her eyes open and fixed on his as she bit her lower lip in the midst of their passion. The bed shook from the intensity of her movement. He shivered from the sudden recollection and pushed it away.

Frederico glanced to the senator — a sprightly looking older man resplendent in a deep blue suit, a black cloak, and a gold, high-collared shirt — and forced a smile. "I'm certain they are the best and brightest of your eligible women," he said. *But no Jazrel would be found among them.*

A bell rang and Frederico lifted his own to reply. Josefus, his Minister of the Interior, pushed his way through the ruby curtain and bowed. "Lord Czar," he said, "I trust that you are well?"

Frederico nodded and lied easily. "I am well. Please sit with us."

The Minister of the Interior sat and pulled a pair of jeweled opera glasses from the velvet case that dangled around his neck. He held the glasses up and picked out the silver tiaras below. "Ah," he said, "are they not beautiful?"

The senator smiled at this. Frederico raised his own glasses and looked again. "They are lovely."

And suddenly, she overtook him again and he smelled Jazrel's perfume mingled with her sweat. The force of it was so overpowering that he spilled wine onto his lap. He leaped to his feet and the sadness, curled like a snake within him all his days, struck at him and its fangs went deep. The tears were near now; he felt them pulling at his eyes. And he felt his heart racing as his hands trembled.

They come upon me faster now. He slipped his opera glasses into their case and carefully placed his wine glass on the small table they shared. He did not have much time. "I am sorry, gentlemen, but I am overtaken by illness."

They each stood, unable to mask the surprise and disappointment upon their faces. The Minister of the Interior found his words the fastest. "Lord Czar, I —"

Frederico cut him off. "Please give my apologies to Espira's finest and assure them that they do not lack in any way."

Then, before either of his guests could speak, Frederico's guards formed up around him in the anteroom just beyond the curtain and they were moving with their emperor, escorting him to his rooms where he could face his demon alone and unashamed.

His shoulders shook as they closed the doors behind him and he let the sob out slowly. Despair and despondency washed him and rather than resisting, he fed them memories of Jazrel. Jazrel fresh from the bath. Jazrel at breakfast on the balcony. He carried himself to his bed, scooping up a bottle of his most potent liqueur. Jazrel beneath him and above him. *Taste and need.* The tears wracked him and he lost all sense of time. He could not tell when he stopped drinking and started clutching at the silver crescent. Drunkenness pressed him into reluctant sleep and he felt the cold metal pressed up to his wet face as he finally fell away into warm gray.

In the distance, he heard the singing of the frogs.

And then something else. Something so amazing and alarming that he suspected he was already asleep.

A voice: "Who is there?" it asked. "Why are you crying?"

Then sleep further folded Frederico inside himself and carried him into dream.

Frederico heard music, distant and metallic. It pulled him awake and he went willingly though his head hurt fiercely from tears and drink. His bed was tangled and the sheets were wet from the fever of his melancholia but he'd come through the night and had not harmed himself, nor had he poisoned anyone else with the darkness in his soul. He could not bear another Sasha. Or another Jazrel.

Relief flooded him. *Music,* he remembered.

A harp, he realized. He stared at the silver crescent and remembered his dreams. A voice. "Hello?"

His voice sounded raspy and afraid. Swallowing the foul taste in his mouth, he spoke again. "Is someone there?"

The music stopped and he suddenly realized that he no longer heard the running water or the frogs. Instead, he heard soft footfalls and then a voice. "Hello?"

It was a girl's voice; she sounded young. Staring at the crescent, he willed his words to form, his mouth to frame them, but both betrayed him. She spoke again. "Hello? Are you there?" Then, as if by afterthought: "Do you feel better now?"

Frederico felt his eyes narrow. "Who is this?"

When she laughed, it was music much like the harp. "I am Amal Y'Zir," she said. "Who else would I be? But surely you know that already, Spirit?"

Spirit. "I do not understand you," he said.

She spoke slower this time. "I am Amal Y'Zir, Spirit, but you should know that." She snorted. "If not, what manner of ghost are you?"

Frederico felt several things at once. Frustration and confusion fought for predominance. "Where are you?"

Now, she laughed. "I am in my rooms, of course. I've been at my music again."

He paced, now, holding the silver crescent to the side of his head. "You play the harp," he said.

"Father tells me that all cultured women of a certain intellect master at least one instrument."

It sounded reasonable to Frederico and he found himself nodding before he realized he was doing so. Then, he shook his head. "Your father sounds very . . . wise. What is his name?"

More laughter. "You are really not much of a ghost. My father is Raj Y'Zir. Surely you've heard of him? He's very powerful."

Her laughter was contagious; he suddenly found himself smiling. "Perhaps you're right; I'm not much of a ghost after all." Of course, he knew there was no such thing.

Her voice took on a note of concern and lowered in tone. "You're not going to start crying again, are you?"

"No," he said.

"Because," she added, "I really wasn't sure what to do. You're my first ghost." She paused and when he didn't answer immediately, she continued. "Are the other ghosts as sad as you?"

He opened his mouth to speak and the bell ringing at his door caused him to close it. He thought for a moment, then lowered his voice to just above a whisper. "I'm going to have to go away for a bit," he told her. "But I will come back as soon as I can."

"Off with you," she said, "to your ghostly affairs." She chuckled again, then added in mock imperiousness: "If I have time, perhaps I will speak to you when next you haunt me."

Frederico hastened to his bedside and put the silver crescent deep beneath the pillows. Then, he rang for his servants and instructed them that he was taken ill and not to be disturbed until the next morning.

Still, after they'd left him alone, he sat for a long while and stared at the silver crescent. The waters and frogs had soothed him, had become a secret calm for him in distress he could not fully comprehend. The weeping took him more often, it was true, but he'd found scarce comfort in times past. The two wives he'd most delighted in had not been able to live with the knowledge of his sorrow — the sorrow that was his family's to bear for reasons no record remained to speak of.

But last night, clutching that slice of moon to his ear as he wept, gentled by the frogs and the brook of some distant place, he'd felt better. As if it had known his need and bent towards it. And now, this new development both intoxicated and terrified him. A voice. A girl by the name of Amal Y'Zir . . . how young, he could not say. Some part of her voice was all the innocence of maidenhood but there was sly intellect — cunning even — beneath the skin of it. He made a note to ask after that House. House Y'Zir; it was not familiar to him.

Could it be as easy as that? And why not? Perhaps this bit of mirrored silver was truly a toy of the Younger Gods, a way to speak across great distance. Some leftover like the hills of their long-ruined cities, or the sighs and groans that leaked out from their tombing caves or those rare lights that swam the deep ocean floors. Their playthings scattered the world. It wasn't unimaginable.

Perhaps this Y'Zir was some minor noble in the Engmark Republic. Perhaps the toy had lain untouched in some shadowed place near a stream until this Amal Y'Zir had found it, drawn to it by the sound of Frederico's weeping.

A chain of coincidence? Frederico thought not. For those not of noble birth, coincidences like that were what life was made from. But not for a Czar. Everything ordered and purposed.

Taking a sip of water from the crystal glass on his night table, Frederico reached into the pile of pillows and drew out the silver crescent.

Amal was at her harp again and the tune was the same that had haunted him awake. He could not see her fingers move over the strings but he heard them as a dream filled with passion and woe.

They weep, he thought.

And Frederico smiled.

*

Frederico lay in his bed and did not feel the weight of weariness he should have felt for having gone without so much sleep. For three days, Frederico hid in his rooms beneath the spell of the silver crescent and the girl's voice within it. He took his meals there, barking for the servants to be quick as he hid the crescent behind his back or beneath the silk sheets of his bed. And when they left, he brought it back to his ear and resumed a conversation days in the making.

For her part, Amal had less freedom than he did and those times that she had to leave at her father's bidding for one lesson or another, Frederico sat at his desk and wrote out from memory what details he could discern from their conversation. There had not been many, but enough to keep him busy for a few hours here or there. Books with titles he did not recognize. References to places he had never heard of. These were the barbs on a larger hook that held him fast and kept him never more than a few spans away from the bauble that had gone from offering strange comfort to defining something empty within himself that he had not noticed before. And it had done so in such a short amount of time that it frightened him but the fear could not compete with the sense of exhilaration.

He had not wept once in those three days.

Now, he lay upon his back and stared up at the moon, waiting for Amal to return. Tonight, he would have to sleep. Tomorrow, despite the strong desire not to, he would return to his work. Still, he would take a few hours with her tonight before giving himself to rest.

Her voice reached him, out of breath. "Are you there, Ghost?"

He chuckled. "I've told you; I'm no ghost. I am Frederico." Then, he chided her gently. "It is more polite to call a person by his name."

He heard the noise of her thrashing her way into bed. He'd noticed the first two nights she'd done the same and in his mind's eye, he saw the girl crawling beneath the covers of her faraway bed, kicking and wrestling them into a more comfortable disposition. "But why should I do that," she said, "when I know of a certainty that you are a ghost?"

There was coquettishness to her voice that played him like a harp. "And what is your certainty of my ghosthood?"

He could hear her smile now around her words. "Because, Frederico, you haunt me so very well." And now, gone was the innocence and in its place, the voice of a woman. "You haunt me when we speak; you haunt me when I am away. I can not escape your voice, even when you are silent. Today, my father scolded me three times for my inattention to his alchemy lesson. He thinks I've fallen in love with one of the Machtvolk boys. He's quite cross about it and has confined me to my rooms." She giggled and the girl was back in her voice now.

Frederico noted the unfamiliar word but lost it when the rest of her words registered. *He thinks I've fallen in love.*

"If I am a ghost for these reasons," he said, "then perhaps you are as well."

"Oh," she said, "I can assure you that I am not."

He smiled. "Then how do you explain my own haunted state?"

"I am Amal Y'Zir, daughter of the Great Blood Wizard, Raj Y'Zir. You are not haunted; you are merely enchanted by my powerful magicks."

They both laughed and Frederico didn't bother to tell her this time that there was no such thing as magick.

After, they fell into another conversation that carried them until dawn touched the sky with pink fingers.

Frederico's ministers waited around the table for him and he came in late to remind them that he did not operate on the schedules they made for him. He smiled at them and noted their surprise.

The Minister of the Interior spoke first. "Is the Lord Czar feeling better? We've been quite alarmed by —"

He started speaking as he sat. "I am quite well, Minister Josefus." He offered another smile and inclined his head first — a rare honor he now granted.

Blushing, Josefus fumbled with the papers before him, then realized he had not returned the nod. He blushed even more and inclined his own head. "Thank you, Lord Czar. I am delighted that you are well."

Frederico opened the portfolio in front of him and scanned the agenda for their meeting. He glanced to Pyrus and Josefus. "I'd like to meet with you both after we're finished here this morning."

They nodded and then the meeting swallowed them all. There was unrest in Espira — accusations of Lunarism that led to violence in the taverns and streets as that region continued to grieve their lost wife. "We believe it will stabilize once you've chosen your new wife," Pyrus said and Josefus nodded in agreement. Frederico smiled at this as well.

The meeting continued beyond the unrest, covering plans to evade increased trade tariffs with Engmark and their other neighbors, intelligence reports of muster fires in the northern tundra region of the Hanh, and an executive session regarding the last action items of the Lunarist Purge and the earliest reports of re-socialization potential among some of the captured cultists.

As the meeting flowed on around him, Frederico found himself engaging as if it were a fencing match. He darted in with a thrust of a sentence here, a parrying question there, steering the meeting to a crisp and quick conclusion.

As the others left, he stood and waited with Pyrus and Josefus. When all but the guards had vanished, he bid them sit.

Frederico sat last. "I have need of your assistance," he said.

"We are sworn to it, Lord Czar," Josefus said.

Frederico glanced to Pyrus. The Minister of Intelligence said nothing but inclined his head ever so slightly.

"I need information on a House Y'Zir and its master, Raj Y'Zir."

Pyrus cleared his voice. "If I knew more, I could serve better, Lord Czar."

"I don't know more. I believe it is in a tropical clime either near or on a sea. Inquire of the Shippers Guild; put the word out to our agencies at home and abroad." He looked up and locked eyes with each of them for but a moment, giving them his most sober stare. "Spare no expense."

Josefus opened his mouth to speak but Frederico rang the bell of dismissal and stood. They turned their eyes down and he paused out of respect.

He resisted the sudden urge to thank them and left the room quickly.

I am changing. He felt more confident; found himself doubting less in his own decisions. The fog of the sadness was lifting from him now.

And it came from the slip of a girl who believed he was a ghost. *Until her*, he thought, *perhaps I was.*

Frederico lay in his bed and stared up at the blue green moon. Over the last month, he'd grown to love these nights and, he thought, perhaps even to love the young woman Amal Y'Zir.

"It can't have been much of an empire," Amal said. "There's no record of it whatsoever, back to the time of the Younger Gods. And it's a small world. I'd have known of it."

Frederico laughed. "It is the greatest empire in the known world — a vast world. My people consider me a god."

"Considered," she said, laughing.

"Considered?" Frederico asked.

"Yes," she said. "Considered . . . past tense. You're a ghost, remember?" She giggled now. "Obviously a mad one."

"Perhaps," he said with as much sarcasm as he could muster, "you could cure me with your so-called magick."

He heard the mock incredulity in her voice. "I'll have you know, Lord Czar Frederico, that I will indeed cure you once I've earned my Alchemy Rankings. And perhaps I'll even restore you back to life so you can serve me better."

Frederico chuckled. "I would indeed serve."

"Aye, you would."

He rolled onto his side, feeling the warm metal against his cheek. "You know I'm looking for you?"

He heard the sound of her skin moving over cloth. "Silly ghost. You'll not find me."

He smiled. "I started some time ago. I've got ships to the nine seas now, asking after you at every port."

Now she laughed. "Nine seas? Don't be absurd. That would be an impossible amount of water."

Frederico joined her in laughing. "Said the girl who believes in magick." Then, he lowered his voice and he heard resolve in it. "I will find you, Amal Y'Zir."

Her voice took on playful taunting. "And what then would you do with me?"

Frederico pondered this. What would he do? Sail the world to make an offer to her father for her hand? Have Pyrus forge papers and establish her in Espira or — bolder still, extend citizenship to her and provide her an estate openly, risk disappointing the populace? He let playfulness enter his own voice. "I can describe several of the things I would do with you, Lady Y'Zir, if you wish it."

But the softness of her moans told him she'd already started imagining those things herself.

Smiling, he joined her.

Frederico pointed to the corner of his bed chamber and watched the servants as they put the harp in place beside its ornate stool. It had been his grandmother's, though she'd never played it. He remembered that it decorated her rooms and towered above him; it seemed much smaller now.

The Palace Steward waited by the door. "Is everything satisfactory, Lord Czar?"

Frederico smiled. "It is, Felip. Thank you."

A momentary cloud crossed the steward's face and he looked away. "I am pleased to serve, Lord Czar."

Frederico studied the man. *He withholds something but does not wish to.* He waited until the servants left, then as the steward turned, he called to him. "Hold, Felip. Come in and close the door."

Paling, the steward did so and when Frederico pointed towards an armchair near the unlit fireplace, he smoothed his saffron robes and sat carefully. Frederico joined him.

"Something disturbs you, Felip. I'd know what it is."

Dots of sweat appeared above the man's upper lip and upon his brow. "It would not be proper, Lord Czar, for me to —"

Frederico chuckled and leaned forward. "It is proper if your Czar asks it of you."

Felip took a deep breath. "There are whisperings, Lord Czar, that you are profoundly unwell."

Frederico smiled. "Do I seem unwell to you?"

The steward shook his head. "You seem . . . happy. The servants comment that they've not seen or heard the weeping in a goodly while."

Frederico sat back in the chair. "I *am* happy, Felip. What else have you heard?"

The old man shifted in his seat, his eyes darting to the left and right. "That Jazrel wasn't truly assassinated by Lunarists but a suicide. That she spent a night with you during your weeping not long before. That you can be heard speaking in your rooms when no one is present, sometimes late into the night." Now, with his tongue suddenly loosened, his words came faster, almost jumbled together. "Some say you've driven yourself mad with grief and guilt over Jazrel, falling into some kind of grinning mania. Some say you speak into a silver mirror. Some say you are speaking with the moon."

Frederico felt the teeth of Felip's first words as they chewed their truth into him, then the last caught his attention, and he looked up. *How I respond is important here*, he thought.

"The staff will always talk," Frederico said as casually as he could. Then, he chuckled. "You can certainly assure them that I am not speaking with the moon, nor am I mad. I know their words trouble you, but don't let them — it means nothing. Still, I would have you keep your ears open and bring any other tidbits of gossip my way that you hear." He leaned even further forward. "And do discourage the staff from that Lunarist nonsense."

Felip nodded. "I certainly will, Lord Czar."

"Thank you," Frederico said. *I have become grateful for what was once my due.* He stood, bowed his head slightly, and when the steward did the same, Frederico did not ring the dismissal bell. Instead, he walked the steward to the door. "Also," he said, "I want you to extend a private dining invitation to Senator Tannen. Pay his house steward handsomely for knowledge of the senator's favorite dishes and spirits. Be certain our chefs can accommodate before the invitation is offered."

Felip nodded. "Yes, Lord Czar."

He locked the door behind the steward and went into the bed chambers. He pulled the lockbox from beneath his bed and spun the cipher into it. He drew out the silver crescent and held it to his ear. "Amal?"

He heard the harp and then the voice. "I am here, Ghost."

"You can teach me now," he said, seating himself upon the stool. He heard the delight in her laugh. "You have it there now?"

"I do, Lady Y'Zir."

For an hour, she talked slowly and quietly to him as he picked notes out upon the strings. It was only later, after she'd left for afternoon lessons — and while he was checking intelligence reports for any news of House Y'Zir — that he realized what the tune was she had carefully walked him through.

It was the song she played upon the night they first met.

He smiled and signed papers authorizing three months of expenses and a redoubled effort to find this woman who brought music to him.

They took their dinner in the private dining room and Frederico waited until they were well into their second bottle of kallaberry wine before he asked his favor. The meal had been perfect — broiled salmon drizzled with a white lemon sauce and decorated with asparagus spears across a bed of peppered rice. Crabbed cucumber salad and garlic steamed mushrooms preceded it and Frederico knew that a pear tart followed, once the kallaberry wine ticked their appetites back to life.

He smiled at the senator. "I have a favor to ask of you. It relates to the matter of my need for an Espiran bride."

Frederico saw the hope come alive in Tannen's eyes. Certainly, the senator had to wonder why he'd been granted this rare dining experience. "Certainly, Lord Czar. Name it. It is no favor — it is my honor." Smiling, Tannen bowed his head.

Frederico returned the bow. "I wish to purchase an estate in Espira. On the coast."

"I am certain we can find a place suitable for you, Lord Czar. Have you met someone of interest there?"

Frederico shook his head. "No," he said. "Not there. It is on behalf of someone else. A Lady Amal Y'Zir. But it would be more proper for the deed to reflect her father's name — Lord Raj Y'Zir."

The senator's brow wrinkled with thought. "I'm not familiar with those names."

"They are from abroad," Frederico said. "I'm not sure of Lady Y'Zir's arrival but I will tell you when I know. It will need a good steward — someone reliable and discreet."

He watched the governor's eyes and when the understanding bloomed in them, it was bright. "I understand, Lord Czar."

"There will be generous remuneration for Espira," Frederico said quietly, "and for you of course. I have a hunting manor for you in the Gaming Wood." He paused. "And once her residency is unquestionable, I will make proposal and settle this matter of an Espiran bride." He raised his glass and his eyebrows. "What say you, Senator?"

There was the briefest hesitation before Tannen smiled and raised his own glass. "Espira is ever yours, Lord Czar."

"Thank you, Tannen. Because of the sensitive nature of this matter I will arrange my gratuity with care."

"I understand completely, Lord Czar."

And with that, Frederico clapped and a servant appeared with the steaming pear tart.

Frederico lay in his bed feeling the sweat dry on his skin. "I bought you a house today in Espira," he told her.

She giggled. "A ghost house?"

He smiled. It had become a game between them. "Yes," he said. "On the coast of my ghostly empire." Images of palm trees and white sands flashed behind his eyes. "It's always warm there."

"Like home," she said, "but not an island."

"Not an island," he agreed.

She sighed and the sound of it was like soft hands upon his skin. "I suppose you think you'll carry me away from my father's tower in a large white ship after paying him some enormous dowry?"

"I suppose," he said.

"And what if he refuses my hand?"

Frederico stretched and stifled a yawn. "I do not think he will. But if he did, I would persuade him otherwise."

Amal laughed. "You do not know my father."

"And he does not know me."

She was silent for a moment and when she spoke, the play was gone from her voice. "Who are you truly, Frederico? I call you 'ghost' and make light of your empire but I've been through the library and I've found nothing. Where do you live? Where are these nine seas you sail in search of me? And are you truly as wonderful as you seem or are you just some whispering memory of a Younger God long dead and captured within this bauble I've found?"

He closed his eyes. "If I am wonderful, I think you've had a part in making me so. And I could ask the same of you. I've spent enough gold searching you out to finance a regional government for two years. I've found no island paradise. No silver tower. No record or recollection of the name Y'Zir in any of a thousand places I have searched. Sometimes," he said, "I wonder if you're not the ghost."

"Maybe we both are," she offered.

"Perhaps. If so, then you'll not mind my ghost house in Espira."

She laughed. "And why would I live in Espira rather than with you in your ghost palace?"

He'd told her little of his wives; truth be told, he'd not thought of them since meeting the girl. And he'd not spoken of Jazrel at all. That loss seemed a private thing to him or at the very least, something to share when their eyes could meet and their hands could touch. "Eventually," he told her, "you would live here with me. But these matters are . . . complicated."

Amal sighed. "I would imagine so. Being an emperor would be frightfully complex, I should think."

"It has its moments."

"So does being the daughter of a wizard."

Frederico laughed. "I'm certain that it does."

"You know I've asked my father's mechoservitor about your empire and your nine seas."

"His mechoservitor?"

"His metal man," she said. "Surely you have mechanicals in your empire?"

A metal man? Frederico thought about the handful of mechanicals he'd seen. Just last week, he'd seen a bird made of metal that could fly and recite verse. "A few," he said. "Mostly small things. Nothing so elaborate as a man."

"He is a wealth of knowledge beyond even our library. I see him infrequently as he's often in the basements about my father's work."

"What did he say?"

She chuckled. "He made inquiries of where I'd heard such nonsense. I told him I'd read it in a book somewhere but could not remember which."

She also hides me from her world, he thought, and he wondered why that impulse was strong within them. Initially, they might think it madness but it would only take a moment to draw out the crescent and prove the truth of it to any who wished to know. *Perhaps we know it changes when it becomes more than the two of us.*

When she yawned and stretched, he heard the sound of sheets moving across her skin and heard the pull of sleep in her voice. "Talk me to sleep, Frederico my Czar, and tell me about my house in Espira."

Yawning himself, Frederico rolled to his side and began describing the estate with its gardens and butterflies, green pools and white sands.

When her breathing became slow and steady, he smiled. "Dream sweetly, Amal my love," he said quietly into the crescent. Then, carefully, he lowered it into its velvet lined box, closed the lid and pushed it back beneath his bed.

Frederico did not announce his visit to the Ministry of Social Behavior but somehow they expected him and ushered him into the Minister's office immediately.

Pyrus was there as well, his anger barely concealed. "This is most irregular, Lord Czar," he said. Still, he stood and bowed his head.

"Quite out of the ordinary," the Minister of Social Behavior agreed, following Pyrus's lead. He looked more nervous than angry and Frederico noted that.

"It may have been once," Frederico replied, "but perhaps you've noticed some recent changes in what was once deemed regular and ordinary." He smiled and went straight to the topic of his visit. "I want to see the Lunar Priestess. I've had a month of excuses and I'll have no more. Broken or not, ill or not, raving or not, I will see her and I will interview her privately."

Though it was not his ministry, Pyrus spoke first. Frederico noted this as well. "But —"

The Czar raised his hand, cutting him off. "Minister Pyrus, is what I ask beyond my right as your Czar?"

There was fire in his eye but the old man bit his tongue. "Anything you ask, Lord Czar, is within your right."

"Very well." He turned to the Minister of Social Behavior. "Take me to her then."

The Minister glanced to Pyrus, then back to Frederico. "Yes, Lord Czar."

They climbed wide and sweeping marble stairs and strode down paneled halls decorated with black and red roses of the Empire, past portraits of the royal family. In the eastern ward, they climbed the corner tower to the midpoint and paused at a walnut door.

The Minister inserted a key and turned the lock while Pyrus tried and failed to disguise the anger on his face. Frederico looked to each of them, then looked to the captain of his Crimson Guard. "I will leave when I'm finished. I will ring if I have urgent need of you."

The captain saluted. The ministers inclined their heads. Frederico opened the door and slipped into the brightly lit room, pulling it closed behind him.

It was a wide open space with a comfortable bed and a small table, a wardrobe, and glass-paned doors that opened onto a caged balcony garden. In the garden, a middle-aged woman with graying red hair sat upon a simple wood chair and hummed at the butterflies that lifted and landed from her naked skin.

Frederico found himself blushing at her nudity, and he turned away from her. "Forgive my intrusion, Lady," he said. "I did not know you were indecent."

She laughed. "I am never indecent." The laughter melted into a smile as she stood. He glanced towards her as she turned to face him and saw continental lines of strength and islands of softness in the curving of her body. He looked away again, a blush rising once more to his cheeks. "You are the Weeping Czar Frederico," she said.

He tried not to notice her breasts. "I no longer weep," he said in a quiet voice.

"Then it's begun." She stopped, then took a tentative step closer to him. "They've given it to you and you've spoken into it." Her eyes were bright with tears. "It spoke back to you and now you are the Last Weeping Czar." She smiled sweetly at him.

There was something compelling and confident in the priestess' words. Frederico felt something like curiosity rising within. Or perhaps it was fear. He heard traces of it in his voice. "What has begun?"

She took another step forward. "The Year of the Falling Moon," she said. "Just as Saint Carnelyin told us."

She started humming again, swaying now to the music. Outside, the butterflies danced with her and Frederico blinked at it all and waited for her words to register. Carnelyin. The storyteller with his fanciful journey to the moon. He opened his mouth to protest, to tell her that the moon was the poisoned garden of gods long fled or extinct, but he was suddenly caught by the song she hummed. He knew it. "Where have you heard that song?"

Her body rippled like a river bathed in light. "He brought it back with him along with the crescent. But you should know this. Your family financed his expedition."

Frederico bristled at the nonsense of her words. "There has never been a Czarist Lunar Expedition."

She smiled. "There has, Frederico. It's the best kept secret of your family and the source of its weeping." Her voice lowered now. "Soon the time for secrets will be past. The Moon Wizard is awake and the end of an age is upon us."

The Moon Wizard. He'd read Carnelyin's story as a boy — most boys had — but it had been many years. He did not remember reading anything about a Moon Wizard. But he did remember something else. It came to him accompanied with laughter and a playful assertion. "I am Amal Y'Zir," she had told him one night long ago, "daughter of the Great Blood Wizard, Raj Y'Zir."

He looked at the priestess. She still hummed the song — the one he'd slowly learned upon the harp under Amal's tutelage — and she danced in quiet supplication. "Did Carnelyin name this Moon Wizard?"

She shook her head. "He did not. And that first, smaller edition of his tale was gathered and burned." She stopped dancing and their eyes met. "He himself was gathered and burned eventually," she told him in a sober voice, "when he refused to recast his perilous tale at the behest of his Czar."

Frederico shook his head. "He died in retirement in Espira, a man of great honor."

"He died in a fire in some basement furnace beneath your palace," she said. "Branded a traitor for telling the truth."

Frederico swallowed. Something in her words held him and demanded that he ask the next question. "What truth did he tell?"

"Sit with me," she told him, "and I will share his gospel with you."

Frederico looked to the door then back to the woman. *They are words*, he told himself. Hearing could not hurt him. But already, this woman struck a chord within him that resonated as true as any upon his grandmother's harp. He'd studied enough of the Lunarists to know they believed a tragic end awaited a faithless world but he'd never cared to know exactly why and what kind of end. It was enough to know that it hung upon mysticism and bordered on madness.

But now, a hunger for the words rode him and he walked slowly to the chair she pointed to.

Folding his hands into his lap, he sat. "Teach me about the moon," he said.

She smiled and in her smile, Frederico saw damnation and salvation dancing together to the strains of a familiar tune.

*

The servants began delivering the manuscripts and documents even before he'd returned to his rooms. He saw them filing past out of the corner of his eye as he silently took his lunch in the small dining room near his suite.

He'd waved Pyrus and the others away when he'd left the priestess's quarters. And the black clouds that gathered within him must have migrated to his face for they did not ask. The Minister of Social Behavior looked concerned. Pyrus looked bemused.

That bemusement had become something else when Frederico started listing off the books and records he wished brought to his rooms. He couldn't tell if it was the tone of voice with which he issued the commands or if it was the documentation itself that he wished to see, but Pyrus had looked almost eager to accommodate him.

And now a stream of men and women flowed into his rooms with arms stacked high, then left for yet more.

He chewed his orange-soaked pheasant slowly and thought about the Gospel of Felip Carnelyin. He could not find the good news in it but he knew it was because the finality of her words were still sinking in.

If her words were true then the world sat at the edge of a great change and there was nothing that could be done for it. And he had played a part in it. He'd sought to cover his shame by blaming the Lunarists for Jazrel and in so doing, he'd uncovered an older shame — the root of his family's tears.

He'd spoken into the silver crescent and it had answered him. He had wept into it and something like joy had found him.

He'd gone in search of truth and found sorrow waiting in its place.

Suddenly angry, Frederico swept the platters and goblets from his table. They clattered against the walls and floor, causing the servants to jump and yelp at his sudden violence. It surprised everyone, including him.

He stood, mumbled an apology, and fled to his rooms and the mountains of paper that awaited him there.

He did not bring out the silver crescent that night. Instead, he kept the lamps up and launched his research. The priestess had given him a long list of places to start and he went to those first, finding her words confirmed with each scrap he read.

The Ministry of Intelligence had been careful, certainly. There were no blatant confessions, no straightforward accounts. But he found what he sought — verification of the priestess's words — in the nooks and crannies of it all. In budget lines and meeting notes, in veiled references and coincidental dates from a thousand years before.

Initially, there was wonder to be found, but beneath it, shame. And as the clues fell into place, the shame gave way to dread.

That dread grew within him until finally, as the sun grayed the eastern sky, it spilled over again into anger, and he went at last to the silver crescent.

"Are you there?" he asked it, rubbing his eyes as if somehow that effort might erase what he'd learned. He heard stirring and then a sleepy voice.

"Frederico?"

He didn't answer at first.

Amal's voice had an edge of panic to it. "Frederico? Are you there? Where have you been? I fell asleep waiting for you."

"How old are you?" he finally asked. He could hear the flatness in his voice. "How old are you *really?*"

"Nineteen," she said. "But I've told you that before."

She couldn't be nineteen and he knew it now. "And your older sister?" His voice was sharper now than he intended it.

"I have no older sister."

No, he realized. She was correct in that assertion.

"But you had one," he said. "There were two daughters."

"I don't know what you're talking about, Frederico. I am my father's only daughter."

"Perhaps," he said, "you should ask him about Ameera." But even as he said it, he knew he should not have. And with the same realization, he knew that the girl he'd spent so many nights with, talking from moonrise to moonfall, had no more understanding of what it all meant than he had just a day earlier.

I should not punish her for knowledge she does not have. Yet he had wanted to and now, just as suddenly, his desire to hurt her melted away at the fear he heard in her voice.

"What's wrong?" He could hear tears just beyond her panic. "What's happened? Have your ships found something?"

He would send word to call the ships back in a few hours. "No," he said. "They've found nothing." There had been nothing those ships could possibly find. Only one Czarist ship could ever have found evidence of Raj Y'Zir and his two daughters and that ship had been dismantled bolt by bolt, broken bit by bit, and buried at sea long, long ago. Its very existence had been hidden so well that the only reference left to it was the gaps in the supply records and the fanciful tale of a man discredited and later murdered by those who sent him to document the journey. Still, he fared better than the rest of the crew.

And far better than the girl he brought back with him.

Amal's voice shook him out of memory. "If not the ships, then what is it, Frederico?"

He looked up at the crystalline ceiling of his chambers. Already, the sky moved toward mauve and the moon had vanished. He remembered the priestess's words to him after he'd finished hearing her tale, after he'd raged and then sobbed there at her feet in her prison. "What do you see in your night sky, Amal?"

"Stars," she said. "Stars and more stars." *He deceives even his own children,* he realized.

"No moon then," he asked. But it would be so much larger than a moon. It would fill the sky and light up the night, brown and green and blue and massive.

"No," she answered.

Frederico sighed. "And nothing else?"

"Nothing else," she said. And as if somehow it added credibility, she added, "I swear it."

Frederico's mouth went suddenly dry and his hand shook. *I should not say more,* he told himself. But at the end of everything he'd learned this night, he could not bear being the only one ambushed and overwhelmed by unexpected truth. "What if I told you," he said slowly, "that your father kept an entire world out of your view?" He waited for the words to settle in. "Could he do that? With his magicks?"

There was silence. He heard the rustle of cloth, then heard the faintest trace of wind, the lingering song of frogs upon it. "Why would my father keep something like that from me?"

"I do not know," he answered. "But couldn't he?"

He could hear the tension rising in her voice. "And why wouldn't he tell me about an older sister?"

"I do not know that, either," Frederico said. But he wondered if he *did* know and if perhaps Raj Y'Zir had hidden both the world he watched and the daughter he lost in order to spare his youngest a grief she was too innocent to bear. But how could Frederico tell her that?

"And why would my father keep *anything* from me?" Amal Y'Zir asked again.

"I do not know," he said once more.

"If you don't know those things," she said now, her voice clearly angry, "perhaps you'll know why I would believe a lying ghost rather than my own eyes and my own father?"

But she did not wait for a reply this time. Frederico heard the softest of cries and knew it was the sound of her sudden, angry exertion. For a moment, his ear filled with the hollow sound of air rushing past and he felt the vertigo as if he himself fell. Then there was a crash.

After the crash, the sound of running water and frogs.

Somewhere above and beyond that, a girl sobbing.

Pyrus swept into the room before the bell of his arrival sounded, his face red and his jaw firm. His black-coat escort fell back before Frederico's Red Brigade guard but not before menacing glances were exchanged.

Trouble brews there.

"Minister Pyrus," Frederico said, putting down his glass of kallaberry wine. He smiled. "You've no doubt seen my release orders for the Lunarists."

"It is —"

Frederico cut him off. "Well within my right as Czar, Pyrus. I've sent word personally to the Minister of Social Behavior." He leaned forward. "We've more emergent matters to address than that harmless cult. War is coming, Pyrus, and we must be ready."

Pyrus looked perplexed. "War? With whom?"

Frederico stood and went to the table. It stood stacked high with volume upon volume — some from his first frantic night of research, more from the last two nights. He'd kept the crescent nearby in case she called out to him while he pored over the records but she hadn't and that was not surprising.

He gestured to the papers there, then swept the broader room with its similar piles of parchment and book. "What if I told you, Pyrus, that there was a threat at least a thousand years brewing?"

The old man snorted. "What do you play at, Frederico?"

One of the crimson clad guards started forward but Frederico waved him off. "I play at nothing but the truth. A thousand years ago we went to the moon and we've wept ever since."

Pyrus had gone from perplexed and angry to starkly surprised. "You believe there is threat of war to us upon the moon?"

Frederico nodded. "I do. We took the Moon Wizard's daughter. We tortured her to death. When Carnelyin got out of hand, we quieted him quickly enough, too." His words came out faster than he intended.

Pyrus began to smile.

"You think I'm mad," Frederico said. "I assure you, I'm not. Mark me: We've preparations to make and still they may not be enough. I've called the War Cabinet together for a meeting tomorrow morning. The Year of the Falling Moon is upon us."

Pyrus laughed and this time, the guard made no move.

Without another word, the Minister of Intelligence spun about on his heels and left quickly, his black-coats falling in behind him as he went.

That fourth night, Frederico fell asleep with his head cradled in the silver crescent. He wasn't sure why; even knowing the threat, he could not stay away. As much as he hoped to never hear her voice again, he longed for it, even prayed for it though he had no god to pray to.

Overhead, the sky was shrouded in clouds that promised coming rain. He heard her voice from far away, calling his name, and he stirred awake slowly.

"Amal?"

Her voice drew closer and was suddenly there, filling the crescent. "Frederico?" She sounded small and far away. Something wounded and broken.

Do not answer her, some part of him warned. "I'm here," he said.

"You were right. I've seen it now."

"Seen what?" he asked, but he knew what. It filled her sky and boggled her.

"I know where you come from now," Amal said. "I know all of it now."

Frederico wanted to speak but didn't know what to say. Instead, he waited and let her continue.

"I tricked my father's mechoservitor into showing me. That was yesterday. Then I spent last night in father's hidden library." He could tell from the rawness of her voice that she'd been crying. "I don't know how he's kept it from me. Or why. But somehow he has." She sniffed. "And now I'm sure he knows I know *something*. I've stayed away as much as I can but he's been asking the servants a lot of uncomfortable questions about how I've been spending my time."

Frederico sat up. "Do your servants know about me?"

She was quiet for a moment, then answered in a quiet voice. "I think they do. They've caught me with you before."

He sighed at the powerlessness that washed over him suddenly. "I don't know what to do."

"There's nothing you *can* do," she told him. She cried for a bit then, and he heard her quiet sobbing as if it were a canticle played out in a minor key, like the song she'd taught him. He felt his own sadness welling up, though he resisted it, bending his focus towards her instead. She sniffed again. "I think I will have to face him soon."

"What will he do?"

"I don't know," she said. "Make me forget again. Like he made me forget Ameera or the world that fills our sky." She laughed and it was bitter in his ear. "A daily glamour with my breakfast."

Frederico closed his eyes to her words and imagined losing himself in forgetfulness. No memory of Sasha or Jazrel to stir his guilt and remind him of loss he brought about by sharing his mad sorrow with them. No recollection of the last months spent with Amal Y'Zir in her imaginary arms, held fast by her voice and her laughter, paralyzed by her tears. "Would that be so very bad?" he asked in a small voice.

"So very bad?" There was an edge to her voice. "To forget you and to forget these times?" She paused. "Even with what I know now, I'd rather remember."

But did she know everything? Did she know what had happened in those bright-lit basements of his forefather? The priestess had whispered that part of the story to him, relaying the only unwritten chapter of Felip Carnelyin's gospel. Eventually, their same questions, repeated again and again, had worn trails into the moon princess's mind and eventually, she had cried out one last breath in despair and hopelessness and every hand in the room shook at the sound of it and dropped what it held, every breath in the room caught and became a sob. A thousand years of weeping.

"I'd rather remember," she said again. Then, after a moment: "Oh, Frederico, I wish your ships could find me here and bring me to you."

"I wish it, too," he said.

They were quiet now and Frederico could hear the sounds of the brook running and the frogs singing against the backdrop of her gentle breathing. He heard something, far and distant, deep and ominous.

"I have to go," she whispered suddenly. "Father calls for me."

Frederico heard her quickened footfalls fade quietly into the other sounds of that lunar night. After she'd gone, he lay there with the crescent and tried to find comfort in the frogs.

But there was no comfort to be found.

It happened sometime in the night and Frederico did not know it. He awakened in the morning, put the silver crescent back into its lockbox, and rang for servants that did not come.

Finally, he went to the door and opened it. The Red Brigade guard was gone; black-coats stood watch in their place.

"What is the meaning of this?" he asked, but he knew without asking. He'd seen Pyrus's face, had heard his laughter, and he'd known even then that this storm had brewed for some time now. Until his interview with the priestess, he might have even welcomed this change, though it angered him that it came through Pyrus. But with war coming, it placed his people and the empire his family had built at tremendous risk.

The black-coat guard did not answer. He stared straight ahead at attention, his freshly-lacquered rifle held tightly to his side. *He's ordered them not to speak.* "Send the servants in with my breakfast," he said. "And congratulate Minister Pyrus on his coups thus far."

He didn't wait for any kind of acknowledgement. Instead, he closed the door and went to his closets to dress for the day.

Pyrus came in with the servants two hours later. He looked

haggard and sleepless, but a satisfied smile played at his mouth. "Well, Frederico," he said, "how go your preparations for war?"

Frederico smiled and looked to the water clock that hissed upon his wall. "I'm afraid we've already missed that meeting, Pyrus. But there is time yet." *Nearly a year if the priestess spoke true.*

These were new servants, Frederico realized, men and women he'd not seen before. They laid out his breakfast table silently, their careful glances taking in their former Czar and the rooms he occupied. Pyrus sat to the table without invitation and Frederico joined him.

"I've spoken with the new Minister of Social Behavior," Pyrus said. "For now, you'll remain here in your quarters, but they will send their physicians later this week to determine just how mad you are and what treatments may help you find your way again." He reached out and broke off a piece of honeyed pastry. "They are doing interesting things with electrostatic pulses and kallaberries these days."

Frederico smiled. "You and I both know I am not mad."

Pyrus laughed. "I know no such thing. The evidence speaks too loudly for me to know it." He started listing his evidence on his fingers. "Your own servants speak of strange goings-on, hidden away in your rooms with that bauble. You've spent the operating budget of a small nation scouring the land and sea for some mysterious family no one has heard of. You spent three hours with the Lunarist priestess and released that dangerous woman and her mad followers without so much as a consultation with your cabinet. And now," he said, leaning forward, "you are ready to declare war upon the moon."

"No," he said, correcting him, "I do not declare it; it has been declared upon us." *And we've earned every last part of it,* he did not say. "And the Lunarists are harmless; we have a much larger threat to concern us."

Pyrus shrugged. "I suppose you've heard about this threat in your little bauble?"

"No," Frederico said, feeling suddenly angry first at Pyrus and his smugness but then, after a moment, with himself for letting any of this come to pass. He'd seen the signs and he'd not cared. He'd played his harp and stayed up nights imagining the touch of a woman whose sister his family had killed, whose father, according to the priestess, would someday avenge himself upon them all. Yet he could not be without her any more than he could be with her and that built his rage even further. *Taste and need.* The anger in him was hot and white and fierce but he forced his shaking hand to put down his cup of chai. He looked up and his eyes met Pyrus's. "I've not heard it in the bauble."

Pyrus waved a dismissive hand. "It doesn't matter where you've heard it. You're unfit, Frederico, and the empire needs leadership." He stood and smoothed the black robes of his dark office. "You'll remain here until sufficient quarters can be arranged for you elsewhere. You'll want to make a list of the few things permitted for you to take when the time comes." He walked to the door and looked over his shoulder as he opened it. "The silver bauble stays here."

Frederico sat, unmoving, for a long time after Pyrus left him there. He bent his mind to his present circumstances and tried to find something beyond the anger that licked at him, chewed on him. Try as he might, he could find nothing past that primal emotion.

He could not even find his tears.

Two days slipped past and Frederico bided time. He gathered up the documents he'd searched, ordered his findings into a logical flow, and stacked everything in a way that the new servants could easily return them to their proper place if the new Czar — or would he go by some other title? — chose not to look at them, chose not to see what Frederico had seen.

He went to the silver crescent less and less, though now he left it out in the open. He'd heard nothing from it but frogs and water since Amal had left to see her father and he wasn't sure he'd ever hear her voice again. Some part of him even wondered if perhaps she hadn't been a ruse, some part in Raj Y'Zir's intricate game of vendetta.

When her voice came through, late in the afternoon of his third day under house arrest, it was muffled but excited.

"Frederico, are you there?"

He stood slowly, eyeing the silver crescent where it lay across the room.

"Frederico, my love, are you there?"

He moved towards it. *My love.*

"Oh, come quickly," she said and her voice was nearly frantic. He could tell she was out of breath.

He paused, then closed the gap. "I'm here," he said.

"I've found a way to you," she said. "I'm leaving my father. I'm coming to Espira."

He blinked back surprise. He'd not expected these words and he found himself not knowing what to say.

She continued. "I'm packing now. I'm taking you with me but I don't know if it will be safe to talk."

Finally, he found words. "How are you doing this?"

"There's a pool in a cave deep beneath my father's tower," she said, the words tumbling out. "It's where he goes to draw up his magicks from the blood of your world." She paused. "It's connected somehow."

A childhood superstition about magicks crept into his mind. "The Beneath Places," he said. The so-called hell of the Younger Gods, where they plundered devils of their souls and slept restless in their sins. *Or bargained for power.* Stories, like the ghosts in the water, to keep children obedient.

"Yes," she said. "We call it that, too. I will swim the pool and come to you." She hesitated. "If you will have me?"

Frederico found her words discomfiting but did not understand why initially. Then, he realized his silence would not be taken the way he intended and he blurted out the first question that came to mind. "But why?" It didn't sound the way he intended and he reframed it. "Why would you have me, Amal, knowing what my family did to your sister?"

"You've wept those tears already, Frederico, and they were never truly yours to weep." There was something in her voice that he could not place and wondered if grace were an emotive quality. "Tears enough are on the way for all of us," she continued, "without borrowing yesterday's."

And in that moment, he forgot about the black-coats outside his door, forgot about the rooms that waited for him at the Ministry of Social Behavior, and forgot even about the wives his grief had slain. All he could hear was the Moon Wizard's daughter as she asked again: "Will you have me?"

"I will," he said.

"Then I will find you in Espira if I can."

And somehow he knew in that moment, without doubt, that he would never hear her voice again.

But before he could reply she was gone. He waited all day

hoping to hear her again but knowing he would not. He took the silver crescent with him into his private dining room and kept it near his tub as he bathed at the end of the day.

He cradled it beside him on his pillow.

That night, the weeping came upon him again but it was different this time because the loss was his own and he understood it. Gone was Ameera's final spell upon his family, replaced now by Amal's first and the force of his bereavement wracked his body in great sobs.

Twice, the black-coats inquired of his well being and consulted quietly with cloaked couriers. Then, sometime in the early morning hours, they came for him and carried the last Weeping Czar out of his palace and loaded him into a carriage bound for his new home.

A sense of time returned to Frederico but he had no way to know how many days he'd lost. How long had he been in this new place?

His new rooms were loftier than his former, overlooking the forests beyond the city. The bars across his balcony cast the sunlight in straight lines across the carpeted floor and though the rooms were much smaller, they were also more comfortable.

He'd fallen quickly into a routine. He read over his morning chai — mostly novels and plays, but sometimes he read poetry as well. He met with his physicians after breakfast, then exercised outdoors under the supervision of disinterested guards. In the afternoons, he practiced his harp.

When Pyrus came to him, his face white and his hands shaking, Frederico had just sat down and raised his fingers to the strings. He looked up. "Minister Pyrus," he said, inclining his head. "Or is it Chancellor now?"

The old man said nothing. He stretched out his hand towards Frederico and in it, wrapped in black velvet, was the silver crescent.

Frederico stood. The sight of it stopped his breath and he saw the look of stunned surprise on his own face, reflected back in its mirrored surface. He reached out and took it, held it to his ear. "Hello?"

"Two daughters have you taken from me out of my own house," a voice like silk said, "and I will have blood for them each." Raj

Y'Zir continued, quietly and with confidence. "When I fall upon you it will shake the foundations of the world. My physicians will cut you for my pleasure."

Frederico looked up and saw the wideness of Pyrus's eyes. "I've not taken your daughter, Lord Y'Zir. She's left you of her own free will."

"You've taken her, whether you know it or not. She's swum the Bargaining Pool, but she was too young to know that her body could not make the journey. Her spirit is yours for now."

Frederico closed his eyes. These were tears he'd already wept but he felt them again at the back of his eyelids.

"You will not hear my voice again until it is in the sky above you," Raj Y'Zir said. "Until then, know that a wrathful father builds his army and his bridge."

After that, silence.

Frederico smiled grimly and looked to Pyrus, returning the crescent to him. "I believe this changes your position considerably."

The old general said nothing as Frederico sat back down and let his fingers find their way over the harp strings. The canticle was upbeat but in a minor key, haunting and yet triumphant.

It is a love song, Frederico realized.

The war production was in full swing when Frederico took to his new estate near Belle-Sur-La-Mer. He left the affairs of state in the hands of his capable Chancellor Tannen and left the gun-fields and navies in the hands of his new Minister of War. Pyrus had taken to the role with gratitude appropriate for a spared life and a treason forgiven.

He found the same routines he'd discovered during his brief stay in the Ministry; they comforted him. And he added new ones. He took to walking the markets by day and the beaches by night, his bare feet shuffling over sand still warm from the sun and bathed blue-green in the light of the moon.

Sometimes, late at night, he even sat on the pier with his harp and played. His servants thought him mad but he was the Lord Czar and could do as he pleased. One night, as the lamps guttered low and his fingers ached from the strings, Frederico stood up and stretched.

He walked to the end of the dock and looked up into the night sky. It had been just past a year now, he realized, and he knew now that the Year of the Falling Moon was not literal after all. He'd wondered. But the anniversary of Jazrel's passing had come and gone more than two months ago and there'd been no shaking ground or raining fire, no booming voice crying out vengeance.

Hanging there, full and bright, the moon waited.

And in that moment, deep in the waters at the end of the pier, something moved.

At first, Frederico thought it was a reflection, blue and green light upon the warm night sea. But then it moved again and he started. He looked over his shoulder to the crimson guard that waited by the front doors of his estate, to the servants stationed near their bell. Crouching, he leaned forward and looked into the water.

It was slender and beautiful and it coiled around the pillar of the dock before sliding off and out — a line of blue-green light moving deeper and away, as if part of the moon had fallen and now sank.

Amal. He couldn't tell if he said it aloud or silently. But a sudden fancy took him. Soft and low, he whistled the tune he'd been playing just minutes ago and watched the light flicker as it turned about and drifted slowly back to him.

What had her father said? *Her body could not make the journey.*

And he realized then that the Year of the Falling Moon was not about conquest and war, vendetta and violence. They'd only had part of Carnelyin's gospel. The angry, broken potshards of loss. Those would still come but they were not the message of promise. No, Frederico realized, this gospel was really about love. A love so strong that it would swim, relentless, at any price. And so piercing that it could be heard in the deepest of dark places.

"You found me," he said quietly.

And with that Frederico stood, returned to his harp, and gave himself to song.

THE NIGHT THE STARS SANG OUT MY NAME

I should have been a runner.

Of course I'm naked. Naked and running full-on. Suit seized up three weeks back. Then captured. So now I'm naked and running under stars that steal my words and warp my sense of size in the vastness of Everything. Using a stolen charstick to burn my way out. A flash. A scream. A smell of burning meat.

I should have been a chef.

CHIB-CHILI, CHIB-PUREE, CHIB-KABOB — That's my jiminy. He chatters endlessly when nervous. His name is Eddie.

My stomach lurches. I haven't eaten in days. Even chib sounds good.

Speak of the devil, one appears. I burn out its face. Chibby Chibby Burning Bright—

I should have been a poet.

My jiminy agrees with this and launches into a litany of children's verse. *Find our way out of here*, I send.

A trisket a — WORKING ON IT, BOSSMAN — a trasket a green and yellow—

Another chib breaks through the foliage to my west. I sweep the charstick over it. Another flash. Another scream. More meat.

Hey diddle diddle , my son John — WEST FIVE LEAGUES, ROVING PACK SEVEN — went to bed with his stockings —

I adjust my course. *Good work, Eddie.*

DON'T MENTION IT.

And he's back at it with the verses. Five leagues more of Eddie's manic sing-song. I tell myself I'm going to have him removed. Upgraded. I tell myself he's been a real pain in the you-know-what for the past thirty years. I tell myself that he's not my friend and I don't need him.

But I do. I really *should* have been a poet. Then I wouldn't need this extra personality piggy-backing my own, watching my six. Then all I'd need is words.

WORDS - BIRDS - TURDS - CURDS —

A moment's peace, is all I ask.

A teacher. I should have been a teacher. An academic, stuffy and proud and (most important of all) without a jiminy.

The whoop-whoop of a Finder goes off somewhere to my left. The moss gives way to ankle-deep swamp-water. Something slimy and soft moves over my foot. God knows what else lives on these far-flung planets. We thought the chibs were bad enough.

THE INNER C'HIBORYAL SYSTEMS ARE HOME TO THOU-SANDS OF DISTINCT SPECIES OF FLORA AND FAUNA, LEND-ING SUPPORT TO FELORIAN'S THEORUM OF —

Enough Eddie. You left me, you fucker.

The jiminy finally, finally shuts up. Lights squeeze past me hissing into the water. Behind me, chib-talk warbles in panting shouts. I spin-drop to one knee, the foul water splashing up into my face. I level the charstick and sweep it left and right. More screams. One of them is mine. A near passing beam opens a welt on my side.

I'm not gonna make it. I'm going back to the camp, I think. That stinking hole where'd they'd taken me. Where they'd hurt me into talking even though I knew absolutely nothing about the battleboats.

I should have been a —

SOLDIER! SOLDIER! ON YOUR FEET, SOLDIER!

And he sounds like my Drilly back Home. Like two hundred fifteen pounds of midnight black meanness poured into a man and force-fed to a brigade of eager young bucks. Drilly's dead, I know, but that voice. That —

MOVE! MOVE! MOVE!

I'm up and running. Somewhere, Eddie is ticking away the long list of what's wrong with me. Chib unbending drugs. Head injury. Dehydration. Exhaustion. All good reasons for me to falter but piss-poor excuses. Did they used to say piss-poor back in the old days?

The things you wonder.

A pop somewhere way back behind. Another Finder? Or maybe a Seeker? Something tangles around my foot. It tightens and pulls. I fall face first and the charstick hisses and sparks out when it hits the water. I lose it, scramble for it and find nothing. I'm being dragged backwards now, my fingers digging into the muck to find some kind of grip. Somewhere behind me a chib is reeling me in and I remember fishing with my father back before the bug-bombs fell. I was eight. It took six months to figure out that we were being poisoned by something other than evolution.

He held up a trout. My Dad, I mean. Held it up and grinned.

"Look, Billy!"

I smile back. "Nice one, Dad."

CHIB PATROL EIGHT CUBITS TO THE SIX, Eddie says.

I push off from the bottom. I flip myself over so that my shoulders and arms leave a wake behind me. Overhead, stars like scattered new pennies glint and shimmer in a thick field of sky punctuated by skeletal trees.

I'm afraid now. My nose is in the wash of rotten water. I escaped once, I tell myself. I could do it again.

NOW THEY KNOW ABOUT ME. YOU'LL BE ON YOUR OWN THIS TIME.

I snarl. *Like before.*

TEMPORARY DISASSOCIATIVE MALFUNCTION.

I know he's right. He came back when he could. Came back and got me the hell out of there.

I see them now. They huddle, hunched over, piles of stinking meat on too many legs with too many arms. One of them works the Seeker and reminds me of my Dad and that trout again. My bladder's dry or I'd have cut loose right then. My body is remembering those arms, those long fingers, the weird tools and needles that made me scream and talk and sob.

PREPARE FOR COGNITIVE OVERRIDE. I've heard of it happening before. I've also heard of it going very wrong. There's a reason why the AIs aren't allowed to drive. Unhinged minds. Atrocities.

No, Eddie, I send. *Terminate override.*

SORRY BOSSMAN.

The chib pain was nothing compared to this. Head squeezed in a vice and popping. Fire underneath the skin spreading. But I do not scream. Roar of water rushing by.

My roar.

And somehow, I am on my feet. Every limb is lashing out and I spin and spin like those gypsies in Mom's shake and whirl dervish glass.

I should have been a dancer.

I yank the reel from the fisher-chib's hands and beat him with it. My foot caves in a soft chib jaw. My other hand finds well-hidden but unprotected genitalia and squeezes out the howls. It's not me. It's Eddie. My jiminy. Raging.

In moments, they are all down. Eddie has another charstick now. He thumbs it to life and burns them into the bloody, boiling swamp-water. Chib-stew. Now I'm the rider in the backseat watching him do something I've done a hundred times on twenty worlds.

LET'S GO, I say.

He doesn't answer. He turns in the direction of Roving Pack Seven and we set out. No more chibs find us and somewhere in the mesh-cap beneath my own scalp I go to sleep.

When I wake up, it's my world again and I think for a moment that I am alone for the first time since I woke up in the chib camp. Before *that* terrible day, I'd spent thirty years with a voice inside my head keeping me safe, alive.

But I am not alone. Hulking suits move sluggishly around me, patrolling the fringe of my vision. I hear the hum of their biomechs. I hear each tiny pebble beneath their feet as it crushes to powder.

"Eddie?" It took a second to realize I'd said it aloud.

One of the suits stops, turns, moves toward me. There is a hiss as the voicemitter engages. "Sorry, Sarge. We've uploaded your jiminy for evaluation. It was pinging pretty high on the stress-check." The PFC pauses, probably wondering where my face went. I want to tell him that it's slid off me and into the dirt of this chib world hell. "I'm sure they'll get him back to you soon."

I swallow back a lump. I try to fight tears. Something breaks in me like one of those pebbles underneath massive metal boots. I am naked and alone in this place.

And I hear my name and look up. Overhead, the stars are moving in a dance like Eddie's dance. Overhead, deep space pushes down on me like a warm blanket. Overhead, a solitary speck of light moves at a different pace than all the others. A transport, full-up, off to find another chib world and punish it for the near extinction of the human race.

I miss the voice inside my head.

I should have been a —

No. I am a soldier.

I miss my friend.

THE GOD-VOICES OF SETTLER'S REST

Mother Holton grieved when the god-voices returned because she remembered what it had cost Settler's Rest the last time, when she was a little girl.

It made her weep.

But they were tears of sorrow, not fear. No, she was not afraid. She knew that it came around like Gussuf's Wheel and that after the god-voices quieted, they would have peace for a season. But this was the second visitation in a century. They would visit sooner and sooner until eventually, they ushered in the next Age of Unknowing.

The Seventeenth Age if the Book spake true. "So many," she heard a dry reed-rattle voice whisper into the darkened bedroom. My voice, she realized.

The room bell chimed and she sat up from the blankets. With each year, they'd piled more onto her. "These winters are growing colder," she would say, "what do you think of that?" And they would heat the blankets near the fire that night and her bones wouldn't ache with the cold nearly as much.

The door opened and a wedge of light pushed into the room. A girl stepped into it.

"Mother, they have started," the girl said. Mother Holton couldn't tell which one it was. Perhaps one of the younger, newer converts. Was that a hint of the Northern Coasts in her voice?

"I know they have," the old woman said. "Help me to prayer, girl."

The girl shook her head. "I am not permitted, Mother."

Mother Holton laughed. "Them that's told you not to answer the voices are already on their knees, I'll wager." She coughed and tasted copper in her mouth. "Whether or not we answer is irrelevant, regardless what you've been taught."

The girl stepped forward, uncertainty in her voice. "Why do we want it so bad?"

For a moment, Mother Holton allowed herself to hear the whispering god-voices. *Comehomecomehomecomehome*, they whispered, *toaplaceyouwillbeloved.* Only the whispers, when they blended, were a choir that balanced perfectly between chant and song. Mother Holton forced the voices back down. "Because we cannot bear to be alone in the Universe," she finally said. "Now help me to my knees, girl."

The girl came to her side and helped her up. There was a time when Mother Holton would have pretended to accept the assistance without resting any weight on her helper. But now, she knew she needed all of the help she could get. The girl gently lowered her to the floor. Mother Holton folded her hands and bowed her head.

"Now pray with me," she said.

The girl shook her head more vigorously. "I can not, Mother."

Mother Holton smiled. "This is your first time, child. You do not know it yet, but you will bend your knee to them that's bidding before they pass. It's better to do it now. It makes what comes later more easy to swallow."

Trembling, the girl knelt beside her.

Then Mother Holton, Settler Priestess of the First Home Temple, answered the voices from her childhood so long ago.

"Oh," she said, feeling the lump grow in her throat, "I've missed you."

When she was thirteen, Abigail Holton loved Enoch Bentley and knew of a teenaged certainty that she would marry that farmer boy and give herself to corn and babies. Her grandmother had raised her on the Book and she knew her part in the Settler's Promise. Grandmother was a seamstress with gnarled hands, doing the best she could by the baby that came into her care in the sunset of her life. Abigail's mother had died following a visitation. And though her grandmother did not speak of it, the other girls in town did.

But Abigail listened to the Book. She would not hate them for repeating the words their mothers whispered among themselves when they thought their children weren't listening. Her mother had taken her own life because the voices never stopped for her.

She was walking in Farmer Bentley's fields, wondering what Enoch looked like with his shirt off, when she heard the voice that changed her life. *Come home*, it whispered and a choir joined in around it. All her life, she'd felt empty and alone until that afternoon as the day stars set hours ahead of the sun. But when the god-voices started there on the edge of her womanhood, Abigail Holton knew that regardless what she'd been taught, she was not alone in the universe.

The voices abated and Mother Holton opened her eyes. She could feel the girl beside her shaking and she looked over to her. Head in hands, she sobbed into the edge of the bed. Mother Holton reached out and put her hand on the girl's shoulder.

"What is your name, child?"

The girl sniffed. "Esther Hopewell," she said. "I am Sister Elizabeth Hopewell's daughter."

Mother Holton nodded. "I remember you." Sister Elizabeth was one of the seven Settler's Daughters who had disappeared exploring the ruins in the southern deserts fifteen years ago. The Temple had been the young orphan's caretaker at Mother Holton's insistence. "Do not be alarmed at the voices, Daughter Hopewell. Their power is in perception alone. They will pass in time. Go, talk with Sister McDougall about it. She can teach you prayers and meditations to help you."

The girl helped her back into bed and tucked the blankets around her. "I will speak to her, Mother Holton. Thank you."

She could see the shame on the girl's face. Shame for having wept or having prayed? It mattered little. Mother Holton reached up a gnarled hand and patted the girl's cheek.

"Remember what I told you," she said. "The voices will pass."

But she fell asleep hoping that they wouldn't, that somehow this time it would be different.

Maybe they will not change this time, she thought, *and the good voices will stay with us*. But she knew from the Book — from a thousand of years of recorded Settlement history — that they would be the same voices they had ever been. And the Settler's Daughters would write the words down, study them, and try as they had for centuries to understand the god-voices.

They had given up on silencing them long ago.

Maybe they will not change this time.
But she knew they would.

The day after the voices changed, Abigail Holton snuck into the Temple and sought out Mother Cassel in her meditation vault.

Her grandmother was a childhood friend of the priestess and she'd grown up in the shadows of the Temple's massive laser-etched cornerstones. At one time, the First Home Temple had been the center of Settler's Rest. But at some point, trade and education had become equally important. Still, her grandmother's friend recognized the need for both and gave her friend regular mending business, paying the high end of fair wages for her skill.

The Book told them that the change would come, but she'd hoped it would be different. When they changed, she spent the day crying, lost and hopeless.

When the voices finally quieted enough for her grandmother to sleep, Abigail slipped into the night to find Mother Cassel.

"Abigail Holton," Mother Cassel said. "Does your grandmother know you're out in the middle of the night?"

Abigail swallowed. "She's asleep."

The old woman smiled. "The change was difficult this time," she said. "This was your first."

She hung her head. "I was faithless, Mother. I didn't believe the Book. I didn't believe they would change." Her eyes came up slowly to meet the old woman's. "I *prayed.*"

Mother Cassel clicked her tongue. "Of course you did. How could you not? The voices are beguiling at first, promising you something better. They gain your trust. But they always turn, Abigail, they *always* turn. They cajole and then they loathe."

"But why?" she asked.

Mother Cassel shrugged. "We do not know. It's always been this way." She smiled. "But with each visitation, we learn more about the voices . . . and more about the world. We will write it down in the Book, and we will take what clues we can from the words between their promises, pleas and threats. We will do what we can *while* we can. And someday," she continued, "the voices will win out for a spell and we will hide our work in the ground until reason comes back into focus again."

Abigail thought about the voices, both earlier and today. When they changed and became angry she had not known what to do. She felt betrayal and yet she felt love, too. She'd known in that instant that she was made for more than Enoch Bentley's corn and babies.

"I want to help," Abigail Holton told her grandmother's friend. "I want to join the Settler's Daughters."

"I know, child," Mother Cassel said, and the next morning she came to Abigail's grandmother and extended her invitation.

Mother Holton took her tea in the Looking Glass room when the voices changed. Her cup rattled when she put it down and she was certain it was from being startled by the angry words that whispered at her.

She knew from the Book and from experience that when the voices changed, they told more in their anger. She had ordered her sisters to listen for this and to double the Scrivener's Watch. It was the only comfort she could take from the change.

The last visitation, during her girlhood, had pointed them to the ruins in the southern deserts. It had taken nearly seventy years to find them and they'd lost many Daughters to the searching. But for the last fourteen years, their excavation there taught them much about the home their foremothers had forged for them so long ago. She listened to the voices until they passed. She had forgotten how bitter they were. *Time will do that*, she thought.

She looked up. "Sister Abernathy?"

Her plump, middle-aged day nurse bustled over. "Yes, Mother Holton?"

"Fetch Sister McDougall for me. I would speak with her in my sitting room."

Sister Abernathy nodded and waddled off to find the woman. Mother Holton finished her tea and tried not to feel sad at the loss. She knew it was an expected response. The voices affected most that way. The change usually disrupted commerce and sometimes even led to violence.

As they occur more and more frequently, she thought, *they will become more adept at handling them. Until the new Age of Unknowing comes to pass.* She said *they* because she knew she would not live to see it. The frequency between visitations increased but not in a way that could be measured and predicted. Hundreds of years of silence, then a smattering that became more regular until finally, the voices did not leave. Teachers would rise up, imparting divinity and destiny to them and slowly, mysticism would consume reason. It was easier than resisting. And, according to the Book, it would eventually undo the work of the Settler's Daughters over decades — even centuries — until the voices finally faded once more and the cycle began anew.

Of course, all of that would be years and years beyond her time. By then, Esther Hopewell's granddaughter, if she were to have one, would be an old woman. And that granddaughter's great grandchildren would be old by the time the world was put right again.

Sister McDougall was perhaps a dozen years younger than Mother Holton. Like the other Daughters, she'd given her life to studying the Book, learning the nuances of the god-voices. Now that they had changed, this would be her busiest time. But she sat across from Mother Holton now and didn't look distracted or annoyed by the interruption.

"Hello, Mother," she said, folding her hands in her lap.

"Hello, Sister. Is your Scrivener's Watch ready?"

Sister McDougall nodded. "It is. We'll get what we can. The change came faster than we expected."

"Yes," she said. Then she changed the subject. "I sent Sister Hopewell's daughter to you."

"I spoke with her," Sister McDougall said. "I've made talking-to's with several of the Daughters. The voices are harder on the younger girls."

Mother Holton remembered. "They were hard on me when I was young. But they brought me to the Daughters." She chuckled. "Before I heard the voices, my highest aim was to be a farm boy's nervous bride." For the first time in years she wondered what had become of Enoch Bentley. Dead by now most likely, but it wouldn't be hard to find out of a certainty . . . if she remembered to ask someone to look into it. *Enough lolligagging in yester-year, woman*, she scolded herself. Fixing her eye on Sister McDougall, she asked the question she dreaded. "How many of them do you think we will lose?"

Sister McDougall shrugged. "None if I can help it. Our coping techniques get better each time."

Mother Holton felt a chill and shivered. "Thank you, Sister McDougall. Please tell Sister Abernathy that I will sit here a spell and ring for her when I'm ready."

The woman inclined her head slightly. "Yes, Mother."

Mother Holton pulled at the quilt that covered her lap and Sister McDougall stooped to pull the heavy cotton patchwork up over her chest, tucking it in behind her. She smiled her thanks and the Sister returned it.

After the woman left her to return to work, Mother Holton sat alone in her sitting room and tried to remember what Enoch Bentley looked like.

He had whispered beneath her window the night she was to leave her grandmother's home to take up her studies in the Temple. The voices had quieted some time ago, but Enoch Bentley couldn't understand. He was a man — or at least very nearly so — and the god-voices passed over most of them. Less than understanding the voices, he couldn't understand her choice to join the Settler's Daughters.

She heard his voice and went to the window. "Enoch Bentley," she said in the angriest whisper she could manage, "you mustn't be here at this hour."

She was fourteen now; he was sixteen. The silver moon lit his blond hair and his eyes were red. "I don't want you to go," he said. Her grandmother slept soundly in the bed across the room, but not for long if the fool farm boy didn't keep his voice down. "Wait there," she said.

She slipped into the calico she'd worn earlier at the small gathering of friends and family her grandmother had hosted. Barefoot, she tip-toed out of the room and let herself out into the night.

She found him crouched beneath the apple tree. Now she could let the anger into her voice. "What are you doing here?"

He blushed. "I . . . I wanted to tell you something."

She crossed her hands over her chest and wondered what she'd ever seen in this awkward boy. Before the voices spoke, she'd been convinced that he was her future. They'd grown up together on the edge of Settler's Rest. She'd helped him with his ciphers and letters; he'd shown her how to trap a rabbit. One year, after the Pioneer Days picnic and barn dance, she'd told him that she would marry him someday and she'd kissed him quickly on the cheek. He'd blushed and run away. A few years later, his mother, a dour farm matron, negotiated dowry with her grandmother. But they had sent the cedar chest back to the farm just last week because Settler's Daughters did not marry.

She looked at him, now, and realized he'd been crying. Her voice was softer. "What do you need to tell me, Enoch Bentley? You know I'm leaving tomorrow for the Temple."

He stammered and his foot dug in the ground. "I don't want you to go, Abigail." His red eyes came up to meet hers. "I want you to stay. I want to be your husband and father your children."

She shook her head. "I cannot marry you. I have to follow my calling," she started to say by way of explanation. "The voices —"

"Gods damn the voices," he said, looking away. The anger in his voice stung like a slap. When their eyes met again, he looked ashamed and tragic. "I — I'm sorry."

When he turned and walked away, Abigail Holton stood and watched him go. *Let him go*, she told herself, *and let some other girl harvest his corn and babies.*

He could never understand, she told herself standing there beneath the apple tree, the grass and scrub around her washed in moonlight.

Enoch Bentley hadn't heard the god-voices; if he had, he would know that she was made for more than him.

Mother Holton stretched out beneath the heated quilts and sighed at another day gone past.

The god-voices had stayed angry until winter bled into spring and then suddenly they had stopped. Mother Holton met with the Sisters daily after that to hear what they'd learned listening for the scraps of truth amid the angry voices. It was long, slow work. Like the work of evolution or the work of the Book.

Between meetings she napped. Sometimes she napped *during* the meetings until someone coughed politely and startled her awake. Mother Holton told her keepers that with the change in weather, she no longer required the heated quilts. But they didn't listen and she was glad for it, though she kept that a secret. She felt cold all the time now.

The door opened and she heard Sister McDougall's quiet voice. "Mother Holton, are you awake?"

She sat up. "I am, Sister."

"I thought I should come to you first," Sister McDougall said, "because you've asked after her."

Daughter Hopewell. Mother Holton felt a stab of loss. She'd known there was something about the girl. "What has she done?"

"She and three of the other younger girls were caught teaching in the city."

It happened every time by the Book. Mother Holton sighed. "How long were they at it?"

Sister McDougall stepped further into the room, her face unreadable in the dim light. "A week maybe. We've gathered up everyone we can and we're working with them now."

Working with them. It sounded much nice than the reality. "And the girls?"

"They are restricted to quarters. I think we're catching them soon enough that we will be able to reclaim them." She paused, looking away for a moment. "But I don't know that of a certainty. I only have word of them that's gone before."

Mother Holton nodded. "You must do your best," she said. "And I will want to speak with Daughter Hopewell in the morning.

Sister McDougall inclined her head. "As you wish, Mother." Then she turned to the door. "I will bid you good sleeping."

"Thank you, Sister." Mother Holton closed her eyes and listened to quiet footfalls and the sound of the hinges whispering. A question struck her and she called out. "Sister McDougall?"

"Yes, Mother?"

Mother Holton opened her eyes. "What were they teaching in the city?"

Sister McDougall didn't say anything for a moment and Mother Holton wondered if something different happened, some new variation of infection that would eventually take them into a time where knowledge and reason meant nothing. But when Sister McDougall answered, it was an old familiar tune. "They were teaching that the voices prove we are not alone in the universe."

Yes. That was how it started. Mother Holton nodded. "Thank you. Good sleeping to you, Sister."

"Good sleeping, Mother," she said as she closed the door.

But Mother Holton took a long time finding sleep that night.

*

Daughter Abigail Holton put down her copy of the Book and stared out of the window at the moonless night. She sighed.

She'd seen him again that day and once again he'd not realized it was her beneath the cowl. It had been two years since they'd spoken and the newness of her calling had long worn off. The glamour she had imagined was mostly housework and cooking, though there were small projects with the Sisters and lots of classroom time. When she'd seen Enoch Bentley and his wagon in the merchant's square she was surprised at the feelings it evoked. He'd been selling corn to one of the produce booths and she had been running a message to the mayor's office for Mother Cassel.

She picked up the Book again but once more couldn't keep her mind upon the words. She tried meditating, but the only image she could conjure was straw-haired Enoch Bentley in his denim trousers and his loose-hanging, stained cotton shirt.

Finally, she gave up and went down to Daughter Henshaw's room. "I need the dress," she said when the freckled girl opened the door, rubbing the sleep from her eyes.

The dress was their best kept secret. Mother Cassel and the others would have had it burned if they knew, Abigail was certain of that.

Phoenicia Henshaw disappeared for a moment and came back with a bundle of cloth. She pushed it through the barely open door. "Now it's your turn to hide it," she whispered.

Abigail nodded. "It is."

She smuggled the dress back to her room and put it on beneath her cassock and cowl. Then, she slipped out her window and climbed into the nearby tree. She'd snuck in and out of the Temple dozens of times to visit her grandmother over the last two years. She easily slipped the gate guard and hid her cowl and cassock in the Pioneer graveyard on the southern side of the First Home Temple before turning west and making for Bentley Farm.

Damn fool girl, she told herself as she stood beneath an alder tree and watched his house. *What are you at?*

The windows were all dark. She moved beneath the one that she remembered was his room and stretched up to tap at it gently. Nothing.

She tapped again and then jumped when it groaned open. Enoch

Bentley looked down, alarm on his face turning to surprise. "Abigail Holton? What are you doing here?"

What *was* she doing here? She looked away. "I . . . I came to see you."

"In the middle of the night?" Maybe he saw the look on her face. Maybe he just didn't want to talk in whispers from the window. He frowned. "Meet me at the barn," he said.

She met him at the large double doors. He wore the same trousers and shirt she'd seen him in earlier, his high leather boots scuffed and cracked. He pushed one of the doors open and went inside. Abigail followed.

After they got inside, he lit the stub of a candle and put it on a tin plate. He opened his mouth, a questioning look on his face, and Abigail swallowed and pushed herself at him. Her mouth found his mouth and she kissed him like the pictures she'd seen in Mercurio's Notes on Human Behavior. At first, he tried to talk, but finally, he started kissing back.

She felt warmth in her belly, a tingling that spread into the rest of her body, out to her toes and fingers and hair.

When his hands moved over her hips and onto her breasts, she did not move them. When his mouth left hers and traced its way down the line of her jaw and along her neck, she shuddered and held her breath. Then, their hands were pulling at clothing as they pulled one another down into the straw.

It hurt fierce and hot when he pushed himself into her and Abigail ground her teeth to avoid crying out. But after a few thrusts, the pain became something like a sunrise that built inside her into light. When he gasped and moaned his seed into her, she imagined that her womb took it and planted it. *Come harvest*, she thought, *I'll give him his firstborn daughter and she will be strong and will not let the voices change her*. She would leave the Settler's Daughters proud of her shame and go to live a life of love in the midst of corn and babies and Enoch Bentley.

Afterwards, she lay in his arms and pretended it was their wedded bed.

"Have you left the Daughters then?" Enoch finally asked.

She turned so she could face him. "No," she said. "I'm going back after you're asleep and you'll not see me again."

He smiled. "Then I will never sleep again."

She said nothing. Instead, she pulled him closer and stroked his face and shoulders and side, pretending she would be there in the morning to cook breakfast while he tended to the farm in the early hours.

But after he was asleep, she stood and wiped herself clean with an old towel she found near the goat stall. Silently, she pulled her dress back on and fought back tears.

She could imagine all she wanted. She could dream a house full of children and a legacy of love. But in the end, she would go back to the voices and what they meant.

And if somehow Enoch Bentley's seed *did* take hold, Abigail would go to Mother Cassel, confess her transgressions and drink the Tander oil to end the pregnancy.

Tonight was a necessary detour, she told herself. A sacrifice was a sacrifice only when its worth was fully understood.

Mother Holton insisted that they take her to the girl's room. They sat her in a chair in the corner and waited outside. Esther Hopewell sat on the edge of her bed, her red-rimmed eyes dark from lack of sleep. "What will happen to me?" she asked.

Mother Holton smiled. "You'll be reclaimed from the voices."

The girl's eyes went wide and her voice trembled. "I don't want to be reclaimed."

They never did. But with time, the voices outside — incessant and reasonable and calm — would offset the internal ones and the girl would find the discipline to hold those ghosts at bay. The old woman nodded. "Nonetheless," she said. She leaned forward. "You've read the Book, child. You understand why."

The young girl's eyes filled with water. "And after that?"

"You'll be watched for a spell. And then you'll be sent home."

A tear spilled over. "This is the only home I've ever known."

Mother Holton reached over and patted her knee. "And so it shall continue to be. But it will be different for you now." She paused. "And your friends will be back to the farms." *Watched for a spell,* she thought, *and kept far apart to keep a resurgence from occuring.* The Seventeenth Age of Unknowing would come soon enough — no point helping it come faster.

When the girl spoke next, Mother Holton heard the loneliness in her voice. "I don't know if I even want to be alive anymore," Esther Hopewell said.

"Of course you don't," Mother Holton said. "But you don't have to know anything right now but this: Sister McDougall and the others will help you if you let them."

I could tell her, Mother Holton thought. *I could tell her that it is the easiest truth of all. That we are not alone in this universe as long as we have each other, as long as we have the Settlement.* But some truths could not be freely given — they had to be slowly revealed because the process of revelation was the true engine of change. They would spend months with her, reclaiming her from the god-voices, and in the end she'd live out her days in quiet service to the Settler's Daughters or marry into the Farming Combine and live among someone's corn and babies.

She realized that Daughter Hopewell had spoken quietly and she started. "What did you say, child?"

"For a moment," she repeated, "I was certain I was not alone."

Mother Holton remembered that feeling. She'd felt it three times. Twice, it was the voices. Promises of home and love followed by threats and wrath and the ranting echoes of a people driven mad long ago. But she'd felt it one other time, that night so long ago, when she'd pretended to be Enoch Bentley's bride.

"You are not alone," Mother Holton said.

The sacrifice gnawed at her for a month. Abigail Holton sobbed at night when no one could see or hear. She found herself oversleeping and unable to focus on her studies. When Enoch Bentley's letter found her, snuck in through an elaborate network of Daughters' errands, it reached her at her lowest point. She'd been scolded twice already that week and she had just realized she was late with her bleeding. She opened his letter, read it and discovered there were even darker basements beneath the lowest places of her heart. Like the voices, Enoch Bentley's letter started with promises of love and home, then became angry and cajoling.

The full weight of the sacrifice didn't strike her until later in the day. When she suddenly burst into tears in the middle of dinner, she found herself in front of Mother Cassel's desk as snowflakes fell outside the window behind, shining silver in the moonlight.

"I do not think you need the Tander oil just yet," Mother Cassel said after Abigail told her story. "You are under tremendous strain. Wait a few more days and then see me if you've not started."

Abigail Holton sniffed, wiping her eyes with the sleeve of her cassock. "Will I need to be reclaimed, Mother?"

Mother Cassel laughed. "Good lords, no, child." She clicked her tongue against the roof of her mouth. "If they made such a way as to reclaim the heart from love, we'd all be better off."

"I do not love Enoch Bentley," she said.

Mother Cassel chuckled again. "You do not know that you do today. But someday you will and it will help you to know that you've chosen well." She leaned forward in her chair. "You *were* making a sacrifice, weren't you?"

Stunned, she nodded slowly. "How did you know?"

"The Addenda speaks of it. It is a common theme among certain of the Settler's Daughters."

Abigail swallowed. "What does that mean?"

Mother Cassel smiled. "Nothing to worry on tonight, child." She sat back in her chair. "But it speaks highly of you, on that you can be sure."

That night, she carefully folded Enoch's letter and hid it away beneath her mattress. From then forward, she read it every night until it faded so badly that she could not read it, holding it in her hands until it finally fell apart.

But even long after that, she lay awake nights and recited it from memory until it simply became some small part of the other voices she remembered.

Mother Holton sipped her tea and looked out on autumn. She sat wrapped in the quilt but near the window so she could see the ducks on the pond. There was a knock at the door and she turned towards it. "Yes?"

Esther Hopewell stepped into the room. "Hello, Mother," she said.

"Hello, Esther Hopewell." She hated that she could no longer call her daughter. "Sister McDougall tells me that you are leaving us."

Esther Hopewell nodded. "I am, Mother."

"What will you do, child?"

The girl shook her head. "I do not know. I will find work in the city. Maybe I will meet a nice boy and bear him a daughter."

Mother Holton nodded. "Maybe you will." Her reclamation had

gone well, but Mother Holton had assumed it would. She'd finally understood what she'd known about this girl but she was certain that the girl did not know it yet. She would know it later when the irony of this sacrifice would make her laugh for years to come. But for now, Esther Hopewell was simply a strong young woman who had once been a Settler's Daughter before the voices changed her life.

I came by the voices and she leaves by them, Mother Holton thought. She raised her hand for the Matriarchal Blessing. "Go ye in grace and peace, Esther Hopewell. Be fruitful and Settle the land."

"Thank you, Mother," she said. She curtsied and then left.

Sister Abernathy came in shortly after, carrying a tray with a steaming bowl and a piece of bread. She helped Mother Holton into bed and then placed the tray on her lap. "I've done that looking into you asked of me, Mother," she said.

Mother Holton lifted the spoon to her mouth, tasting the sweet corn chowder. She couldn't remember any *looking into* that she'd needed recently. But she'd learned not to show it, to simply nod and wait.

"He died six years ago," Sister Abernathy continued. "I talked with his daughter when I was in South Hold last week. He left many children and grandchildren behind." She laughed. "There were Bentleys all over down there."

Mother Holton nodded. She vaguely remembered hearing that he'd gone south with the earlier expeditions more years back than she could count. "He lived a full life then," she said in a quiet voice.

Sister Abernathy leaned forward. "Who was he, Mother?"

"Someone I wanted to have a happy life," she said. "And it sounds like he did."

She finished her corn chowder, soaking the bread in what little remained to soften it for the teeth she still had. When she was done, Sister Abernathy took the tray away just as the linen boy entered with her stack of heated quilts.

They tucked her in and left her to nap, but instead of sleeping, she laid awake and remembered that night long ago, the night she'd given herself to Enoch Bentley in order to understand what she was giving up to serve the Settler's Daughters, to give her life to the mystery of the voices in the quiet halls of the First Home Temple. Words came back to her, a voice that spoke promises of love and home, and for the first time in years, she found herself reciting Enoch

Bentley's letter. She was surprised that she still remembered most of the words, and she spoke them now quietly as if they were a prayer of great power. She moved slowly through the first half, telling herself that it was to savor the beauty of them. *Lie to yourself, old woman, see what it will get you.* She recited the first half slowly so that she would be asleep before the voice changed. She did not want to hear the angry voices tonight — not the voices that had driven her to Temple so long ago. Not the voice of Enoch Bentley that had given her calling a value beyond a young girl's fervor. She closed her eyes and smelled the fresh-plowed earth.

In her dreams that night, Abigail Holton raised corn and babies. Beneath it all was a whispering she could just barely discern.

God-voices assuring she would never be alone.

THE MUSIC OF THE SPHERES

A bie finally gave up on the radio when five passes yielded nothing but shit-kicking music and indignant talk show hosts that tried too hard to be a cool they would never attain. Silence was preferable to that so he gripped the wheel and watched the headlights swallow highway.

When he saw the hitchhiker ahead, he considered it well-timed kismet. At least, he thought, it would be someone to talk to.

He edged the Ford to the shoulder and hit reverse. The dark clothed figure stepped into the scrub, out of the way, as he braked.

The door opened and Abie adjusted the guitar on the back seat to make room for a rucksack and what looked like a cello case.

"Climb in," he said. "Toss your stuff in the back."

Without a word, the hitcher pushed the gear into the back seat and pulled the passenger door closed.

"Where you headed?" Abie eased the car forward and back onto the road.

"Tahoe," the girl said.

Abie went for a second look. Maybe it was her height, maybe the way she carried herself, but with the hood pulled up and the bulky overcoat, he'd been convinced it was a guy. Maybe that was the goal, he thought. Out alone on a Nevada highway, truly the middle of nowhere.

"So where you from?"

She stared out of the window away from him. "Could we listen to the radio?"

The shit-kickers still ruled the airwaves. He sighed and drove in silence.

Thirty minutes later, he picked up another hitchhiker. This time he wasn't exactly sure why. He intended to drive past the dark clothed figure but found himself pulling over. He even climbed out of the car and moved his guitar to the trunk.

This one climbed in with a rucksack and a violin case.

"Where you headed?" he asked this one over his shoulder.

"Tahoe," she said. Both were dressed alike. Both hid their faces in shadowing hoods and looked away.

He shook his head, trying to shake off the strangeness. It *felt* strange, like an uncanny deja vu, and yet *he* felt calm. Almost like that slight floating feeling after his first cigarette in two weeks.

Thirty minutes later, he stopped again. This time, he moved everything to the trunk and even helped the newest addition load her harp case. He had no idea how it all fit. It seemed like something out of a bad commercial with clowns and cars, only in reverse.

"Let me guess," he said. "Tahoe?"

The slightest nod of the hood and he climbed back into the car.

Abie Kincaid still felt too good to wonder much. Three tall girls, each with musical instruments, each dressed alike, twenty miles apart on a deserted highway in the middle of the night. No big deal. Instead, he daydreamed about the shows he would play. Someday. He had a pack of songs he'd written along with the covers he'd learned. He'd fed himself a solid diet of folk and alternative rock. Dylan and McLean, the Goo Goo Dolls and Matchbox 20. It was, he thought, only a matter of time.

So what if Jessica thought he was terrible. She'd be the first in the line, he knew, when Abie Kincaid shoved the shit-kickers over far enough for him to have his own corner of the airwaves.

His daydreaming ate up an hour.

"We need to stop," all three hitchhikers said in unison. When they spoke together their voices were liquid, blending into a tone that ran over his entire body like a warm, soft tongue.

They gestured to a small roadside bar. He pulled up and parked. "How long ladies?"

The first one he'd picked up turned towards him. "We've been untruthful. We are not going to Tahoe."

He suddenly thought that perhaps this was their stop. His stomach sank as the bizarre well-being drained away like so much bath water. "Where are you going then?"

"Midway."

He scratched his head, remembering senior history three years ago with Mr. Frunk. "The island?"

The second one shook her head. "No. Northern Idaho. On the border."

Relief flooded him and he smiled. "Oh. I can take you there."

"Yes," the third one said. "We thought so."

The slight buzz became a full-on drunk. "We might need a map," he said.

"And currency," the first said.

"And a new car," the second said.

"Bring your guitar," the third said.

So he did. They all walked into the bar and when they pushed back their hoods they were each uniquely and stunningly beautiful. Each wore their hair short, one copper, one brunette and the last blonde. Their eyes wouldn't allow him to find their color — they were deep and wide and undulating.

Every man in the bar stopped what he was doing and watched, slack-jawed. Every woman did the same, only with hard glances that said *step-off* or something like it.

One hitcher moved to the wall of slot machines.

Another headed towards the pool table.

The last took Abie's arm firmly and steered him towards the stage. A country western band was wrapping up an old tune about cheating hearts.

The owner came over in a hurry.

"My friend is a performer," the girl said.

"Sorry miss. We already have a band for the night."

Abie watched the magic work. A slight smile pulled at the corners of the owner's mouth. His eyes glistened, too. He was catching whatever drunk she had tossed Abie. "They can play later," she said.

"I reckon so," he said, grinning. He walked over to the amp cord and yanked it. The lead singer came over, red faced. The room buzzed anger.

"What the hell you doing, hoss?"

"Change in plans."

The girl laid her hand on the singer's arm. His face remained red but the anger left it. Now he blushed.

Then Abie was on stage, tuning his guitar and doing a mic test. The girl opened his guitar case at the foot of the stage and fixed her gaze on him.

Abie lost everything in the room except for that pair of eyes. He lost the music. He lost the lyrics. He lost his soul. But he sang. Christ Almighty, for the first time in his life he truly sang.

When he finished, the guitar case overflowed with bills. The line of people, red eyed from crying, hoarse from screaming his name, slipped out of the bar into the dawn.

"We have to go," the girl said, dumping the cash into a whiskey carton the owner had provided.

The other two joined them, each with plastic sacks. Near as he could tell, everyone including the owner must be going away with empty pockets. The slot machines were dark now, too, and silent.

They pulled onto the highway as a nondescript sedan with tinted windows pulled in.

They helped themselves to a used Chevy at Slim's Quality Pre-Owned Cars and Wedding Chapel just outside of Reno. They left Abie's car and two thousand dollars cash in the space where it had been, then turned north.

The girls talked more now. But still not much. They also left their hoods down.

"Where are *you* headed?" the redhead asked.

Abie's high had peaked with the show. His face hurt from the grin. "Midway."

The blonde laughed. "Before you picked us up."

Abie glanced at her in the mirror. "Seattle."

The brunette chimed in. "Home of Nirvana."

They all sighed. Even Abie.

The miles spun away beneath them. They stopped for food, for gas, and for restrooms. They ate in the car, on the road, occasionally looking backward.

"Why are we going to Midway?" he asked as they passed through Sand Point.

"We're not. We're going just past it," the blonde said.

"But why?"

They answered in unison again. "We have a performance there." Abie laughed as their combined voices washed over him and enjoyed the growing lump in his jeans for another forty miles.

Twice in Sand Point and once in Bonner's Ferry he thought he saw more nondescript sedans conveniently waiting at intersections. At one point, during a more secluded stretch of road, he thought he'd seen a black helicopter in his side mirror, low over the trees and silent.

His traveling companions seemed quieter. They'd seen, too, he thought.

They turned off for Midway, a small, out-of-the-way border crossing. It was choked with black sedans. The helicopter was there as well. Men and women in dark suits milled about.

"Do I turn around?" Abie felt panic eating away at his calm.

"No," all three said.

"We don't have time," the redhead said. She sat beside him in the passenger seat and looked at the sky, studying it carefully. "We only have an hour."

Abie pulled up to the stop sign in front of the guard station. The border patrol officer stood behind a man and a woman wearing dark suits.

"Where are you from?" asked the man.

"Where are you headed?" asked the woman.

Abie saw the snipers on the roof now, saw the men against trees just inside the forest. All this side of the border. The other side appeared to be business as usual.

He started to say Nevada, but the blonde touched his shoulder from the backseat. The redhead leaned over him. "I'm just a poor wayfaring stranger," she said, "a-traveling through this world of woe."

"But there's no sickness, toil, or danger," the blonde said, "In that bright world to which I go."

The man and the woman backed up. "Please step out of the vehicle," he said, reaching under his jacket.

Three car doors opened. Three voices joined together: "I'm going there to meet my mother, she said she'd meet me when I come." It became song. "I'm only going over Jordan. I'm only going over Home."

Abie watched as the three women converged on the two suits. As they took slow, deliberate strides, he watched rifles raised and pistols drawn. He held his breath. They continued singing. One by one, the guns dropped. Then the hands that held them. And then the bodies attached to the hands until the asphalt, roof and forest were a kindergarten classroom strewn with sleeping children.

They climbed back into the car. Abie felt the draw of the song and felt his euphoria battling the drowsiness that stole over him. He also felt the words. The desire to join in had gripped him from the start but he'd held back.

"Drive," they said. And he did.

They left the highway not far into Canada and drove down a dirt road until it ended in the forest. A creek murmured past on their left and a trail wandered off on their right. The hitchhikers grabbed their packs and their instruments.

"This is it?" Abie asked. "Your performance is here?"

They nodded.

His soul became a leaking balloon, elation rushing out from it.

"You're more than welcome to watch." The redhead smiled at him.

"Bring your guitar," the blonde said.

"Fifteen minutes to curtain." The brunette broke the fern barrier and moved down the trail.

They went at a good clip; Abie followed after. Somewhere behind him, he thought he heard a car door slam but he ignored it. They walked for ten minutes, then stopped in a clearing.

The instruments came out with practiced speed. He sat on the edge of the clearing.

"Three minutes," the blonde said.

Silence. Stillness. The sound of beating hearts. The sound of wind rustling leaves. Of grass bending beneath the weight of bugs. Of footsteps on the trail behind.

And then music exploded.

It burst from the instruments in a perfect unified chord. It burst from the throats in a honeyed tone that permeated the air. They began to sing and play and Abie watched.

The suited men watched, too, from where they stood at the end of the trail. They were helpless to act.

In the beginning was the song. They sang it, each voice strong and blended with the others. A song about long ago and far away, vast distances in space and time. A song about the Four who became Three because of terrible war far from home. A song about a song; one sung to bind the darkness in the Cosmos and halt the Hater's spread. Abie had never heard anything like it.

And yet he knew it.

A song about long traveling in night to find the next binding place.

The words pushed at his lips and pulled at his tongue. His fingers fumbled with his guitar case. Still he held back.

A song about a Fourth found in the desert.

"Join us," they said and he gave in to it.

Drawing his guitar like a great flaming sword, he strummed and added his note to their chord, added his voice to their choir, joining their war. He stood with them now in the clearing and watched the suits watch them. Their faces were washed with love and hope and wonder.

The Three spoke into his mind now. *This binding will hold ten thousand years,* they said. *If we but sing true.*

The ecstasy burst within Abie like a hundred collapsing suns, the heat pouring in on itself. He felt his sneakered feet leave the ground and saw that they too were lifted up. White beams shot from their instruments now and from their mouths and eyes. As the Four raised, their hair flowed upwards as if caught in a waterfall of light that defied gravity. The performance reached a crescendo and Abie knew, just as the girls did, that it had been a success. He also knew of other scheduled performances waiting ahead of them. Other worlds locked in the raging war. But first, to rest in the place that he was made for and made from.

He smiled and they smiled too.

Then light took the Four and carried them Home.

FOUR CLOWNS OF THE APOCALYPSE
AND THE MECCA OF MIRTH

Bunko the Clown died in the arms of a New Vegas hooker. It was an un-discussed contradiction given his full title: Bunko the *Gospel* Clown. After a quiet burial, Stan promoted into the vacant position and the Three Clowns of the Apocalypse held open auditions in the spacious back room of the Two Headed Lizard. Their sole applicant arrived, passed through the hoots and whistles of the noisy main room, and stood waiting in the doorway.

Giggles spoke first. "A girl."

"Yowza," Cuddles said and nervously twisted a balloon into a five-legged poodle.

The new Bunko kept quiet.

"I'm here about the position." Not just a girl; a slip of a girl. Young, but old enough to attract the attention of the bar.

Giggles pointed to the pile of clown-gear. "Do you know what to do with it?"

She nodded and walked to the table. She started separating the gear with practiced confidence while the Three took notes and whispered among themselves.

"A girl," Giggles said again.

"The Good Lord works in mysterious ways," Bunko finally said, testing his new vocabulary. "And she seems to know what she's doing."

Cuddles spoke last. "Yowza." The balloon popped in his hands.

They watched the girl pull her long hair back into a bun. She opened a jar of cold cream and rubbed it into her face, then wiped it off with a floral-patterned towel. Next, she opened the Captain Jangles White Number Twenty Seven and smeared the greasepaint over her skin. She didn't look at them, her attention fixed on the table. Powder. Brush. Ignoring the mirror, she deftly etched the bright red star over her left eye and forehead with a grease-stick, then drew out and filled in her mouth until it formed a banana smile. Stan the Clown took shape before them.

She dropped the carpenter's apron with its multitude of pockets over her shoulders, fastened it, and pulled on the baggy pants and bright yellow shirt accented with pink puff balls reminiscent of cotton candy. Leaving on her low-cut boots, she pulled the purple bread-loaf shoes over them. Then the Crazy-Perm Sparkle Wig with its little beanie propeller cap sewn onto the top. Putty nose and last, the gloves.

Giggles looked at his oversized pocket watch. "Fifteen minutes."

"Twenty-five is goal," Bunko said. "Jehovah bless me."

"Yowza."

Giggles pointed to another table. "Show us what you've got."

Nodding, the girl picked up three brightly painted frag grenades and juggled them, turning them into a rainbow above her moving hands. Without warning, a click, a clank and the blue grenade shot forward to land easily in Cuddles' outstretched glove. The Three stared at it. They looked up at a whizzing sound and watched her work two razor yo-yos with careful precision, slicing bits off the test dummy with each throw and pull. They nodded.

She tied and floated three gas balloon bunnies. She stripped down and re-assembled a napalm tuba. She pop-gunned stuffed chickens from the back of a tricycle while playing "Damn Those Baptists" on a kazoo. Gracefully, she flowed through the regiment.

"Take a seat." Giggles pointed to the stool.

She flipped it over, sealed the saw-cut leg with Insta-Hold, and then sat.

Thick gloves muted their applause. "Nicely done, Praise the Lord," Bunko said.

She dipped her head; a slight bow.

Now the questions. Bunko went first since he'd most recently held the position. "What is the chief end of Stan the Clown?"

The girl looked him in the eye. "To gladden the hearts of the innocent, bring hope to the forsaken and death to the lovers of chaos and wrong."

"And his secondary, thank *you* Jesus?"

"Knock-knock jokes."

Bunko nodded.

Cuddles went next. "Yowza?"

"Yowza Zammy Bam Bim Boo," she said with the beginnings of a nervous smile.

Cuddles nodded. He and Bunko both turned to Giggles.

His words were slow in coming and carefully selected. "We are the Four Clowns of the Apocalypse —"

Bunko interrupted. "Three, actually, at the moment."

Giggles glowered. "Our peril is often dire, our laughter is often long and our tears are never seen. Why do you wish to join our ranks?"

She stared at him for a full minute. "Knock knock?"

"Who's there?" Giggles and Bunko asked, taken aback.

"Iva."

"Iva who?"

She leaned forward. "Iva seen the Great Clown-Maker and I know where he lives," she said, slow and nearly a whisper.

They looked back and forth between themselves. "You're hired," they said in one voice excepting Cuddles. But everyone knew what his *Yowza* meant.

Giggles, Cuddles, Bunko and Stan set out for Clown Mountain that afternoon. They rode hot wasteland winds in their pedal-action mini-blimp.

"We use the mini for local gigs," Giggles told Stan by way of explanation. They pedaled at an easy pace high above the fused glass, sand and rock of the man-made desert.

Stan nodded. "How long is the ride?"

"We'll be home by morning, praise the Lord," Bunko said.

Just before sunset, the ground below shifted to scrub. The sky purpled like a bruise and stars poked tentative, faded fingers of light through the tapestry. As the moon lifted, its silver light etched the landscape below and outlined the shape of a mountain in the distance.

They rode in silence, the *whup whup* of the mini's four large propellers like a heartbeat in the night. Sometime after midnight they passed over the watch-fires of a mutie tribe. A few shouts, a few flaming arrows peaking and dropping a full ten feet beneath them. Then stillness.

"Bless their hearts," Bunko said.

"Yowza." Cuddles slipped a frag grenade back into his pocket.

Giggles looked over his shoulder. "Tell us about the Great Clown-Maker. Does he still live?"

Naturally, they'd heard legends. Five hundred years of storytelling passed from clown to clown. How the First Four had traveled the madness on the heels of the Last War, sent out by Captain Jangles to make the world safe.

"Of a fashion," the girl said. "His soul lives. His wisdom lives. But trapped in a dangerous place."

"And does he still make clowns?"

"He made me." She paused. "Knock knock?"

"Who's there?"

"Juana."

"Juana who?"

"Juana see him for yourselves?"

"That," Giggles said, "is precisely why we hired you."

The sun rose over the forested foothills of Clown Mountain. Giggles pulled a retractable wand from his pocket, extended it, and keyed a switch. Red light blinked from its tip like an allergic eye. Hidden in the trees below and ahead, laser cannons and hunter missiles hiccuped and went back to restless sleep. In occasional grassy fields, Electric Death Cats the size of ponies stretched in the morning sun, recharging from the night's patrols.

Clown Mountain, once named simply SAP Center 3, filled their forward view, a balding head of stone ringed by Evergreen hair on its lower slopes. Legend told of three Self-Sustaining Armageddon Preparedness Centers. The first, a radioactive gravel pit by either malfunction or malfeasance, somewhere in the lost east. The second, far north in the Domain of the Claus. That cult of red-suits had long ago diverted its weapon production capacity in the direction of food and tools delivered regularly by jet-sleigh throughout the reach of their territory.

The original Giggles, centuries ago, had learned of the SAP Centers from a grandfather who'd once commanded the Corps of Engineers. The general, on his burn-blackened death bed, passed the wand to his only surviving heir while the other Three stood guard outside. Then, after fighting their way across the ruins and chaos of a dying world, they finally knew they'd found a home and headquarters beneath the growling mountain.

The mini-blimp descended gradually, Giggles and Cuddles working the levers that, in turn, worked the flaps and ballast. A large blister of stone peeled back and they settled into the hangar.

Stan looked around wide-eyed. The others followed her gaze as she took in the massive Vertical Lift Battle Wagon, its steel hide bristling with armament and painted in the colors of the rainbow.

They unstrapped themselves and Stan walked over to it. Giggles followed. "The Clown Around," he said.

"I've heard of it," she said. "I've never seen it."

Bunko walked over. "Now by the grace of Holy God you'll fly it." He clapped her on the back.

"Yowza," Cuddles said in agreement.

"Here's the plan," Giggles said. "First, sleep. Cuddles, you show Stan her room. Tonight we'll pull the maps. Tomorrow morning, we'll load up and head out."

"What are we going to do?" Stan asked.

Giggles looked thoughtfully at the girl. "We're going to see Captain Jangles, the Great Clown-Maker."

"Why, Dear Lord?" Bunko asked. "Why?"

"To bring him home."

"Yowza?"

Giggles remained silent for a moment, watching the light flicker over their white-caked faces. "Because he's our father. Because, besides each other, he's the only family we have."

Stan the Clown looked down. Her quiet words held sadness. "No one should have to be alone in this world."

"Amen," Bunko said.

The Clown Around's engines whined them into the air. They lifted two hundred meters before Giggles dropped the nose and engaged the thrusters.

After much-needed sleep they'd gathered in the Playroom, faces scrubbed pink and hair wet from showers, loose-hanging fatigues fresh from the laundry-bot and smelling like soap. The beginnings of wrinkles and receding hairlines contrasted with the new Stan's youth. She'd pointed to the place on the map and there had been brief conversation. Supplies they would need. What they might encounter along the way.

"How long ago were you there?" Giggles asked.

She shrugged. "A year or two back."

"How did you get in?"

"By the grace of —" Bunko started.

She interrupted. "I fought."

Giggles' eyes narrowed. "Why?"

"I wanted to be a clown. I . . . I'd heard stories."

"Yowza?" Cuddles pointed to the map.

"The Mecca of Mirth," she said by way of answer. "Proud sponsors of Captain Jangles and His Clown Brigade."

They rocketed east, strapped tightly into the Battle Wagon's crew seats. They were back in costume again. Behind them, piled high in the cargo hold, were the tools of their trade. Tricycles with rear-mounted machine guns. Oversized spray pumps of various gases. Self-propelled pie throwers with whipped Qwik-Die cream. Exploding paddle balls and phosphorous Easter eggs. And for Bunko's benefit, box upon box of gospel tracts to fulfill the secondary of his new position. They'd fill the pockets of their Kevlar-lined aprons when they landed.

Stan sat in the co-pilot's seat. Giggles looked at her after they were two hours out. "Want to try it?"

Stan grinned. "Sure."

"Take the stick."

She did and he hit a button. The Clown Around bucked and listed momentarily as she adjusted to the controls.

"Nice, eh?" Bunko said. "I remember my first time."

"Me too," said Giggles, his wide smile broadened by the make-up.

Cuddles unbuckled his harness, leaned forward and flicked several switches. Calliope music filled the cabin as interior and exterior speakers vibrated to life. Below, a herd of mutie cows scattered as the Battle Wagon's shadow chased them across yellowed prairie.

"Knock knock," Stan said.

"Who's there?"

"Yeah."

"Yeah who?"

Her whoop drowned out the circus music; Giggles and Bunko joined in and Cuddles honked the horn on his lapel. "Yahoo!"

*

They landed in the late afternoon near the center of a burned out city. The ruins seemed deserted. The bright colored Rad Patches blended into their costumes and immediately tilted towards yellow but held. They checked one another's gear after stuffing their pockets with equipment and set out. Stan rode the electo-trike; Bunko stood behind her and manned the gun. Giggles and Cuddles rode scooters. They moved silently in the shadows of twisted metal and piled stone, dodging debris as they went.

"Are you sure you're ready for this, second day on the job and all?" Bunko asked Stan. "Shall I lead you in a prayer or perhaps quote you a bit of edifying scripture?"

Her hands tensed on the handlebars. "I'm fine."

They rolled to a gate set into the side of a massive half-blasted concrete dome. Scattered across the dome, bulbous outcroppings and spires thrust against the sky in various states of decay. Bits of paint flaked colorlessly away. A large Perma Sign over the gate proclaimed that the Mecca of Mirth was Closed Due To Holocaust.

"The automations are still working," Stan said in a low voice. "And they're deadly. We'll be safe once we get to the Great Clown-Maker's Big Top."

Giggles checked the gate, pushing and pressing in various places. He looked at Cuddles. "Explosives?"

"Yowza."

Stan slipped past. "I can get us in. First time, I went in underground. But Captain Jangles gave me his code."

She whistled the first few bars of "Margaret's Methothist Mother" and with a whir and a click the gate spun open.

The Three nodded, impressed.

"Secure the rides," Giggles said. "We're on foot from here."

They did. Cuddles tied a gas balloon kitten and held it ready. Bunko sailed a Light of the World Self-Combusting Sparkle Plane into the dim courtyard ahead; illumination dripped from its wings. Deep beneath their oversized shoes machinery thrummed to life.

The first few generations of Apocalypse Clowns had written down much of their memories of Before Times. Very little had been written about the Meccas of Mirth. They were the life-work of that Great Baptist Liar and Cheat, Reverend G. Spenser Rowl, the man who had tricked Captain Jangles and a dozen others into selling their namesakes for a pittance. Originally, there were three Meccas of Mirth but one in a place called Eastern Europe was firebombed in the Second Revolution. The other two were lost in the Apocalypse ninety years later.

"Here's the drill," Giggles said. His secondary was tactics and covert operations. "I'll take point. Cuddles, you've got the rear." Stan and Bunko filled out the sides of a narrow, diamond-shaped formation. They moved cautiously forward together.

The courtyard was a labyrinth of collapsed stone and iron ringed by cartoonish, dilapidated storefronts. Tinny speakers guttered to life and lights flickered tentatively, remnants of an automated holo-program.

A hand of blue light waved, interrupted by the piles of rubble. "Welcome to the Mecca of Mirth," an announcer said. "Home of Arnie Aardvark, Philo P. Ferret and . . ." Here a chorus of kids chimed in: "Captain Jangles and His Clown Brigade!"

A crackle, a hiss and they saw caricatures of themselves in the air above. The images juggled, danced and pantomimed. "Giggles! Cuddles! Bunko! And Stan!" Applause and cheers throughout.

Then the system shut down.

A smell of burning fur reached them, despite the filters in their Mark III Gas-Away Noses.

"Rad-rats?" Giggles asked. Stan nodded.

The odor grew. Initially, they heard the scrape of claws. Then the gasp of ragged breath. Then the crackle of fried skin rubbing against itself. A green glow punctuated the air.

The Four Clowns of the Apocalypse stood silent and still. A rad-rat scuttled into view, its pale light illuminating melted fur, black eyes and yellow teeth. Cuddles launched his balloon. It shot out and slowed over the dog-sized rodent. Bunko's Flaming Dart of the Evil One pierced it easily and the skillfully tied kitten burst into a haze of nerve toxin.

The rad-rat twitched and vomited, gnashing its teeth as it buckled. A second, just behind it, scurried backwards as the small cloud dissipated.

Stan's fingers flew over the keys of her napalm tuba. Liquid fire arched out and the second rad-rat collapsed beneath burning rain.

Giggle's razor yo-yo shredded a third as it tried to flank them. Bunko obliterated a fourth with a Thus Saith The Lord Exploding Bible.

"Yowza," Cuddles said after the ringing in their ears stopped.

"Let's go," Giggles said.

They left the courtyard, their shoes gently slapping the ground. As they drew closer to the center of the complex the Four picked out rays of sunlight slanting through the hole in the dome above. Light played over motes of dust that swarmed like angry gnats. As they passed monolithic rides and collapsed attractions, a distant voice ahead gradually rose to an electronic bellow.

"P-Popcorn, p-peanuts, cotton c-candy." They heard the clanking and clunking and stopped. A monstrosity loomed in the shadows of Pirate Pete's Lagoon of Luck. Sparks flashed beneath metal joints. Three electric eyes the size of soccer balls cast beams of light that swept over the Four.

Stan the Clown drew three grenades, tossing them lightly in an arch of color between her hands. "Snack-Mack."

The Snack-Mack snorted smoke and stomped towards them. It smelled of burnt sugar. "Popcorn, peanuts, cotton candy." A large funnel-ended tube worked its way free of the tangled wires and metal, pointing itself at the Four. "Or maybe," the Snack-Mack said, "Caramel covered clowns?"

Hot brown goop shot out of the cannon. Stan ducked. Giggles dodged. Cuddles rolled. The sticky wad engulfed Bunko and he fell beneath it, paralyzed as it hardened on impact.

Stan's first grenade bounced off the metal and exploded somewhere to its left. The second tore off the cannon. A bit of shrapnel raggedly parted Giggle's wig.

"Careful," he said as he backed up.

Stan looked sheepish. "Sorry."

Cuddles drew his slingshot and aimed. One of the eyes shattered. The acid jawbreaker began its long journey, melting its way deeper into the Snack-Mack's head.

The machine turned broadside, small doors flipping open. Peanuts blasted them, cutting through their costumes and lacerating what their aprons did not protect. Their arms, faces and legs stung from the salty cuts.

Pop. Another eye flashed out. Hiss. Another trail of acid traced its way into the Snack-Mack's system.

Stan's third grenade took out a leg. Giggles fired his peel-rifle at another leg and the monster slipped.

A hot blast of cotton candy knocked Cuddles over. His shot went wild. The jawbreaker clipped Stan's left earlobe. She howled and dropped her fourth grenade. Giggles lunged in, kicking it away and beneath the falling Snack-Mack. Its massive weight muffled the explosion.

They stood panting, blood and makeup running together.

"Could someone," Bunko's muffled voice said behind them, "for the Love of God get me out of this?"

They fought their way forward for hours. Rad-rats, Cleaning Bots, and even Automatic Dwarves complete with Laser Pick Axes from the Under The Mountain Mining Mystery ride. At last, weary and wounded, the Four Clowns of the Apocalypse stood before the Big Top.

"We made it," Giggles said.

"Yowza," Cuddles said.

"Can I hear an Amen?" Bunko asked.

Stan said nothing at all.

The doors opened automatically and hissed shut behind them after they'd walked through. The air inside smelled musty. The Big Top was empty and completely intact, row after row of bleachers ringing a built-up stage. High above, trapezes and hoops hung still. A hum filled their heads. Overhead, speakers crackled to life. An announcer's voice overlaying excited murmuring.

"What time is it, kiddies?"

A crowd of children: "It's time for Captain Jangles!"

"What time is it?"

The children's voices were replaced by a theme song: "Time for Captain Jangles and His (hyuk hyuk) Clown Brigade!"

The lights dropped. The air chilled. Movement flickered in the center ring. The Four Clowns of the Apocalypse walked forward slowly.

An old man in baggy clothes guttered and hissed as he stood up from his chair. The chair was real. The old man, however, was a projection. He turned to them, his face suddenly alarmed, his mouth opening to speak. There was an unspoken warning in his eyes. Then he vanished momentarily and blurred back into focus. He smiled.

"My Sons," he said, stretching out his arms. "You've come home to me."

"Who are you?" Giggles asked with narrow eyes. "Or should I ask *what?*"

"I am the Great Clown-Maker. I am Captain Jangles. Or at

least, all that remains of him." He smiled widely. "And you are what remains of my Clown Brigade."

"We thought you were dead. The First Four wrote that you died just after the Last War."

"My body died. My soul lived on . . . here in the Mecca of Mirth. That damn Rowl bought me and kept me."

"So you sent the girl?" Giggles asked. "Why did you wait so long? It's been five hundred years since the Sending Out of the First Four. There have been eighty seven Clowns of the Apocalypse since then."

"I slept long and dreamed, my Sons. Only recently have I awakened."

Cuddles stepped forward. Skepticism was his secondary. "Yowza?"

"I trained her in the same Clowning Ways of your predecessors. What further proof could there be?" The hologram sighed.

His movements jerked like a puppet on strings. He flashed in and out. "We have little time."

"Why?" Giggles asked.

"Because I'm dying. The end of me is near. The reactor below us is failing. Madness has crept into the subroutines. I've asked you here to grant a tired old man his dying wish."

Giggles stepped forward. "What do you want us to do?"

"It's . . . complex," Captain Jangles said.

Three soft, simultaneous snicks behind them. Three brief stings as darts pierced the backs of three necks.

"Hey," said Bunko. "Where's Stan?"

Then he fell to the floor with Giggles and Cuddles, already fast asleep.

They awoke to low laughter.

The Aunty Clowns stood over them, black painted faces glistening in the light, file-sharpened teeth clacking together. Giggles, Cuddles and Bunko lay tied on the floor.

Of course they'd heard of Aunty Clowns, but hadn't believed the rumors. Leftovers from a crazed cult long ago. Anarchists and evil-doers bent on chaos and destruction.

Mama Aunty Clown stood with her fat arm around Stan. "Look what our little Sasha brought home."

"Why?" Giggles asked Stan. She looked away but Mama Aunty Clown took it as her cue.

She stepped forward, hitting a switch on her Electro-Puppet-O-Matic Body Harness. The image of Captain Jangles took shape before them, perfectly imitating her stance and movements, perfectly parroting her words as she spoke. "The reactor below us is failing. Madness has crept into the subroutines." Mama Aunty Clown laughed, her massive breasts jiggling beneath her purple jumpsuit. Captain Jangles laughed with her until she turned off the projection.

"So there is no Captain Jangles?" Giggles asked.

"Oh . . . there is," Mama Aunty Clown said, fingering a bright gold hand-crank that hung from a chain around her neck. "But these days, when he works at all, he works for us." She nodded to Stan. "After all, he *did* train our little Sasha."

"Yowza," Cuddles said.

"Bless me, Jesus," Bunko said.

Giggles looked at the four Aunty Clowns and Stan. "What do you want?"

"The key. Now."

"What key?"

"The key to Clown Mountain."

Giggles gulped. "I don't know what you're talking about."

"Yes, you do," said Stan. "Tell her where the key is."

Mama Aunty Clown drew a Blaze of Glory Self-Propelled Rocket Pistol from her cleavage and leveled it at Cuddles' head. She worked the action. "The key?"

"In my pocket," Giggles said.

"Try again. We've already emptied your pockets." She raised the pistol and fired it into the bleachers. The small explosion on impact sent up a shower of metal and plastic dust.

Giggles blanched. "Bunko?"

"Not me. You had it last."

"Cuddles?"

"Yowza."

This time, it was Giggles turn to look around. "Hey," he said. "Where's Stan?"

Mama Aunty Clown looked. "Sasha?" Her jaw set with anger, accentuating the white greasepaint frown. "Let's have no foolishness. Your initiation is nearly complete."

"Looking for this?" Stan asked from high above. She held up the wand, fully extended and blinking red.

Mama Aunty Clown and her three Sister Aunty Clowns spread out, all watching the girl on the trapeze. "Now be a good Daughter Aunty Clown and bring Mama the key." She stretched out a fat-fingered hand.

"I'll trade you," Stan said. "A key for a key."

Mama Aunty Clown pursed her lips. Again, she touched the small gold hand-crank. "You want the Captain?"

Stan nodded. Bending her legs, she gained momentum on the trapeze.

"Come get it," Mama said, raising her rocket pistol. She fired three quick rounds as the Sister Aunty Clowns drew weapons of their own.

Stan leaped; the trapeze burst into smoke and dust behind her. She caught the bottom of a hanging hoop and used it to propel herself up and away, catching another trapeze one handed, still waving the blinking wand.

"Fine," Mama said. She yanked the chain from her neck and hurled it across the platform.

Stan giggled. She pulled back her arm and let loose. Giggles, Cuddles and Bunko winced where they lay watching. Only instead of the wand, a bright red Smoke-Cracker pinwheeled down to explode at Mama Aunty Clown's feet. A pink cloud engulfed her and she fired wildly.

The three Sister Aunty Clowns let loose with automatic rifles but Stan was a bright blur in the air. She leaped, spun, twisted, cannon-balled, and finally landed lightly on her feet. Whizz and snickety-snack, dual yo-yo razors slashed through Giggles' and Cuddles' plasti-cord bonds.

"Knock knock," she said.

"Yowza?" Cuddles asked.

"Tank," she said.

"Tank who?" Giggles asked.

"You're welcome." She tossed him the wand and flashed away, cartwheeling towards a Sister Aunty Clown. He caught it and slipped it into his apron while he freed Bunko with his other.

She moved through the first Sister in twelve seconds. Exploding gumballs shredded feet. Razor yo-yo's shredded arms. Clown shoes collapsed the nose deep into the fat face and Stan bounced away.

Giggles, Cuddles and Bunko followed.

Bunko and Cuddles each took one of the remaining Sisters. Stan raced for the key. Giggles closed on Mama Aunty Clown. Each of them moved into free-form Clownfighting positions.

Mama Aunty Clown wasn't watching. Instead, she sighted in on Stan and fired. The rocket struck the back of Stan's shoulder but did not detonate. The impact flipped the young Clown; she dropped heavily and lay unmoving.

Giggles launched himself at Mama Aunty Clown. His feet connected with her wide posterior. She jiggled but did not fall. Instead, she threw aside her empty pistol and seized his feet with both hands. Sharpened teeth glinted through her snarl. She twirled and with each rotation gathered speed before tossing him easily into Bunko.

Cuddles flying-clown-kicked, arms stretched gracefully, snapping back his Aunty Clown's head. He followed up with a rolling-clown-head-butt to her solar plexus. As she staggered, he pulled Bunko to his feet and they finished her off together with dual-clown-spinning-fists. Then they tag-teamed the last of the Sisters as Giggles squared off once again with Mama.

Mama Aunty Clown backed away, watching the last of her sisters fall beneath a combination of Cuddle's accordion-clown-swooping-down and Bunko's clown-elbows-scissor-death. Her eyes narrowed. "Another day, Apocalypse Clowns."

The floor disappeared beneath her and she was gone.

Giggles ran to Stan. She lay in a pool of blood, blinking back tears. But she held the gold hand-crank and its chain.

"Sorry, Giggles," she said, not moving. The rocket had entered from the rear. There was no exit wound. Maybe it had been a dud; there was no way to know.

Giggles squeezed her hand; she pressed the crank into his palm. It looked like something that went with a toy. "Why, Stan?"

"Captain Jangles. He told me."

"But why?" The hand-crank grew warm and hummed in his closed fist.

"Because," Captain Jangles said, shimmering into life and light. "I wanted to come home, boys." He broke into a broad electronic smile that flickered with static beneath his mop-head wig and bright green helmet. No longer a tired old man, he wore his full uniform bristling with medals, pins and bells. "Now get over here, Cuddles, and take care of Stan." The Great Clown-Maker pointed at Giggles. "You . . . come with me. And bring my key."

Cuddles knelt beside her and gently rolled Stan onto her side. "Yowza." He drew a bobby pin from his wig and went to work disarming the embedded rocket.

"Bless the Lord Oh My Soul," Bunko said.

Giggles followed his Captain out of the Big Top.

They lifted off well past dark. Giggles and the Captain had returned with a small golden box; the hand-crank fit it perfectly. Then, Bunko and Cuddles carried Stan out on a makeshift stretcher. Captain Jangles led the way, his ghostly projection shimmering ahead like portable moonlight. The silence seemed to signal the Mecca's surrender; the park gave them back to the ruined city, which in turn gave them back to the Clown Around.

Now, the Great Clown-Maker hung in the air between their seats, watching Giggles turn the crank in the box. "That's everything," he said. "All that's left of me." The box popped open revealing a vortex of light within. "Thanks, boys."

"No problem, Dad." They looked over shoulders, checking on Stan.

"She'll be okay," Cuddles said.

Bunko and Giggles stared at him.

"What? You think 'Yowza' is the upper limit of my vocabulary?"

They continued to stare.

He shrugged and slapped his foot against the floor. "Yowza," he finally said with a grin.

Then he hit the switch, flooding the night with light and music. The forward thrusters engaged; Captain Jangles and his Clown Brigade rocketed westward and home.

THE BOY WHO COULD BEND AND FALL

They called him Slinky Boy because he could bend and fall from the top of the stairs all the way to the bottom with no serious injury and much to the amusement of others.

"Amazing," someone said.

"Look at him go," another added.

"Yee-haw," Ninja Bob shouted. Then he and Larry Sue and Longhair Eddie hauled their toy back up to the top of the stairs for another go in that small gap between classes at the end of the day. Slinky Boy's real name was Focus Jones; it reflected his parents' most wishful thinking. They were in real estate and had met (and conceived their son) at a Personal Effectiveness conference while they were both married to other people. Focus showed up nine months later. Fourteen years later, his classmates at Thomas Jefferson High School renamed him in honor of his new exploitable skill.

"Wow," someone said.

"Look at him go," another added.

"Yee-haw!"

What they liked most about it was that he didn't seem to mind at all. He went down making only a slight whooshing noise, then lay still at the bottom. The first few times, of course, he'd sprung to his feet with a bit of a flourish. But after that, when he realized that it was going to be an ongoing fete, he just laid there and waited for Ninja Bob and an ever-changing gang to scoop him up and haul him back to the top.

It had been a daily occurrence for as long as he could remember.

"You're weird," Angelica told him after the others left for fifth period.

"I know," he said.

She studied him from behind her thick glasses. "I've never seen anyone as weird as you."

"Me either," he said. Then, as an afterthought, he shrugged.

Angelica smiled. "Do you want to go to homecoming with me?"

That's the first time Slinky-Boy realized knowing how to bend and fall could come in handy.

The second time was different.

It was fourth period, a year later. He'd been staying on his own for the week — his parents were at a Self Leadership in America Life Skills Conference and they had decided he was old enough to stay home alone.

The secretary's tinny voice summoned him over the intercom accompanied by the snorts and eye-rolls of his classmates.

His Uncle Joe and his Aunt Margaret waited in the School Guidance Counselor's office with the Principal, Ms. McPherson. The long tile strip of hallway smelled like lemon floor cleanser.

"I can't believe you don't have a *real* counselor here," Uncle Joe was saying. Focus noticed right away that his eyes were red from drinking or crying or both. Aunt Margaret's eyes were red, too, but she was Presbyterian and did not drink.

The Guidance Counselor shrugged in an apologetic way. So did the Principal.

Everyone looked up when Focus walked in. They closed the door. They started to talk in somber, quiet tones.

Slinky Boy didn't remember much of what they said. He caught bits about the plane crash, about his new home with Uncle Joe the Alcoholic and Aunt Margaret the Pious, but after the first five minutes, he was bending and falling, bending and falling, bending and falling.

"What on earth is that whooshing noise?" Aunt Margaret asked.

"What the hell is he doing?" Uncle Joe added.

"He didn't learn that here," the Guidance Counselor said.

The pain rolled on; Slinky Boy bent and fell around it.

Years later, in the last conversation Focus Jones had with his wife before she left him, she asked him about it.

"Where do you go, Focus?"

Slinky-Boy looked up at her. She still tugged at his heart when he looked at her but he'd never quite learned how to say so. "I don't know," he said. Her eyes told him she wanted more. "Someplace else," he added. "Someplace not here."

The force of her sigh signaled exasperation, like the last breath slipping out of a love grown old and tired. "I can't live with you anymore."

The rest of the conversation faded into whooshing.

When the world reconstituted itself around him, Slinky Boy sat alone in his half-empty house.

At one point, someone suggested therapy might help.

The counselor — a real one, not a guidance one — sat on a comfortable chair, and Focus Jones sat on a comfortable couch. It was a simple room with a desk in one corner, mood lighting, a bookshelf filled with an odd assortment of titles: *You CAN Learn to Fly, Bartley's Guide to Living Well*, and *Parent-Blaming for Dummies*. The room smelled like peppermint.

On the third session, she asked about the bending and falling.

"So this started back in high school?" She sipped her tea and waited.

Focus nodded. "Yes."

"How did you feel about it?" She sipped her tea again and waited.

Focus shrugged. "I didn't feel anything about it."

She set down her tea, picked up her pen, wrote something down. She set down her pen, picked up her tea. "Really?"

Focus felt like a child caught playing with his mother's underwear. It must have shown on his face.

"Do you think maybe this —" she looked at her notes "*bending and falling* — could be a way of dealing with your parents' death?"

"I was doing it before they died."

Down went the tea, up came the pen. "Really?"

"Yes," he said. But he couldn't remember exactly when he'd started.

An uncomfortable pause settled in. The counselor watched him and sipped her tea.

"Where do you go, Focus?" the counselor finally asked.

"I'm not sure. I never open my eyes."

"Why don't you open your eyes?"

He thought for a moment. When no words drifted up, he shook his head.

"Maybe," she said, "you're afraid that if you opened them, you'd see that you were back where you started? That you hadn't gone anywhere at all?"

He deflated. He melted into the couch. He groaned inwardly.

The counselor smiled. "We'll come back to that next time. Why don't we talk a little about your mom?"

Slinky Boy saw her lips moving but all he heard was *whoosh* as the world spun away.

Speaking of worlds:

The end of the world landed on a Tuesday just a few years later and no one knew to roll out a red carpet by way of greeting. That is to say that it was painfully sudden and terribly unexpected.

This group had bombs. That group had diseases. The other group had airplanes and missiles and multiple payload delivery systems. It was an apocalyptic cluster-fuck of global proportions.

But terribly effective.

Look, up in the sky! Exhaust streaks like fuzzy spaghetti noodles draped over Grandma's Blue Quilt. Then a sky the color of amber under rainbow clouds that roiled and twisted and burned the eye. Bacteria rumbling in the thunder; viral rain — at first a sprinkle, then a downpour.

Slinky-Boy turned off the news and went out to his yard. Others were gathering to watch it all go, but not him. They turned to him with white and wild eyes.

Whoosh. "Wow," someone said.

Whoosh. "Look at it go," someone added.

Silence. Eyes tightly shut, he bent and fell.

More silence, oppressive and ominous and safe.

I can do this, he told his eyes.

Slinky Boy forced them open and looked out on a whole new world. Purple trees and lemon skies and peach grass. The smell of the circus and fresh cut lawn. The sound of glass flowers tinkling in the breeze. The taste of chocolate and cinnamon on the air.

He reached back, far back, into himself to find some word to express this latest discovery.

"Yee-haw," he said to no one in particular at all.

THE SECOND GIFT GIVEN

Go-on-all-fours-sometimes-upright tracked the three-horn spoor alone. He moved along the ridge in the red of the day when the Greater Light swallowed the sky and heat danced over stone.

Below, the big waters licked at the land. In the days when he was young, Go-on-all-fours remembered eating swimmers the People used to pierce in the shallows while the children played on the shaped rocks that the Oldest People had left behind. But the swimmers were rarer now than even the three-horns and the big waters drank those rocks long ago. Rememberer-of-forgotten-days said some-day the big waters would drink all of the land and the People as well. But Rememberer-of-forgotten-days also said that the People had walked *across* the big waters before they were so big, in the days before the sky burned red. And Rememberer-of-forgotten-days had difficulty remembering where (and sometimes when) to make water.

Go-on-all-fours picked up a pebble and put it in his mouth. Hunger chewed at him; there'd been no meat for twenty days. He clutched his piercer, its sharpened tip burned hard in fire, and went on threes with his nose to the ground. His hackles rose. He crested the ridge and stopped. The scent of blood made his tight stomach rumble.

Now he went upright, stretching his neck, working his nose, darting his eyes over the place where the broken rock became gray scrub and spider trees. Blood. The three-horn lay in the shadows, sides heaving, a small piercer protruding from its neck. Go-on-all-fours-sometimes-upright growled a warning in the speech of the People, raising an octave into inquiry. No response.

He shuffled forward cautiously, piercer ready. Laying beside the dying three-horn was a bowed stick, the ends tied together with a strand of dried gut, and a pile of small piercers. He sniffed them, inhaling a strange, sweet smell like nothing he'd known before.

Turn.

The compulsion spun him around, a panic boiling in his chest. He lost his footing and fell.

Compassion. No fear.

A female upright walker stood a throw away. Her hairless skin radiated in the copper light and she stood straight and very tall. She held a similar bowed stick in her hands and her mouth curved liked the stick, her teeth shining white.

Go-on-all-fours scrambled backwards, dropping his piercer. Her smell — strange, sweet — overpowered the three-horn's blood-smell.

Watch. Learn.

She pulled the string, holding a small piercer point facing out. The small piercer blurred across the ground, sinking into the three-horn's throat beside the other piercer. The three-horn bleated and died. She lay the thrower down, then turned and walked away.

Frozen and whimpering, he watched her go and tried to re-member what she looked like.

Go-on-all-fours-sometimes-upright pounded the dirt and howled to be heard. Rememberer-of-forgotten-days handed him the horn and he spoke. "Scared. Not harm. Golden-upright-walker *People*."

"Harm," said Best-maker-of-fire, gesturing at the two throwers and the bundle of piercers. "*Not* People. *We* People. Upright walker eater of People."

They had argued long after the last of the three-horn had been devoured, the women and children banished to their caves. As night drew on, the mountains cooled and the Lesser Lights throbbed and sparkled overhead. Rememberer-of-forgotten days taught the People they were dead hunters guarding them while the Greater Light slept. He also taught that the Greater Lesser Light, fat and white in the night, was a mother who chased her young to bed. Perhaps the upright walker gave the gift because *she* was a mother, too, taking care of her young. Go-on-all-fours wondered about this and poked a stick into the fire, despite Best-maker's growl of protest.

Rememberer coughed. He was the oldest of the People, and blind now though he once had been their best hunter. "Uprightwalkers make gift." He smiled toothlessly at Best-maker-of-fire. "Not eat Go-on-all-fours-sometimes-upright. Could."

No-child-in-stick laughed and made a spitting sound. "Go-on-all-fours-sometimes-upright too skinny."

Everyone else laughed, except for Best-maker. He scowled, picked up one of the throwers and tossed it into the fire. Go-on-all-fours leaped to his feet and burned himself pulling it out. "Not people," Best-maker said. "Eaters of people."

When the angry growls died down, they all went to bed. He had not told them about the voice in his head: they would never believe him.

Come.

He came awake, instantly alert, and untangled himself from his woman, Best-maker's sister. She mewled a question in her sleep and rolled away.

Outside. Come.

He picked up his piercer and left the cave silently, careful not to wake his young. The upright walker waited at the edge of the clearing and the sight of her hurt his eyes. Easily half-again his height at his tallest, she stood with her hands hanging loosely at her sides. Long golden hair spilled down her shoulders and over her heavy breasts. Her eyes shone bright green.

Compassion. No fear. Follow.

He followed her, going upright until his back and legs ached from the effort. They hadn't gone far when a chittering sound stopped him.

No fear. This voice was heavier. He knew it came from the monster that separated from the shadows, but he raised his piercer anyway. *No fear.*

Fear, he said back. The eight-legged monster — almost a spider but even larger than the six-horns Rememberer told stories of — scuttled closer.

No fear, the woman said. She put a hand on his arm. Cool. Soft.

He pushed the piercer into her belly as far as it would go and screamed as the monster leapt.

*

His first awareness was the fullness of his brain. His second awareness was the coolness of the grass beneath his bare skin. He opened his eyes on golden light playing in the boughs of upward-sweeping trees. He sat up and looked around. He had never seen so much green in one place.

Pleasure. "You like my garden?" The naked upright walker strode into the clearing, a piece of fruit held loosely in each hand. *Confusion. Anxiety.* "I've never seen anything like it." The memory of attacking her jarred him. *Fear. Surprise.* The golden skin of her flat stomach showed no mark from his piercer. "You're . . . well?"

She laughed. "Of course I am. The Seeker would not have allowed me Outside had the risk been real."

"The Seeker?"

"Ra-sha-kor, the Firsthome Seeker. I am the Seeker's Lady, Jadylla-kor. We have traveled vast distances to find you, cousin." *Dark. Alone. Searching.*

"I do not understand."

She offered him a piece of fruit. *Trust.* "Of course not. You're not fully recessed, cousin. When you are, everything will become clearer."

He took the purple globe and studied it, rolling it around his fingers. He looked up at her and their eyes locked. Raising her own piece, she bit into it and its golden juice ran down her mouth, dripping onto her breasts. *Trust. Eat.*

He took a bite and his mind expanded. As if she stood in his mind speaking, words formed without sound as they stared at one another. She answered questions before he could ask.

I name you cousin because you and I are of the People.

Long ago, before the Seventeen Recorded Ages of Humanity, our cousins flung themselves out from the Firsthome like scattered seed. Outward and outward they spread away and away to find new homes among the stars. Long travelers into dark, they warred and loved one another in those distant days and fled so far from home to have lost their way back to it. This was the Darkest Age, marked by the absence of history and the presence of myth. Then, in the Fifth Age, came Yorgen Sunwounder, the first Firsthome Finder, who searched and found the cradle of the People, of Humanity.

But the Firsthome did not know him for time and technol-

*ogy had changed him, and in his rage he smote their sun and
thus began the Cousin Wars that brought about the Second
Darkest Age. Humanity rose and fell again and again and once
more the Firsthome was lost . . . .*

He stopped her with a blink. "What is happening to me?"

She placed her hands on his shoulders and drew her face nearer,
her stare unbroken. *Recession. A return backwards to what you
once were, cousin. A human. One of the People. Truth: all life
changes over time. Truth: the clock-spring can be unwound
carefully, carefully, we have learned. Infinitely small workers
live in the nectar of this fruit, each unwinding you, recessing
you to what you would have been millions of years ago had
time not taken you on a different journey. Infinitely small teachers
in this fruit fill your mind with language and comprehension.*

Another voice now in his head, deeper and stronger: *Enough,
Lady. His recession is as far as you may take it. Bring him to
me.*

She released him and he realized that the closeness of her mind
and body had aroused him. He blushed and moved to cover himself.
The Lady smiled sympathetically.

Peace, she said with her mind. "It is time for you to meet the
Seeker and to taste the root." Turning, she strode out of the clearing
and Go-on-all-fours hurried to keep up with her, surprised at how
easily he now went upright.

They entered another clearing after darting in and out of wet,
hanging foliage. Twice, he thought he saw the monstrous spider-
thing that had captured him. Once, they brushed against a wall of
blue crystal, warm to his touch, and stretching up, up, up, lost far
above in light.

In the center of the clearing stood a massive tree, its branches
bent low with heavy purple fruit.

"I'll leave you now," the Lady said, squeezing his arm. "I will
return when the Seeker calls for me."

This time, she did not walk away. Instead, her shape began
to shimmer and then melted into the ground too fast for him to
respond.

He heard a chuckle in his head. *She is fine, cousin. Bending
light rather than moving feet. Welcome. I am Ra-sha-kor.*

"You are the Firsthome Seeker. The Lady said —"

I am the Firsthome Finder. I have sought you, cousin, through deeps of space and time that you cannot begin to comprehend. It is my great Joy to have finally found you.

"I am —"

You were Go-on-all-fours-sometimes-upright. Again, the chuckle. *You now need a new name. May I have the honor of naming you in my own tongue?*

The People gave names when a child was old enough to hunt — now he understood that it was an important coming-of-age ritual. "Yes. I would be honored, Lord."

You shall be called the Firstfound Cousin, the Healer of the Broken Distance, Sha-Re-Tal. Tal.

He did not know why exactly, but he knelt. After a respectable silence, he looked up. Other than the tree, the clearing stood empty.

I am here, Tal. The tree. Tal stood and took a step towards it.

"You —"

The People, over time, have learned to make themselves into what they will. My roots run the length of this craft, nourishing it, powering it, carrying the wisdom and knowledge of the People in its sap. Even as the Lady chooses her form, I have chosen mine. As has Aver-ka-na, our Builder Warrior. The branches behind him rustled and the huge spider sidled tentatively out.

Compassion, it said. *No fear.*

The Finder's mind joined in. *You have nothing to fear, Tal.*

With everything in him, Tal fought the panic as the creature came closer, its mandibles clicking. It raised a hairless arm and lowered it onto his shoulder.

Peace, cousin.

Then, it turned and scuttled away. Tal released held breath.

Sit with me, the Finder thought. Tal sat, his head suddenly hurting. "We will make words in this way now," the Finder said, its deep voice drifting down from somewhere lost above. "You are young in understanding yet and I would not wound carelessly after so long in the finding of you."

"I am grateful," Tal said. And he was. He felt himself expanding, stretching, his awareness filling like the hollow of a rock as the tide gentled in.

He sat in the shade of the tree until the Finder spoke again. "You express gratitude for our shame."

Confusion. Uncertainty. "Your shame?"

"It is not our way to force," the Finder said. "The Rul-ta-Shan — the First Gift Given — was choice. The Lady gave of the fruit while you slept."

Tal nodded slowly. "I would have chosen so."

"We hope so. Still, the ages had robbed you of choice and so we made our own on your behalf, trusting our cousinhood to cover a multitude of transgressions. Thus we brought you to this place, your choice restored."

Love welled in Tal's heart and brimmed his eyes. The power in it made his life with the People, his life as Go-on-all-fours, seem small and far away. Breeding. Hunting. Foraging. Starving. Led by appetite and instinct to survive. "I was an animal," he whispered. "I was not of the People. Now I am of the People. You have made me —" he struggled to find the word — "whole."

The mighty tree shook. "No. You were always of the People, Cousin. You were as whole as you could be." *Freedom.* "And now you possess the First Gift Given. What will you choose, I wonder?"

The grass at the base of the tree rustled, exposing thick roots that pulsed with life and possibility. Tal crawled forward. "I wish to know," he said.

"Then taste the root and know what you will."

He put his tongue to the root; it was bitter and sweet, the tang of earth and grass, and it swept through him, over him, into him. Tal collapsed inside himself, his eyes slamming shut as his brain pried open.

Understanding. He saw. *Loss.* He knew. *Endings.* He wept. *Beginnings.* He slept.

He awoke to the Lady cradling him against her warm body.

"Lady," he said. "How long?" But he knew that too.

She offered a sad smile. "Years. But not many. The sun swells from its wound. Slowly, it swallows the Firsthome."

"And the People will end," he said in a quiet voice.

"No," she said and he remembered. *Beginnings.* "You have choice now if you will make it."

Her fingers lightly stroked his skin. The smoothness of her pressed against him and he was smooth now, too. The smell of her filled his nose, overpowering the scent of flowers and grass around them. He swallowed, sensations overwhelming him. "I choose."

"It is a great gift," Jadylla said.

He stretched out a nervous hand to touch her. "I am grateful."

She brought her face close to his. "No." Her breath was warm. "*You* give the great gift, Cousin, and the giving of it heals the broken distance between the Peoples." Her mouth touched his. *Heat. Unity.* "The life we make together will satisfy our deepest longing for Home."

He'd never mated face-to-face. He was nervous and awkward as his hands sought her out. Her own hands moved lower on his body and, learning from her, he imitated her caresses. Slowly, they touched one another with hands and mouths and when he could no longer wait, he gently crawled onto her and let her guide him into her. He pushed into her warmth and wetness and her eyes went wide for just a moment. Then she smiled and pushed back against him, moving her hips in time with his own.

When they finished, he lay back in her arms. Her sweat and her scent mingled with his own. They were silent for a long time before he spoke.

"Why me?" he asked.

"What did they call you? Before the Finder found you?"

"Go-on-all-fours-sometimes-upright," he said.

"Sometimes the past returns in small ways. Of your People, who else ever went upright?"

He shook his head.

"We watched for a year. We watched you hunt. We watched you mate. We watched you all and you were chosen."

He thought of the others. With no sky overhead, he'd lost all sense of time. He wondered if his mate slept or if she foraged to feed their young. He wondered if they wondered where he was, if perhaps they even searched for him.

Thinking of them prompted a question. "Could they also be . . . recessed?"

She shrugged. "We do not know. And we could not find out without further shame."

"But I am grateful. Wouldn't they be grateful as well?"

She rolled away from him. "It is not a matter for discussion."

Something sparked in Tal's memory. "I have young. When they choose to crawl into the fire, I do not allow their choice. Does that shame the First Gift Given?"

"It is not the same," Jadylla said.

"How is it not the same?"

"It is not the same," she said again. She disentangled herself from his arms. "You have honored me, Cousin, but I must leave you now." She stood and touched her stomach. "This life must be nurtured at the root and my husband calls."

Tal lay back and watched her leave. He thought about his mate and his young at home. "When my young crawl into the fire, I do not allow their choice," he said to himself. Because, he thought, the parent chooses for the child until the child can do so for themselves.

An unhealthy line of thought. Aver-ka-na scuttled towards him, its naked belly dragging the ground, its eight legs moving slowly.

"Not unhealthy," Tal said, his brain spun to bring down exactly the right word. "Love."

Not love, it said, mandibles clacking. *Love respects the First Gift Given.*

"Love," Tal said slowly, "pulls young from the fire."

The Builder Warrior chittered, its eyes rolling.

Tal stood, stretching himself fully upright and raising his fist. "I will return with fruit for my People." No answer dropped into his mind or drifted into his ears. He started walking and kept walking until he saw the tree, heavy with its purple fruit.

Anger. Sadness. The Finder stirred. *I can not permit it.*

The ground at the foot of the tree peeled back, exposing Jadylla where she lay wrapped in roots. Her eyes opened. She was different towards him now, her voice cold and far away. "We came for you. Not them."

Tal swallowed. He felt anger building. *Falseness.* "You did not come for me. You came to take life from me."

Neither answered.

"I will take life, too. Life for my people." He paused. "It is *my* choice."

The Firsthome Finder's Lady looked at the Firsthome Finder. Her tongue slipped from her mouth, touching the root, moving over its surface. Finally, she nodded. The tree shuddered and fruit fell like rain.

Jadylla's eyes were narrow. "You may take what you can carry. We will not wait long for you."

Tal picked up a piece of fruit. "And you will take us all with you."

Only those who choose, the Finder said into his mind.

Tal picked up more fruit, cradling it in his arms. "Only those who choose," he repeated.

Light swallowed him and sent him spinning away.

Tal stood on the rise overlooking the fires and the caves. He watched Best-maker-of-fire argue with No-child-in-stick. Young played around the fire, moving quickly on all fours in a game that imitated hunting and mating behavior. He saw his own young among them. His mate, Soft-voice-sharp-bite, sat with the other females, grooming one another.

Compassion, he sent. *No fear.*

They looked up quickly as if struck, all wide-eyed.

He lifted a piece of fruit. *Watch. Learn.* He bit into it, letting the juice spill onto his naked skin. He took a step forward, extending the fruit though he was still two throws away.

They moved, scrambling back toward the caves. "Don't go," he said. "It's me — Go-on-all-fours-sometimes-upright. I've come back for you."

"Not People," No-child-in-stick growled. "Upright walker eater of People." His eyes rolled wide and wild.

Peace. "No," Tal said.

Abandoning their fire, they fled into the caves.

He spent the night trying to coax them out. He fed the fire for them, hoping somehow it would show he meant no harm. He placed a piece of fruit outside each cave entrance. He called to them. He waited.

As the sky reddened and the swollen sun crawled out, he heard his young whimpering in the dark.

Come. Eat.

Deep in the back of the caves, they growled and moaned.

Finally, he took a piece of fruit and went into the cave that used to be his own. His mate yelped and hissed as he moved quickly toward her. She clawed and kicked at him as he grabbed her, biting at his hands as he tried to force the fruit into her mouth. She shrieked, her nails and teeth drawing blood, her eyes wide in terror. He shoved her away from him, turning toward his children.

She fell on him before he could take a step and he went down beneath her, the air knocked from him as her thrashing feet connected with his testicles and her gnashing mouth found his ear.

"Not People," she screamed. "Eater of People."

Tal wanted to fight back but couldn't. Suddenly he knew that it didn't matter anymore. He yelled again and again. His young were fleeing now and other forms were moving into the cave waving piercers and hefting rocks.

He heard his own bones breaking and smelled his own blood on the air, the tang of iron mingled with the sweetness of nectar.

He closed his eyes and waited for the end.

Not love, the Lady's voice in his mind said, heavy with sorrow. Tal's eyes opened. He lay wrapped in the ground, tangled in the Finder's roots. "No, not love."

"You are well now."

He nodded. "I am grateful."

She touched his arm. He still felt the distance but no longer cold. He saw now that her belly curved slightly outward, his child growing there quickly, nourished by the Finder's sap.

Come to Newhome with us, Ra-sha-kor the Firsthome Finder said. *Come, cousin, and meet your Other People.*

Tal twisted himself free from the roots, goosebumps forming on his skin as he remembered the stones and fists and fire-sharpened sticks. "What would I do at the Newhome?"

Jadylla smiled and rubbed her stomach. "You would care for your daughter. With me and with the Firsthome Finder."

He saw that the Builder Warrior hung from his legs in the tree branches, weaving three silk hammocks. His mind told him that these were to let them sleep for the long voyage.

"My daughter will not need me." Tal bent, placed his lips to the root, letting knowledge and emotion wash through him. "She will be cared for."

Understanding. Acceptance.

Love, he thought.

Tal stood on the edge of the big waters in the cool of the night. Far above, a fleck of light moved away, crisp and clear among the pulsing stars. He waved though he knew they could not see him.

He picked up the thrower and the pouch of little piercers they had left with him. He tested the string and calculated in his mind exactly what he would need to make more of them. He also thought about ways to go out onto the big waters to find the swimmers and ways to capture the three-horns and breed them for food. Ways to plant the good berries and tubers and to dig them at his leisure. He even thought about ways to take his People to a new place — far to the north or south — where life could be better for them until there could be no life and the sun finally swallowed the world.

Perhaps someday they would let him do these things for them . . . *with* them. Certainly not now, but maybe with time.

For now, he would hunt. For now, he would keep what little he needed to survive and leave the rest where his People could find it. He would do this every day for as long as it took because he knew that if choice was the First Gift Given, love must indeed be the second.

Sha-Re-Tal, the Firstfound Cousin and Healer of the Broken Distance, found the three-horn spoor and broke into an easy run. He ran upright, his feet steady and sure beneath him, his eyes and nose and ears remembering their work very well.

A silver moon rose over the big waters.

He howled at it and dared it to chase him.

INVISIBLE EMPIRE OF ASCENDING LIGHT

Tana Berrique set down her satchel and ran a hand over the window plate in her guest quarters. The opaque, curved wall became clear, revealing the tropical garden below. She'd spent most of the past six years living in guest quarters from planet to planet, inspecting the shrines, examining the Mission's work, encouraging the Mission's servants. But the room here at the Imperial Palace on Pyrus came closest to being her home.

She sighed and a voice cleared behind her.

"Missionary General Berrique?"

She didn't turn immediately. Instead, she watched a sky-herd of chantis move against the speckled green carpet of vines, trees and underbrush. "Yes, Captain Vesper?" The bird-like creatures dropped back into the trees and she turned.

She'd heard of this one. Young but hardened in the last Dissent, Alda Vesper climbed the ranks fast to find himself commanding the best of the best, Red Morning Company of the Emperor's Brigade. He stood before her in the doorway, one hand absently toying with the pommel of his short sword, his face pale. "I bring word, Missionary General."

"So soon?" She glanced back at the window, ran her hand over the plate to fog out the garden's light. "By the look on your face, I must assume that he's now Announced himself?"

The captain nodded. "He has. Just a few minutes ago."

Sadness washed through her. She'd known he would Announce; she'd just hoped otherwise. And now Consideration must be given. Afterwards, the path to Declaration could follow. And along that road lay death and destruction unless he truly did Ascend. She'd overseen four Considerations since taking office six years earlier. All had led to Declarations; all had ended in bloodfeuds. She'd discouraged all from Declaring, had seen the obvious outcomes clearly despite their blind faith and inflated hopes. None had listened. Millions dead from men who would be gods.

"Then I will Consider him," she told the captain. "We must move before the others consolidate and shift their allegiances. Ask the Vice-Regent to petition his father for a lightbender to take us. Tell him I specifically requested Red Morning Company to assist the Consideration."

He bowed his head, his smile slight but pleased, fingertips touching the gold emblazoned sun on the breast of his scarlet uniform. "Yes, Missionary General."

He spun and left, ceremonial cloak billowing behind him.

I've only just arrived, Tana Berrique thought as she picked up her satchel, and yet once more I depart. She brushed out the lights to her guest quarters and exited the room and its heaven-like view.

The lightbender vessel *Gold of Dawning* took three days to reach Casillus. One day on each side to clear the demarcation lines under sunsail, one day to power up and bend.

The Missionary General boarded the Captain's yacht with Vesper and a squad of brigadiers. She'd exchanged her white habit for the plain gray of the Pilgrim Seeker and let her hair down out of respect for Casillian custom. She and Captain Vesper took the forward passenger cabin just behind the cockpit and forward from his squad.

Gold of Dawning spit them out into space. The vessel's executive officer piloted them planet-side himself. There were no viewscreens in the passenger cabin, but Tana knew vessels under many family flags took up their positions around the planet. They waited for her to do her part as she had done before, and they waited for the Declaration.

She thumbed the privacy field and turned to Vesper. "Where is he, then?"

"They've taken him to the local Imperial Shrine for safekeeping. Once he Announced, word spread fast."

They'd watched this one for some time. The Mission had seen the potential in his humble birth, in the calloused hands of his lowborn parents, in the scraps of data they'd fed into the matrix. By age seven, they'd known he would match in the high ninetieth percentile. Now at fifteen, he was easily the youngest to score so near the ideal and the second youngest to Announce before reaching his majority. She'd seen some of his paintings, some of his poems. She'd heard a snippet from a song a year earlier. Now, she reviewed his results and charted them on the divine matrix.

"At the moment, he's only a ninety-eight three," she said out loud.

"Only?" Vesper asked. "Has there been higher?"

She nodded. "When I was an Initiate years ago we saw a ninety-eight six."

His surprised look and indrawn breath made her smile. "A ninety-eight six? I've never heard this."

"There are many things you've not heard," Tana told him. "And you have not heard this either . . . from me." She raised her eyebrows in gentle warning.

Vesper nodded to show agreement. "What happened to him?"

"Her," she said. "This one was a girl."

He scowled. "A girl?"

"Yes. A young woman. Quite rare, I know, considering our understanding of the matrix. And in answer to your question: She died."

"No surprise there," he said. "The disappointed can be quite unforgiving. And the unforgiving can be quite brutal."

Tana nodded. "True. But this one never Declared. She Announced and then took her own life shortly after her Consideration."

She wasn't sure why she told him this. By the letter of the law, it was a breach in the Mystery. But by the spirit, Tana felt drawn to the young man. Or perhaps, she thought, it's been too long since I've trusted anyone outside the Mission.

Vesper seemed surprised. "Took her own life without Declaring? That seems odd." He chuckled. "Why?"

"I think," Tana Berrique said, "she saw something the rest of us couldn't see at the time." Now she hinted at heresy and treason and backed away from the words carefully, studying the sudden firmness of the captain's jaw, the tightness around his eyes.

He looked around, shifting uncomfortably in his seat. The question hung out there like forbidden fruit and she knew he would not ask it.

She patted his leg in the way she thought a mother might. "Pay no mind to me, young Captain. I'm tired and eager to be done with this work."

He relaxed. Eventually, she closed her eyes and meditated to clear her mind for Consideration. The yacht sped on. Somewhere in her silence, she fell into a light sleep and woke up as the atmosphere gently shook her.

He waited in a vaulted chamber in the lower levels of the Imperial Shrine. Captain Vesper's men took up their positions around the shrine, supplementing the Shrine Guard. A duo of Initiates accompanying the shrine's Pilgrim Seeker escorted the Missionary General through room after room.

"We are honored to have you," the Pilgrim Seeker said.

"I am honored to attend," Tana said, following the proper form. "Though I face the day with dread and longing."

The Pilgrim Seeker nodded, her eyes red from crying. "Perhaps he will Ascend."

"Perhaps he will not," Tana Berrique said. "Either way, today will be marked by loss. For one to Ascend, another must Descend."

"In our hope, we grieve." The Pilgrim Seeker quoted from an obscure parameter of the matrix. "And we are here."

They stood in a small anteroom, watching the boy in the chamber through a one-way viewscreen. He sat quietly in a chair. A plain-clad couple stood near the door. The man had his arm around the woman. They looked hopeful and mournful at the same time.

"His parents," the Pilgrim Seeker said.

The Missionary General felt anger well up inside her. "He's very young," she told them. "Who encouraged him to Announce?"

"He did it himself, Mum," the father said.

"And how did he know?"

The mother spoke up. "We didn't even know ourselves. I swear it."

Tana frowned. "Very well. I will give him Consideration." She lowered her voice so that only the parents could hear. "I hope you know what price this all may come to."

The mother collapsed, sobbing against her husband. He patted her shoulder, pressing her to his chest. When his eyes locked with Tana Berrique's she saw fire in them. "We didn't know. Have done with it and let us be." Now tears extinguished their ferocity. "If we had known, don't you think we'd have fled with him years ago?"

The despair in his words stopped her. She felt their grief wash over her, capsizing her anger. She forced a gentle smile, too late. "Perhaps your son will Ascend."

"Perhaps," the father said. She drew a palm-sized matrix counter from her pocket and thumbed it on. She felt it vibrating into her hand, ready to calculate his responses and add them into the equation as she gave Consideration. Tana Berrique nodded to the Pilgrim Seeker, who opened the door into the chamber. She walked into the room and stood above him. He sat, eyes closed, breathing lightly.

One of the Initiates brought a chair and set it before the boy, then left. She sat, placed the matrix counter on the floor between them, and waited for the door to whisper closed. When it did, she smiled.

"What is your name?" she asked.

The boy opened his eyes and looked up at her. "I would like a privacy field, please."

She flinched in surprise. The counter chirped softly, flashing green. Ninety eight four, now. "A privacy field? It's not done that way."

His eyes narrowed. "It's done any way you say it is, Missionary General Tana Berrique. This is your Consideration."

Surprise became fear. The green light flashed him a solid Ninety eight six now as his words registered against the equation. She waved to the hidden viewscreen and a privacy field hummed to life around them. "You know a great deal for someone so young."

The boy laughed. It sounded like music and it washed her fear. He leaned forward. "Perhaps I'm not so very young," he said.

"That's what I'm here to Consider," she told him. "May I follow the form?"

He nodded.

"What is your name?"

"I am called H'ru in this incarnation."

She raised her eyebrows. "This incarnation?" she repeated.

"Yes."

She watched the counter. He was nearing ninety nine. "And your other names?" she asked.

He shrugged. "Are they important?"

"They may be, H'ru. I don't know."

He shook his head. "They are not."

Tana changed the subject. "What led you to Announce?"

His young brow furrowed. "I was told to."

"By your parents?"

He chuckled, the brief laugh ending in a secret smile.

"By one of the Families?"

The smile faded. "By myself," he said.

She shook her head, not sure she heard correctly. The counter did not chirp or hum, no light flickered from it. "Could you say that again?"

"I told myself to Announce," he said.

She felt her stomach lurch. "That's not possible."

"Ask me. Return to Pyrus, wake me, and ask me yourself." His smile returned. "After you are finished with the Consideration, of course."

"The Regent would never allow it. And even if he did —" She suddenly realized she had lost focus, lost composure, spoken aloud. The counter still did nothing. She scooped down, picked it up to see if it still hummed. It did.

"I've stopped it," he said.

"How?" she asked.

"I willed it to stop and it stopped."

"What else can you will?" she asked.

He shook his head. "We'll not talk around circles, Tana Berrique. You do not need a counter to know who I am."

She let the air rush out of her. He was right. She didn't need it to know. The four before had been betrayed by either humility without strength or arrogance without power. Their equations had tested the matrix, to be sure, but they could not Ascend. After Declaring, the house-factions and bloodfeuds had undone them and they'd died on the run from followers turned vengeful from disappointment and fear. But this one was different and it shook her.

"You've not met me before," he said. "The others were near but false. Except for one."

She nodded. She blinked back tears, fought the growing knot in her throat.

"You're wondering why I took my life before," he asked. "It's what you told the Captain on your flight in. I saw something the rest of you could not see at the time. But you see it now, don't you?"

She nodded again and swallowed.

"Your god, your Emperor of Ascending Light, has lain near death for too long while the Regent and his kin hold power in wait for another god to rise. But they intend no new Ascendant be found. They use this trick of Announcement, Consideration and Declaration to extend both hope and fear. But in the end, no one Ascends. The Dissents tear out the heart of the Empire and only strengthen the aspect of a few."

Her hands shook. Her bladder threatened release. She shifted on the chair, then pitched forward onto her knees. "What is your will, Lord Emperor?"

He touched her hair and she looked up. He smiled down, his face limned in the room's dim light. "Take your seat, Tana Berrique."

Mindful to obey, she returned to her chair. "My Lord?"

"H'ru," he said with a gentle voice. "Just H'ru."

Tana felt confusion and conflict brewing behind her eyes. "But surely when you Declare, you shall Ascend unhindered? How could they prevent you?"

"They will not prevent me," he said. "*You* will." He paused, letting the words sink in to her. "And I shall neither Ascend nor Declare."

"But my role is Consideration. I take no part in —"

"I will tell you to," he said. "And because I am your Emperor, you will obey."

"I do not understand," she said.

"You will." He patted her hand. "When the Regent calls you out, say to him *S'andril bids you to recall your oath in the Yellowing Field*. He will admit you to me. And I will tell you what to do."

She sat there before him for a few minutes, letting the privacy field absorb the sound of her sobs as he held her hands in his and whispered comfort to her.

At long last, she stood, straightened her habit, and waved for the privacy field to be turned off. The counter stopped at Ninety nine three. She looked down at the boy. "This Consideration is closed," she said. "You may do what you will."

The boy nodded. "I understand."

Without a glance, without meeting the eyes of the Pilgrim Seeker or the parents, she strode from the chamber, passed through the anteroom and said nothing at all to anyone else.

*

Back at Pyrus, she spent her time gazing down on the garden while she waited for the Regent to call her out. No Declaration had swept up from Casillus and the pockets of ships, loaded with troops, continued to deploy strategically around that world and others while everyone waited.

Captain Vesper finally came for her. She had not spoken to him since before the Consideration but she knew that he could see her unrest. He fell back into his official role though she saw his brow furrowing and his mouth twitching as unasked questions played out beneath his skin.

She followed as he led her into the throne room.

The Regent sat on a smaller throne to the left of the central dais and its massive, empty crystalline throne. To the right, his son, the Vice-Regent, sat. He waved the Imperial Brigade members away.

After they had gone, he motioned the Missionary General forward.

"Well?" he finally asked. "There has been no Declaration from Casillus. Then I learn that you made no report on this Consideration." He scowled, his heavy beard, woven with gems and strands of gold, dragging against this chest. "What do you say for yourself?"

"I say nothing for myself, Regent." She intentionally left off the word *Lord.*

"I find that highly unusual, Missionary General."

She shrugged. "I'm sorry you find it so."

"Can you speak about this child H'ru and his Announcement?"

"I can. He Announced and I Considered."

"And?"

Tana Berrique paused, not sure how to pick her way through this minefield. Lord help me, she thought, and I will simply be direct. She met the Regent's eyes. "What do you want me to say?"

"What I want," the Regent said in a cold voice, "is to know when the Family warships and armies will either stand down or take action. Something that will not happen until this boy makes up his mind. We do not need another Dissent. We do not need another false god Declaring and moving our worlds into civil war."

She continued to stare at him. "I find it interesting, Regent, that you did not at any point mention wanting a new god to Ascend and bring all this uncertainty to a close."

His face went red and he growled deep in his chest. "If you were not the Missionary General," he said in a low voice, his hands white-knuckling the sides of his chair, "I would have you killed for those words."

She smiled. "So you do want the new god to Ascend, for our Emperor of Ascending Light to sleep at long last, knowing his people are safe for a season?"

"Of course I do," he said. "We all do."

Now she took her moment. "Very well," she said. "*S'andril bids you to recall your oath in the Yellowing Field.*"

His eyes popped, his face went white and his mouth dropped open. "What did you say?"

"You heard me quite well. And I assume that you know what it means."

Shaking, he stood up. "It can't be."

"It is."

His son looked pale, too, but clearly didn't understand what was happening. Tana Berrique wasn't sure herself, but she felt the power from her words and their hard impact.

"He told me this day would come. He told me those words would come." The large old man started to cry.

"Father?" The son stood as well. "What does this mean?"

"An old promise, son. Go gather your things."

Tana watched the son's face go red. "My things? What are you saying?"

"Our work is done," the Regent said. "We're going home now."

"But this *is* my home. You said so. You said —"

In a bound, the old man stood over his son, hand raised to slap him down. The son buckled and cowered on the floor as his father's voice roared out: "What I said doesn't matter. We leave now and hope for mercy later."

"I'll let myself in," Tana Berrique told him.

Behind the throne room, in his private bedchamber, the Emperor of Ascending Light lay beneath a stasis field, attended by scuttling jeweled spiders that preserved his life. Tana Berrique stood at the foot of the massive circular bed, her body trembling at the sight of him.

He'd been a big man once, muscled and broad-shouldered, but the years had withered him to kindling. His white hair ran down the sides of his head like streams of milk spilled onto a silk pillow. His hands were folded around his scepter. She stepped forward and dropped to her knees beside his bed, thumbing off the stasis field to awaken him from long sleep. The spiders clattered and scrambled, unsure of what to do with this un-programmed event. The paper-thin eyelids fluttered open and a light breath rattled out.

Tana Berrique bowed her head. "You summoned me, Lord."

"Yes." His voice rasped, paper rustling wood. "Are my people well?"

"They are not, Lord. They need you."

The tight mouth pulled, thin wisps of beard moving with the effort. "Not as such."

And she knew what was coming now. The reality of it settled in as she recalled the boy's words. They will not prevent me, he had said, *you* will. "What would you bid me, Lord?"

"Kill me," the Emperor of Ascending Light whispered. One hand released the scepter and thin, dry, brittle fingers sought her hand. "Let it all change." He coughed and a spider moved to wipe his mouth. "It is time for change."

"I don't think I can." She felt the tears again, hot and shameful, pushing at her eyes and spilling out. She wanted to drop his hand but could not. "I don't think I can. I can't."

He shushed her. "You can. Because I am your Emperor." His lips twitched into a gentle smile. "You will obey."

Tana Berrique stood and bent over her god. She felt the sweat from her sides trickle forward tracing the line of her breasts as she leaned. She felt the tears tracing similar paths down her cheeks. She shuddered, bent further, and kissed the dry, rattling lips. She placed her hands gently on the thin neck and squeezed, the soft hair of his beard tickling her wrists. The eyelids fluttered closed. She kept squeezing until her shoulders shook. She kept squeezing while the spiders panicked and climbed over one another to somehow complete their program and preserve a life. She kept squeezing until she knew that he had gone. Her hands were still on the throat when heavy boots pounded the hallway.

"Missionary General!" Captain Vesper's voice shouted from outside. "Is the Emperor okay? The Regent's retinue is packing for a rapid withdrawal and no one is telling me any —" She heard him clatter into the room. "What are you doing?" he screamed. She turned quickly to face him. Panting, eyes wild, face drawn in agony, the young officer pulled his sword. "What are you doing?" he asked again, pointing its tip at her as he took a step forward.

"I'm doing what I'm told," she said. "And by the Ascending Light you'll do the same or watch all our Lord worked for crumble and decay."

He paused, uncertainty washing his face.

"You already know, Alda." She gestured to the bed. "He wanted more than this for his people."

The sword tip wavered. "I thought we were working for more," he spat.

"We are. He was." She waited. "I'm doing what he said."

"What proof have you?"

She shook her head. "None but his words to me and me alone. And something about the Yellowing Field. I don't know what — it meant something to the Regent, though."

Alda went paler. The sword dropped. "The Yellowing Field? Are you sure?"

"You know of it?"

His shoulders slumped. "I do. It's a Brigade story from the forging of the Empire."

"I've never heard this," she said.

He walked forward, looking down at the Emperor. "There are many things you've not heard," he told her. "When S'andril was young he saved a boy who swore he would repay him. 'I have saved your life today,' the Emperor told this boy, 'and one day I will bid you repay me by not saving mine.'" He looked up at her. "I am at your service."

She sat on the edge of the bed. "We're not finished yet," she told him. "There's more."

He nodded. "The boy?"

He understands, she thought. *He truly understands.* Her words came slowly. "It will be bloody. Many will die. But after this, we can rebuild. There will be no further Dissents. The Families will burn out their rage and then we can have peace." Because, she hoped, if the god is truly dead then the idea of that god can live on without harm.

His voice was firm. "His family, too?"

"No. Spare them but keep it quiet. Just him. He won't struggle. It's what he wants."

"And after?" Alda Vesper stood.

She played the words to herself, then said them carefully. "After, I will Declare the boy myself and give witness to his Ascent." An eternal emperor, she thought, on the throne of each heart. An invisible empire of Ascending Light.

"God help us," Vesper said. He spun on his heel and left.

She sat there for a while and wondered what her life had suddenly become. And she wondered what would come after the lie her god bid her tell?

She would return to her guest quarters. She would clear the window and sit in front of it and stare down into the garden, wondering what it would be like to breathe the hot air of Pyrus, swim the boiling rivers of its jungles, pluck the razor flowers by the water's edge. She would address the Council of Seekers and dismantle the Mission. She would write it all down, this new gospel, for the generations to come after and go into hiding from the wrath of the disappointed and unforgiving.

Finally, she stood to leave.

Vesper's words registered with her. God help us, he'd said.

She looked down at the Emperor of Ascending Light one final time.

"He already has," she whispered.

THERE ONCE WAS A GIRL FROM NANTUCKET (A FORTEAN LOVE STORY)

with John Pitts

M exico City glowed for Agnes — called to her in her dreams like a lover, sultry and full of heat. Here, her mother had assured her, she could gain strength.

The frailty of her childhood had lingered into adulthood. Her parents blamed the New England winter and the rigor of college life for her exhaustion. They didn't know about the affair with Martin — Professor Ellesby to them — or how badly it had ended for her. They didn't know she was lovesick and soulsick and lost in her own head, sorting through memories of stolen passion and unrequited love. And they certainly didn't know that forcing her into this hot, bright, living city compounded her longing for something she couldn't quite name.

Her father John Barnham, New England's preeminent architect, and Mary Barnham, her socialite mother, returned to Boston, packed her things, and forcibly relocated her with them in Mexico City.

For well over a year, John Barnham had overseen the construction of the first cathedral built since Mexico's revolution. Mary Barnham kept to her bed during the day, avoiding the oppressive heat and the news from Europe. At night, she proved to be the life of the party for the expatriate community. While war raged across Europe, and men died in the trenches, Mary Barnham drowned her misery in scotch and shallow encounters.

This was fine with Agnes. At night she attended the functions expected of the daughter of visiting dignitaries. But the days — oh the glorious days — she reveled in her solitude, lost and alone in a city of millions. Surely, here, she would compose the poem that haunted her dreams — find the words to express the ache in her soul.

Agnes walked along the cobblestone streets that twisted and turned through the old city. She swung her leather satchel with her pens and paper in her left hand and skipped over the puddles from the morning's rain. Her thin, tanned legs kicked out the edge of her long white dress with each hop.

Beethoven's "Ode to Joy" played in her head, remembrances of the previous night's concert. Heat from the strong summer sun washed into her, filling her hollow places with warmth. A smile played across her lips, brief and bittersweet. Martin had loved Beethoven, the bastard.

And so had his gaunt and pinched wife.

Perhaps today she'd find the inspiration that had eluded her since the frigid December afternoon she encountered Mrs. Martin Ellesby at the symphony.

She'd fled Wellesley then, reeling from shock and deep shame. What else could she do? The scandal would devastate her family.

In the end, her muse flew before the burning ridicule of her peers, ripping from her more than the sweet memories of Martin, of the innocence of her love, but also the joys of Elizabeth Barrett Browning and Walt Whitman.

Instead she found herself enfolded into the stoic propriety of her father's house, affirming his long-held bias toward women and education.

But here, with the long winter a painful but distant memory, she had no fear of meeting the knowing glances and judging stares of her mother's inner-circle. In Mexico she could lose herself in obscurity.

A myriad of people flowed through the city. The Europeans and Americans were easy to spot in their drab clothing and pinched faces. The Mexicans, comfortable in their city, wore bright colors, celebrating life. The dark, weather-worn faces greeted her each morning with smiles as she purchased fresh-picked melon, halved and dripping, the juicy meat exposed to the world, or thick-crusted bread and gloriously rich goat cheese for her mid-day repast.

A Spanish mission stood out amongst the mud-brick houses that lined the lane. Up ahead, growing against the startling blue sky, rose the new cathedral. She and her parents had been in Mexico City since May, and the cathedral's slow transformation had transfixed her. Despite her best intentions, and well-laid plans, she inevitably found herself drawn toward the spire rising over the belly of the city.

As she wound in and out of the streets, the growing spire winked in and out of view. Each time it came into view, a tightness crept into her belly, only to subside again when the view became obscured by other, closer buildings.

Shame had overwhelmed Agnes since the encounter with that horrible, shrieking Mrs. Ellesby. The hope that had been snuffed out inside her heart had given her something in return, a curse, it seemed, to seek answers. It drove her from sleep and haunted her waking pauses. Now the sight of that cathedral spire brought the feeling of expectation and dread.

Today she'd started south of the cathedral to visit a woman she had heard made beautiful wooden rosaries. She thought of her childhood in St. Ignatius' school for girls in Connecticut. How the nuns had showed her the path to Jesus the Lord, through His Mother, Mary. She'd long since given up on the strictures and confinements of the Catholic church, but deep down, under the mousy brown hair, the glasses and the meekness, she felt the dread of the Christ.

The anger and righteousness that threatened her, the judgment that would be meted out to her one day.

She purchased a rather plain rosewood rosary with tiny veins of pink swimming through the creamy wood — each bead linked to its brother with a hand worked bit of silver. She slipped the rosary over her head, felt the heavy silver crucifix nestle between her breasts.

The square in front of the cathedral bustled with a mid-day crowd larger than normal. The benches surrounding the fountains where she usually ate her lunch held gawkers and photographers, quite a few more than normally lunched here. The usually quiet murmur of the city had been replaced by a rising cacophony. Shouting erupted near the cathedral. Obviously something of note had drawn these people here.

She craned her neck above the crowd as best she could, but nothing out of the ordinary struck her. A small, rotund local, poncho and sombrero brightly colored, pushed past her, his mandolin clutched in his fat little hand. The usual "excúse me" she received in such situations did not appear.

"Hmmmph," she sniffed, wrinkling her nose. "Rude and odiferous."

Then an ancient woman, dressed from head to toe in black, shawl wrapped over her thin graying hair, stumbled forward, nearly knocking Agnes to the ground. Agnes spun around, confused. The crowd swelled, and more and more people began to push toward the cathedral.

Agnes, tall and thin, moved along the edge of the crowd like a small twig rolling along the crashing waves. Just as she felt she would fall under the swelling onslaught of bodies, a firm hand appeared, an offering in the growing madness. She took the hand and found herself lifted out of the tide of bodies and raised onto one of the tall, flat tables that surrounded one of the ministerial buildings like barriers.

The hand belonged to a man, an Anglo, by all signs.

He stood above the crowd, his clothing disheveled and his fingers stained yellow from nicotine. Agnes looked up into his face, strong chin covered in a thick black beard. Several curly locks flowed down the sides of his face, escaping the twisting braid that lay across the back of his neck. She stared into his piercing gray eyes, marveling at the gold flecks that seemed to draw the light around her, focusing her attention into the depth and concern.

"Are you quite all right?" he asked, still holding onto her hand.

The breath caught in her throat. Something in his touch, in the splash of blue that lay across his left cheek, and the seriousness of his gaze, broke something inside her. She giggled. Not a demure, proper little laugh, but an outright trill of released tension and pent-up annoyance that escaped her like the effervescent bubbles in a fine champagne.

Bemusement painted his features.

"I'm fine, thanks to you." She smiled at him, feeling the muscles in her face tugging upward.

She looked down at her hand, still clasped in his. His eyes followed, and he released her suddenly, a rosy flush creeping up through unkempt whiskers.

Agnes then noticed, his left hand held a palette. To his left, facing the cathedral, stood an easel.

"Oh, you're a painter?" she asked.

"Yes, I pretend to be," he said, nodding his head slightly.

She looked at the painting. The brush strokes were quite delicate, the colors blending pleasantly. The starkness of the cathedral's spire shone against the inexplicably chartreuse sky. "It is lovely."

He blinked at her for a moment. "You think so? You don't find the sky off-putting?"

"I find it a wonderful compliment to the gold and tan of the cathedral."

His blush deepened. "Most people find my color choices too unrealistic, unnatural."

"Most people are boors."

They stood in silence then, looking at one another in wonder.

"Quite a day, eh?" he said, finally.

She turned to see the square awash in a human sea. The crowd moved in a great swirling circle out one end of the square and back in the other, all revolving around the nearly completed cathedral. "What is happening?"

"Oh, haven't you heard?" he asked. "They've had a visitation."

"A what?"

"Apparently a young boy fell. He had been delivering supplies to those who worked at the top of the scaffolding. He would have most assuredly died from his injuries, but the foreman, a burly Romanian fellow, began yelling for the men around him to fetch a doctor. Then, out of the sky, a lady descended. She came in a cloak of roses, alighted near the boy's cracked and bleeding form. The men fell to their knees, making the sign of the cross. The chant went up, spreading through the city, Virgen de Guadalupe."

She turned, taking in the scene, watching the swell of humanity surge forward, hearing the murmuring of the prayers and the chants. How had she missed this washing through the city? "And you were here when it happened?"

He shook his head, a wry smile slipping from his face. "Alas, no. I was at a coffee shop arguing politics with a rival of mine when the word spread. The bastard came and went, his camera capturing what events he could. I had to dash to my room and get my canvas."

She cocked her head to the side. "Your friend captured this on film, and you decide to capture it on canvas?"

"Yes, I know," he said. "Wholly inadequate to the event, but it is what I know to do."

"I think it captures the scene splendidly."

They stood together, watching the crowd slowly converge on the cathedral.

"Do you mind?" he asked. "My paints are drying out, and I can't afford to waste them."

"No, please. Continue." She waved her hand toward the cathedral. "If you don't mind me watching."

He smiled. "It would please me to have a woman as fair as you watching me paint." He turned toward the canvas, knelt and lifted a small jar of paint from a valise at his feet. He used a small silver blade to daub out a bit of yellow onto the board and mixed it with the paint already there. Once satisfied with the consistency, he carefully scraped the remaining paint from the instrument and replaced the stopper into the jar. He pulled a brush from the valise and stood. He stuck the fine hairs of the brush into his mouth, twisting it a half turn as he extracted it, creating a fine point. Then he tipped the brush into the bright yellow and turned toward the canvas. With a deep sigh, he slowly drew the brush upward from the uneven spire, creating a splash of light that erupted from the center of an empty square.

She watched him, mesmerized by his creation — admiring the deftness of his strokes, the surety in his hand. The emergence of something from nothing, a miracle of creation in oil and fiber — it stirred something within her.

And with that, her muse burst forth.

> *"Like the sundering of a lover's embrace*
> *The lady erupted over the crowd*
> *Leaving the body hale*
> *And the spirit renewed."*

She stumbled as the words trailed off, the sky a spiral of chartreuse and gold. She felt his strong hands catch her, heard his voice through a cottony wall of murmured prayers. "Oh, my fair one," she thought he said. Then the world went black.

This city's drab winter threatened what little of her muse remained. And the drab people in their drab clothes did the same.

Agnes grieved for Mexico City in the months after they left. She missed the bright colors, the bright people, the lavish meals and high ritual.

Naturally, her mother had been sleeping when the painter brought her home. Her father was working. The housekeeper had not thought to ask the young man his name. The physician called it heat exhaustion, and she kept to the shade for three days, but those days had been glorious, her pen moving over page after page, some deep part of her triggered by the remnants of visitation or the firm hands or the mad, swirling sky of the painting. For the rest of the summer,

Agnes wandered the plazas and cafes around the cathedral hoping to find him, perhaps to thank him for bringing her home, perhaps to thank him for finding her muse. She didn't know for sure. Regardless, he was nowhere to be found. When summer ended, she returned to Boston with her parents but did not return to college. Her father insisted that she take a year to think through her choices, given her early withdrawal and poor marks at Wellesley. Autumn in New England bled into a winter in New York, the close of the War to End All Wars punctuating the season with relief.

"Champagne, Miss?"

Agnes turned to the server with his tray of fluted glasses, smiled and shook her head. "No, thank you."

He moved on and she watched him go, then watched the crowded room, eyes moving over the gowns and tuxedoes as New York's upper crust mingled with the intellectuals. Her father had insisted she attend though she would've preferred remaining in Boston for the holiday.

She stood at the edge of the party now, listening to a string quartet playing Mozart. A few couples danced. Most split off to gather in small groups, clusters of men and clusters of women scattered about the ballroom.

Agnes walked the room, picking up bits of conversation. The widespread devastation in Europe, the latest Chaplin film, the new Nash 681 touring car on the streets. Nothing here for her.

A voice rose above the others and she gravitated towards it for some reason that she could not fully grasp.

"Russia," the voice said, "is just the beginning." She moved towards it. "Certainly it's not perfect. But the idea is there. By God, I hope they pull it off. I hope it spreads like a fire. We could all use some idealism that works for a change."

Agnes reached the edge of the conversation. She saw a plain suit, dark hands, but a small knot of men obscured the speaker's face.

"Not 'by God' if your Marx is correct about religion."

"Being the opiate of the masses, Father Reynolds?" the voice asked. "Mark my words, inside thirty years cinema will replace it as such."

The group laughed. Even Agnes stifled a chuckle. The heads moved and she nearly didn't recognize him with his neatly trimmed beard and his short curly hair. The eyes and smile gave him away. He looked up at her, surprise registering on his face. "Miss Barnham?"

She took a step back, a sudden heat rising to her cheeks.

"Miss Agnes Barnham?" He stepped toward her, nodding to the priest. "Please excuse me, Father Reynolds."

"Ah," she said, "So I see you've turned up again." She smiled and offered her hand. "Mister . . .?"

"Schonfeld," he said. "Jacob." He grinned. "What a nice surprise."

"Indeed," she said, recovering. "You quite vanished, you know."

"Mysterious of me, yes? Unfortunately, my visa ran out rather . . . unexpectedly." His eyes smiled. "But I'm glad you looked for me."

She snorted. "You flatter yourself, Mr. Schonfeld. I merely wanted to thank you for returning me home safe and sound."

"Ah," he said. "That's all?"

She nodded, eyes tracking the waiter with his bobbing tray of glasses. She needed a drink. Quickly. "How's the painting?"

He shrugged. "It passes the time suitably. Annoys the parents adequately. And the poetry?"

She felt her cheeks grow even hotter, remembering that spontaneous stanza so many months before. "Poetry?" The waiter dodged by. Her hand snaked out and grabbed a drink as he passed.

"It's quite good," he said. He reached into his jacket pocket and pulled out the last issue of the *New England Poet*. It had been only out two weeks; how could he possibly know? Her knees went to water. Then she remembered the rest of the poem, scribbled out furiously in a cafe near the cathedral in the weeks that followed.

No, she thought. Not this; anything but this. Involuntarily, she started looking for an escape route.

"I was hoping," he said, as he opened the digest to a dog-eared page, "that you would grace me with an autograph."

Those flecks of gold in his eyes danced with amusement. She swallowed. "How in the world did you —"

He interrupted. "Actually, it really *is* quite good. Especially this bit." His finger traced a path down the text and he cleared his throat:

"Arms strong to save and eyes to pierce
A smudge of sky on olive cheek
The Virgin's Son in Mexico my
Lost soul to seek."

He looked up from reading. "I've never been in a poem before." That trapped feeling of embarrassment took on sharpness that spilled over into her voice. "Again, you flatter yourself."

He held out the digest and a pen. "As a Marxist and a Jew I was terribly offended," he continued, grinning. "But as a man, I was quite captivated."

She took the pen, scribbled a few words across the page and handed it back to him.

He read it and laughed. "'You're an ass. Affectionately, Agnes Barnham.'" He bowed his head. "Thank you."

She curtsied and tried not to look smug. "You're quite welcome."

He shifted now to stand beside her. "So what brings you out tonight?"

"Why, Mr. Schonfeld," she said, "haven't you heard it's New Year's Eve?"

"Not for me. Again, Jewish."

"So perhaps the real question is what brings *you* out tonight?"

"Why, my calling of course."

"To embarrass young women with your own pomposity?"

His sudden laugh tingled down her spine. He cocked his head. "That's an added benefit. But actually, the ideological potential for embarrassing the folks is astounding."

She didn't want to ask but had to. The coincidence weighed on her. "And the poem?"

"Ah. That." He started looking around the room. "That was quite a happy accident. I have a friend who spends a lot of time down at the library reading up on strange occurrences, fanciful events, lights in the sky and what-not. We'd been talking about the visitation in Mexico City, he did a bit of looking, and your poem got clipped."

"I find that highly unlikely. It came out not two weeks ago."

"It is his work," he said. "He's here tonight. You can ask him."

"Sounds like a bit of a crank to me."

"Ah, but a well-connected crank to be sure. He's here as the guest of Theodore Dreiser." He took her elbow and warmth fled out as his fingers brushed her skin. "You'll love him. Full of all kinds of amazing information. Besides, he's actually responsible for me finding you."

She raised her eyebrows. "Mr. Schonfeld, you seem to be mistaken. I found you. Twice now."

He shrugged. "Believe what you will." Then he patted the pocket with the concealed journal. "'Miss Agnes Barnham,'" he quoted from memory, "'daughter of preeminent architect John Barnham, currently makes her home in Boston, Massachusetts, with her family and her cat, Hezekiah. This is her first professional publication.'"

He smiled at her, slipped his hand into his pocket and withdrew it. A single train ticket to Boston. "I was leaving tomorrow."

She opened her mouth to say something, then closed it. She felt something odd moving from her stomach toward her throat, as if she'd swallowed a moth that now wanted out.

He put the ticket away. "Still," he said, "it's a hell of a coincidence."

She blinked. "You're telling me that you were coming to Boston tomorrow to find me?"

"Yes," he said.

"Why?"

He cleared his throat, looking around the room at everything but her. "Well. That's a damned good question."

"And?"

Jacob shrugged. "I think it was the poem. I'd never felt so . . . Messianic . . . before."

Agnes felt a giggle rise but fought it down. She wanted to be annoyed. "So it's really his fault, then," she said.

"Whose?"

"This friend of yours who spends his days in the library studying poems about unexplained phenomena."

"Oh, not just poems. Newspapers, magazines, the works. But yes. His fault." He grinned and offered her his arm. "Do you think," he asked, "that all of these coincidences are . . . coincidental?"

She rolled her eyes, letting him steer her through the crowd. "Are all Marxists this funny, or are you an exciting new prototype?"

"Just the Jewish ones," he said. "Let's meet my friend."

Agnes couldn't help but smile. "Let's," she said. "I'm really quite cross with him."

They navigated the room in silence now. With his free hand he waved to a group of men huddled in the corner. "There he is."

A tall, heavy-set man wearing a gray tweed suit who seemed out of place laughed loudly. He looked a bit like Teddy Roosevelt, Agnes thought. He swept off his glasses and rubbed them clean with a cloth. "— and I suspect only four or five people will actually pick it up," the man was saying.

"Going on about that again?" Jacob asked as they approached.

"Charles Fort, may I present to you Miss Agnes Barnham."

"Ah," Fort said. "The Mystery Poetess of Boston I've heard so much about."

"Nantucket, originally," she said, extending her hand. "Mr. Fort. A pleasure to meet you." He took her hand, squeezed it.

"Nantucket?" Jacob asked. "Really?"

She nodded slightly. "Born and raised." She turned to Fort. "So what *were* you going on about?"

"His book," said another of the men. "And he'd best stop, considering the limb I've climbed out on for him."

Fort released her hand. "I told you, Dreiser, you needn't bother."

A bespectacled man with a greasy comb-over and wide lips inserted himself between them, taking her hand. "Miss Barnham."

"Mr. Dreiser," she said, a smile playing at the corners of her mouth. The fingers of his other hand lingered a bit long on her wrist. She gently pulled away, craning her neck to see around Dreiser. "What's it called?"

He stepped aside. "*The Book of the Damned.*"

"Fantastical or spiritual?" she asked.

"Neither, actually," Fort said. "Or perhaps both, I suppose."

"Fort here chases down the unusual and extraordinary," Dreiser said.

"Yes, Mr. Schonfeld told me as much," Agnes said. "Do tell me a bit about it."

Fort's smile widened. "I'd be happy to, Miss Barnham. What strikes your fancy? Strange markings on meteorites that have fallen from the sky? Artifacts found within rocks? A rain of fishes in a cornfield?"

Agnes shrugged. "Anything, really. Just tell me the most amazing thing you've seen."

Dreiser laughed. The others in the group chuckled as well, except Jacob. Jacob stared at her, a strange look on his face. Charles Fort blushed.

"Fort here hasn't actually *seen* any of the amazing things in his book," Dreiser said, clapping the man on the back. "He gathers them up from the library."

"Not so, Dreiser," Fort said. "I've seen the most amazing of the amazing."

"Pray tell," Agnes said.

Fort put his hand on her shoulder, turning Agnes slightly. "Do you see the piano there?"

She nodded. The group became quiet.

"Are you watching carefully?"

She nodded again, squinting intently.

"Now . . . move just to the left. The woman there, in the blue dress? Do you see her?"

"Yes." She was a short middle-aged woman talking with a group of matrons. She glanced over, smiled and gave a subdued wave.

"That woman is my wife, Annie Fort, and *she* is the most amazing thing I've ever seen." He chuckled and dropped his hand from her shoulder to glance back at his friend. "What do you think of *that*, Dreiser?"

"Fort, you devil, I'm speechless," Dreiser said.

"And *that*," Charles Fort said to the group, "is the second most amazing thing I've ever seen."

The conversation moved on around her but Agnes couldn't hear anything. It was as if someone had stuffed cotton into her ears. The music faded. The voices drifted and the room slowed down. She watched as Jacob talked with his friends, watched his hands move, watched his eyes move. Light came from him and suddenly he seemed very much the same larger than life figure that stood against the sky in her memories of that plaza in Mexico City.

Maybe, she thought, visitations happen every day. She opened her mouth to say so, to somehow add something to all of the words she could no longer hear. Then Agnes realized suddenly that Jacob's eyes were fixed on hers, his lips forming a surprised and nervous smile, his hands limp at his sides with no further point to make.

A quiet miracle rustled but refused quite yet to be born.

On a rather dreary Friday evening in late May, the phone rang unexpectedly. Her father answered, grumpily thrusting the phone toward her after a few minutes of listening. "Some editor." He screwed his face into a twist, as if he smelled something foul. "Wants to talk to you about your poem."

They'd never phoned before, usually corresponded by mail. Agnes accepted the phone, took a quiet breath and held one hand against her breast. "This is Agnes Barnham."

A familiar voice, tinny and distant, filled her ear. "Miss Barnham, lovely to hear your voice."

She glanced at her father, one hand covering the phone, eyebrows raised.

Mr. Barnham rolled his eyes and shambled out of the parlor, mumbling.

Agnes grinned. "Mr. Schonfeld, how nice of you to call. You're buying poetry these days?"

"Listen, I haven't much time," he said. His words tumbled fast. "Do you fancy snakes?"

"Not so much," she said. She paused, waiting for him to continue but he didn't. "Why do you ask?"

She heard other voices in the background, equally excited. She heard Jacob's muffled voice as his hand covered the receiver. "Please, can you keep it down? I'm on the line with Boston here." Clearer now as he answered her question: "A chap up in Maine rang Fort to say there's been a snake-fall near Portland. Would you like to see it?"

She wasn't sure she'd heard correctly. "A what?"

"A snake-fall. A rain of snakes. Would you like to see it with me?"

She looked around to make sure no one was in earshot. "Where are you?"

More voices. "Oh. I'm in New York. But I'm leaving in a few minutes and wondered if I could swing by and pick you up."

Formality slipped her mind. "Jacob, you're over two hundred miles away. Portland is at least another hundred miles from here." Her mouth wanted to smile. She fought it back as if somehow he'd be able to hear it in her voice. "You're just going to *swing by*?"

He seemed embarrassed now. "Well, only if you want to see it."

"Mr. Schonfeld," she said in her sweetest voice, "you're either batty or drunk or both."

He ignored her comment. "I should hit Boston easily by morning. Shall I pick you up at eight?"

She thought for a moment. "Oh, I should think eight-thirty at the earliest. At the train station, please."

"At the train station?"

"It's easier that way. Trust me."

"I'll see you then," he said and rang off.

Agnes stood for a moment, holding the phone in her hands. A snake-fall in Maine. For a moment she wondered if this was some odd courtship she'd happened across, then wondered if calling it a courtship presumed too much and wondered exactly why some part of her felt afraid and hopeful all at once as memories of his eyes, his hands, his mouth flashed silently past.

Last, she wondered what lie she'd tell her father about to-morrow.

The field of snakes stretched on and on before them. Agnes poked at one with her foot, ready to jump back if it moved. It didn't; it seemed all the snakes were dead. "You do this often?"

Jacob looked up from unloading the Model T. He smiled, pulling out a collapsible chair. "When I can." He unfolded the chair and steadied it.

Agnes shielded her eyes from the late morning sun. "This must explain why there is no *Mrs.* Schonfeld."

He laughed. The sound of it still made her feel warm. "I suppose it does." He unfolded a second chair and set it up near — but not too near — the other. Then he worked the easel free.

She sharpened her pencil while Jacob set up his easel and squeezed paint onto his palette. She sat down and drew her notepad from her satchel. She scribbled:

> *Caught up, cast down in a courtship of snakes*
> *A carpet of corpses unmoving, unliving*
> *Untethered at last from past mistakes*
> *Free from the unloving and unforgiving.*

She lined it out and stole a glance at Jacob. His eyes flashed merriment and his mouth twitched into a grin. She fell back into the last several hours and returned his smile.

The jostling of the car and the easiness of his voice had drawn her out. They'd talked about everything. Movies and music. Last week's vote in the House to approve the new amendment, the one that would finally expand America's democracy to her and millions of other women. ("If we're going to drink to that," he had said, "we'd better do it quickly.") Eliot, Frost, Van Gogh, Marx, Sanger, and the surprising popularity of Fort's book — they moved from subject to subject, eventually settling into their childhoods, their fears, their frustrations and even a bit of their dreams.

His brush darted now from palette to canvas, his eyes wandering over the field.

After an hour of more random scribbling, more random lines to somehow capture this time, she looked up at him. "Why do you do this again?"

He glanced at her, his brush never losing its stroke. "Bored so soon?"

She chuckled. "Not bored. Curious."

He smiled, his white teeth gleaming in the light. "It awes me. I like how that feels. So I paint that feeling."

"You do this a lot?"

"What? Lure young women into fields of dead snakes?"

Now her chuckle became a laugh. "No. Paint oddities."

His brows furrowed. "Not oddities, Agnes. Unexplained and unexpected wonders." For a moment, he paused, his brush hanging in the dead space between paint and painting. Then he remembered her question. "I paint what I see."

She looked at the field of dead snakes. "But always after the fact? You'd said in Mexico City that you'd arrived *after* the visitation. And these —" she waved at the snakes — "they fell yesterday . . . maybe even the day before."

"I'm usually appallingly late to miracles," he said.

"Usually? So you've been on time before?"

"Once or twice."

"Only twice?"

Their eyes met. Something danced in his. "Three times, now that I think about it."

She raised her eyebrows. "What were they? Strange lights in the sky? People vanishing and reappearing?"

"No. Missed all of those." He went back to painting.

"Are you going to tell me?"

"Maybe later," he said. "For now, my paints are drying."

She rolled her eyes. "I've heard *that* one before."

He didn't answer. After a few minutes, she pushed herself back in the chair, lowered her hat, and closed her eyes.

It was late afternoon when she awoke. The sun had vanished, dark clouds spreading across the sky.

"And the lady awakens," Jacob said. "I think we're going to have muddy roads home if we don't pack it up soon."

Agnes stood and stretched. "Did you finish your painting?"

He nodded, standing himself. "I did. Just now."

She took a step closer to him. "May I see it?"

Jacob blushed and stammered. "I . . . I'm not sure you'd —"

"Oh, don't be silly." She walked around the easel to stand by him. Her mouth opened and shut and she looked from the canvas to him and back.

It was the most beautiful painting she had ever seen. A stunning girl stretched out, asleep in a collapsible chair, her hair cascading from beneath an off-kilter hat. She followed the line of the neck, the curve of the breasts, the sleek, coltish grace of the legs. The girl's feet rested on the shore of an ocean of rainbow-speckled serpents while overhead, a sky colored by a thousand dreams swirled and twisted like a silk canopy above.

Agnes did not know what else to say. "You've been painting me."

He turned to face her, shuffling his feet slightly. "I did."

"But why?"

"I paint what I see."

And suddenly it struck her. Three times, he had said earlier, and she realized now that those had been the only three miracles she'd been on time for, herself. Mexico City. New York. Now here.

"Is it okay?" he asked her.

The sky above rumbled and opened. Something bounced off her shoulder but she ignored it. Dark shapes fell into the field, thudding softly as they bounced off the car.

Her eyes searched his. She didn't know what to say so she did the only thing that came to mind. Throwing herself into his arms, she kissed him and kept on kissing him while frogs fell around them. Beneath their feet, the ground hopped and croaked, rolling like a living sea. Overhead, the sky turned a shade of ochre that neither paint nor poem could capture.

THE TAKING NIGHT

The little boy looks out through five-year-old eyes, safe in his hiding place beneath the table. He's supposed to be in bed — it's dark outside. But the ringing doorbell called him and no one saw him sneak down the hall. Those men in blue are still here, talking quietly in the living room, and he doesn't like them one bit because they make Mama cry.

"... so sorry," he hears one say.

"... a hero," the other says.

Mama nods and sniffles and stares at the yellow piece of paper shaking in her hands.

He wants to tell them to go away, wants to do what Daddy said before he left to fight the bad men. "Take care of your mother, Victor," he said. But he's afraid. Instead, he wipes his nose on his pajama sleeve and tries not to cry.

Vic Adams peed himself in the night and woke up foul-tempered. He rang and rang for the nurse, and when the small, attractive blonde came in, he was too ashamed to tell her why he called. She checked the bandages for seepage and left frowning. At least I won't be pissy alone, he thought, and watched her swish through the door.

His left leg itched and he chuckled at it, imagining it laying in some medical waste bin somewhere begging to be scratched. He'd read stories about amputees, and now he knew they were true. He looked over to the button that would drip morphine into his veins. Just one push, he thought, then didn't.

Instead, he pushed himself back in the pillows and switched on the room's wall-mounted intervision — a Japanese job going back a few years and slower than a fat guy in a foot-race. He pulled up his mail, skimming each item, looking for something more personal than a bill or a pitch. What he really wanted to see wasn't there. Something from her. Something saying goodbye, or better yet, I'm not going after all. Nothing new from her waited there in the electric mailbox; just the same old messages, piled up in the SAVE bin.

But when he switched from mail-mode to news, his granddaughter was there, big as life, broad-smiled, eyes flashing. Her dad's eyes and smile, he realized with a pang of loss. She wore the blue jumpsuit well, with pride, her hair neatly pinned up off her collar. A sharply dressed reporter sat across from her.

"How do you feel today, Captain Adams?" Vic cringed; even before the divorce, she'd only used her maiden name. It didn't seem right, not sharing her husband's name. At the very least she could've hyphenated it. But she *was* the last of the line, once Vic went.

"Great." Captain Charlene Adams radiated life and the cameras caught it, throwing it around the world by satellite. "I've never felt better."

"Tomorrow's the big day. Are you ready for it?"

She looked into the lens with a cocky grin. "I've trained and waited for four years — I'm as ready for tomorrow as I'll ever be. But tomorrow isn't the *big* day." She paused and Vic could see her taking pleasure in the reporter's confused look. "The *big* day is about three years from now — for those of us going, anyway — if old Einstein parsed right."

The reporter nodded. "Senator Caroway has openly expressed her concerns about sending such a young crew on this mission. As a matter of fact, she's led the opposition to this mission from the start and has used it to garner a great deal of support for her campaign from the Christian Fundamentalists Coalition. Do you have anything you'd like to say about that?"

This will be good, Vic thought. Give 'em hell, Tatertot. Instead, the young woman shook her head. "I don't want to comment on political issues, Bob. I'm not really following the Presidential race — it's not as if I'll be voting in it." The reporter and those standing around laughed. "I do have great respect for Senator Caroway, though. She's had a tremendous influence on my life."

A male orderly came into Vic's room, his bulk momentarily eclipsing the screen. "Breakfast, Mr. Adams. Hey, is that her . . . is that your granddaughter?"

Vic nodded, waving impatiently for the man to move. He did, setting down the steaming tray and turning to the screen. "Hmm. She's a total frib, ain't she? How old you say she was?"

"Twenty-eight." He didn't like it when men ogled her that way. And he had no idea what frib meant, but also knew he didn't want to know.

"That means she'll be about what . . . thirty-two . . . when they get there?"

He nodded, trying to catch the last snatches of her voice. There had been another question and he missed it. Now it was an outdoor shot, and the angle widened to take in the nine others, none older than thirty-five. They even *looked* like a team, at ease with one another, standing so close that their arms and shoulders touched. Which one would she end up with, he wondered? It was impossible to tell — they were all young, attractive. Five men, five women. On a one-way trip that started tomorrow morning.

Swallowing his pride, he asked the orderly to change him, and when he was finished, Vic Adams ate his breakfast quietly and scanned the channels for more of her.

The man watches his bedroom ceiling through forty-nine year-old eyes, knowing the call, expecting the call. The phone rings and he reaches for it.

He knows what questions to ask, fighting back the tears.

"When? What time? She was asleep when she went?" He doesn't hear the answers, just the questions and the rushing behind his temples. Time to get up. Time to get dressed. Time to call Jerry and tell him about his little sister. She was so young, his second wife, Marybeth says, pulling on her clothes and crying. Only twenty-five. His little girl, he tells himself, his only girl.

Who could have known that husband of hers went both ways? No one did until he got sick. And that bastard died first and left Vic with a little girl who, after fighting for three years, was resting now.

Just resting, he told himself.

*

Still no mail at lunch time, and no flashing light to indicate an incoming vidcall. Vic Adams stirred a puddle of mashed potatoes and gravy around a forkful of meatloaf and shoveled it into his mouth.

"Mr. Adams?" The doctor was a young man, but the best, everyone told him. "How are you feeling this afternoon?" Padding softly to the morphine dispenser, he checked the meter and smiled. "Not using this anymore at all now, are we?"

Vic managed a grin. "I don't know about you, but I'm not."

Dr. Jacoby laughed. "Good to see your humor's returning. Mind if I sit down?"

Vic nodded to a chair nearby. "Help yourself."

Sitting, the doctor's fingers flashed over the e-chart. "Your blood sugar's down where it needs to be. That's good. How's the leg?"

"Gone." Vic chuckled. "Itches some, still."

"Well, the physical therapist will start in with you tomorrow, get you up and in a chair, start working those other muscles. It'll be a few months before we can fit you with one of those new Kawasaki prosthetics, but there's no reason why you can't be out of here and into a care center in say . . . a week?"

Vic felt himself deflating, even though he'd known all along. They'd told him before the surgery, when they saw the deteriorating bones and the infection creeping up like purple ivy from his left foot. Without Dolores around to nag him, he'd become neglectful. He skipped his shots, missed his appointments and ate whatever he damned well felt like eating for a bit too long this time, and now it had cost him. The leg was a significant loss, but not the most significant. Hell, he was eighty-seven years old. How much longer would he have walked anyway? The trip to the Cape to see her off — that's what gnawed him most.

The doctor stood. "I'm really sorry, Vic. I know you wanted to be down there tomorrow morning. There just wasn't any way so soon after the surgery."

Nodding, Vic turned away. "I understand, Doc." When Dr. Jacoby slipped out of the room, he changed channels again and sipped his lukewarm coffee.

"Sorry, Tatertot," he told a grinning face on the intervision. "I want to see you go or make you stay, but I don't have a leg to stand on."

He laughed at his own joke and then took a morphine hit.

*

He's a little drunk, seeing the world through sixty-five-year-old eyes. He's just come home from his retirement party. Thirty years at CARECO, helping people with their auto, fire and life, and now his third wife, Dolores, is waiting for him in the bedroom, her dress, nylons and underthings a bread-crumb trail for his eyes to devour. He's trying hard not to think about the war in Eastern Europe, about Jerry and that Goddamned stratobomber he flies over there. Instead, he wants to think about having wild, drunken sex and celebrating his sunset years. But the vidphone hums to life in the hallway and he stops to activate it with his voice.

"Hello, Grandpa," she says and he can tell she's frightened. She's in the dark, in Jerry's den, talking very quietly but very clearly for a six-year-old.

"Who is it?" Dolores shouts from upstairs.

"It's Charlene." He turns on the hall light. "Hello, Tatertot. Your mom know you're up at this hour?"

She shakes her head. "I'm scared, Grandpa."

"Why?" In the background he hears quiet voices. He looks at the time: One o'clock. His stomach begins its long ride down.

"The men in blue are here, Grandpa. They're making Mommy cry."

Please God, don't let it be so, he prays. No one should outlive their children, he tells himself. It's just not fucking fair.

That evening, he shut off the intervision and picked up an old-fashioned paper magazine, savoring its slick surface in his hands, its inky smell in his nose.

The article on First Contact was very good, spanning all the way back to the late eighties, when the Reagan Administration had first pulled voices down from the stars and bottled them up tight under a lid of secrecy. It followed the slow development over the decades that followed, even published the three messages that had come to us and our three responses. Then, the article concluded with an outline of The Plan.

Ten for ten, to pass without meeting somewhere in the long night between systems. We knew the basics — they were humanoid . . . even human, unless you listened to those clowns in the Christian Fundamentalist Coalition, who insisted that it was all a Satanic hoax or a plot to create the New World Order they all feared.

And my Tatertot's one of our ten, Vic thought. First ambassadors . . . maybe even first colonists . . . to Procyon. He tried not to think about her so far away. He was eighty-seven now. He'd be dead before she arrived, but for her it'd only be three years — and that spent asleep. He never did grasp relativity, and even the article's layman simplicity made little sense to him.

He remembered watching Armstrong step onto the moon, his children on his lap. Their mother, drunk again, was passed out in the bedroom. His daughter had wriggled, always bored by anything that did not involve rapid movement. But Jerry was all rapt attention.

"I wanna fly, too," he had said.

Later, when Caroway stepped out onto Mars, Vic held his granddaughter tight and watched it on their very first intervision. Charlene, then eight, had been just as engrossed as her father had, thirty-five years earlier. She'd come to live with Vic and Dolores after her mother died. Pills, the doctor said. His daughter-in-law barely lived past the anniversary of Jerry's death in Yugoslavia.

"I wanna fly, too," Charlene had said. For the next ten years, pictures of Leslie Ann Caroway skipping across the Martian landscape plastered her walls.

Vic never told her that her father had said exactly the same thing.

He fell asleep with the magazine open on his chest and dreamed of a far away world.

He looks into the open casket through eighty-three-year-old eyes that are too dry for tears now. Charlene slips up behind him and her hands come around him. "I'm sorry, Grandpa," she tells him and he's glad she's stopped calling him Vic for the moment.

He shrugs. "Life's for the living, Tatertot. I'll be okay." He's quiet for a moment. "She was a good wife. The best."

Behind him, his granddaughter is crying and she's holding him so tightly that he can feel the ribbons and bits of metal from her uniform pressing through his sports coat. "I just don't understand. Everybody I love keeps dying."

He hears the little girl in her voice and he reaches up a liver-spotted hand to pat her own, slender woman-hand. "I know," he tells her. "Me, too."

She loosens up her grip. "Why?"

He doesn't have an answer. He wants to say that death is just a part of life, but part of him believes that it's just a pithy funeral home marketing pitch to keep the dead coming. "Night always comes," he said. "The sun's never up forever."

"At least we have each other." He's surprised she doesn't mention her fiancee, Ted, the gangly pre-med student she's been dating for three years, but he says nothing.

"Yes we do," he answers. For now. Until the night takes one of us, too.

He awakened as a shaft of light grew over his face. "Vic?" The shaft disappeared as the door shut. "Vic?"

Vic opened his eyes, seeing the dim room through eighty-seven-year-old eyes. The voice sounded familiar. "Ted?" Charlene's ex-husband.

"Yeah. How you feel?"

"Like a one legged man in an ass kicking contest. What the hell are you doing here?"

Ted grinned, lopsided. Vic always liked that grin. "Char sent me with a message."

"Well, why didn't she just mail it over?"

Ted shook his head, grin widening. "She'd have brought it herself, but they're all tucked away for tomorrow's launch."

Vic sat up. "So what's the message?"

"*Get your lazy butt out of bed, Grandpa.* Or something to that effect. You and I are going to the Cape for a little fireworks show."

"Well, it's about Goddamned time." He tried to make it sound gruff, but his voice cracked with emotion.

With expert hands, Ted dressed him quickly and shifted his weight into a waiting wheelchair. Then, at the last possible minute, he disconnected the monitors and IV. "We don't have a helluva lot of time," he hissed, slipping the chair through the door and racing it down the hall, its wheels a rubber whisper along the tile floor.

Once, somewhere behind them, Vic thought he heard someone

shouting, but the elevator doors hushed shut, cutting off the sound. Ted hit the ground floor at a trot and in less than five minutes, he was racing his Mercedes up the freeway ramp, nose pointed toward the coast.

The two men were quiet for the longest time, and finally Vic spoke. "So she put you up to this? I thought you two had split?"

Ted nodded. "We have, on paper at least. She thought it was best that way, her going and everything." Vic noted the bitterness in the man's voice. So he'd been right — it wasn't mutual, after all.

Sounded like his Tatertot, so narrow in her focus, every corner of her life coming under submission to the dream. For her, divorcing Ted would be a necessary cog on the gear that turned her toward space. She couldn't justify leaving a husband behind and couldn't conceive of coming back to him.

"I'm sorry, Ted," Vic said, reaching over to pat the younger man's arm. "I wish she weren't so damned headstrong. She's really going to miss out on some things."

Ted scrunched down in the seat, eyes scanning the star-speckled night. "Yeah, but so are we."

Sometime between the middle of the night and earliest hours of the morning, Vic Adams peed himself again, but didn't notice and didn't care. Ahead, the massive tower loomed on the tarmac, the shuttle hugging its booster rockets like drunk friends. She's suiting up now, he told himself, going over the last details.

They parked where all the others were parked, mingled in with spectators and reporters, all hoping to get a glimpse of the ten before they left forever. Ted wheeled him up as close to the fence as possible and stood by.

A voice caught his ear and he twisted, seeing her face fill a film crew's relay monitor. "It's her," Vic said excitedly.

". . . last thing you'd like to say, Captain Adams?" the reporter from the day before asked. They were re-playing the interview, and this was the part Vic had missed.

"Yes," she said, her eyes soft and looking out into the world. "I want to say something to my Grandfather. I won't be able to see him before I go. I —"

But Vic stopped listening and turned back toward the shuttle. He could play the tape back later, but now the clock wound down and gouts of smoke belched from beneath the massive rockets, now the ground shook and a roar filled his head. The great leviathan lifted off the ground, burning up the air as it plowed upwards to make its rendezvous with Armstrong Station and the Orion Class starship, *Ulysses*, that waited there for its maiden crew.

Vic watched it disappear, his wonder drowning out the whoops and hollers of the human sea around him. He followed its arching line against the azure sky, the sun warm on his tear-streaked face. There was no night here now, he told himself, but there was night where she went. A cold stretch of night between islands of life.

Raising his hands in supplication, he gave her to it.

ON THE SETTLING OF ANCIENT SCORES

Another." The stranger in town pushed his empty glass forward. He sat at the bar, smoking and watching the room through the mirror as the pretty bartender scurried from customer to customer.

"Right away," said the bartender. She didn't smile much. Not once in two hours. Her hand brushed a strand of hair from her face.

"No hurry." He crushed out the cigarette, watching the last of its smoke curl tightly upward to open like a fist in the air. She bustled off to get his drink.

"Hello. This seat taken?" A man in a white suit. A man wrapped in a suit as white as a snowstorm, right down to the white carnation in his lapel and the scruff of his white beard. It was the Lord.

"Not lately," the stranger said.

"And this one?" A woman. A redhead, tall, leggy, in a tight black miniskirt and an equally tight blouse. Her tan breasts spilled out of the low neckline. She nodded to the Lord. "Heya."

He nodded back. "Long time no see."

The stranger looked from one to the other. She was the Devil. He didn't need to see her tattoo to know it. He coughed politely to get their attention. "So. You both made it. Good."

Her smile split her face, and the bared teeth shone. "Of course. I never turn down an invitation."

God tugged the stranger's sleeve. "Neither do I." His eyes were warmer than Satan's, but mysteries and secrets still swam in them; unexplained management practices danced inside. Neither's gaze was particularly comforting.

"Well," the stranger said. "I'm glad. We need to talk."

The bartender returned, sliding a glass of bourbon into his waiting hand. "Something for your friends here?"

"Not exactly friends, but sure . . . whatever they're having."

"Merlot," God said.

"Sounds good," the Devil said.

"Two merlots," the stranger said.

She left again.

"Let's move to a table." The stranger picked up his drink and then picked his way past redneck loggers and pool-shooting bikers to a table in the corner. God and Satan slid into one side of the booth. The stranger took the other. "Let's get down to business," said the stranger. "The universe is a fucking mess, and you're both responsible for it."

A stunned look crossed God's face as his mouth opened and then shut.

"Don't look at me," Satan said, batting her eyes. "I'm not responsible for anything. He made me who I am, and when I tried to set things right, he cast me down with the rest of Heaven's Free Thinkers."

"Well, I —"

The stranger cut them off with the stab of a fresh cigarette. "Enough. You're *both* responsible." He turned to Satan. "You can call it what you want, but evil is evil and you are the origin of it. You are the Father of Lies and —"

"Mother," she hissed.

"Fine. Whatever. It started with you. You *chose* that road for yourself. And you knew what you were doing." He leaned in. "Regardless of what happened in Heaven, there *was* that bit in the Garden."

A dreamy smile played Satan's lips. "Oh . . . *her*. She was delicious. So young, so innocent, so . . . *easy*." She laughed. "And he was yummy, too."

God shook his head sadly. "You see what I deal with?" He sighed.

The bartender zipped in with two wineglasses and then zipped away. Satan and God sipped.

"You're both responsible. You —" he pointed at God. "You created this mess. And despite free will, you created Satan knowing full well what he . . . *she* . . . was going to do."

God nodded. "You're absolutely, completely, correct."

Satan leaned forward. Her voice whispered like fingers on his thighs. "I've never seen him step up to the plate like this before. Bravo!"

"Well, it ends now," the stranger said. "It changes today. We're fed up. We're tired of being played against each other. We're tired of having to figure out the music we're supposed to dance to. So . . . kiss and make up."

God choked in mid-sip. Satan spilled her wine, splattering it on the table like blood.

"I beg your pardon?" God checked his white suit for red stains.

"You heard me. Kiss and make up. Right here. Right now." He stood. "You two think about it a minute. I gotta pee."

"What a coinincky-dink," Satan said. "So do I." She showed a lot of leg climbing out and made a great show of stumbling and grabbing the stranger's arm. He didn't flinch, though her touch was cold on his bare skin.

She stopped him outside the men's room door. "You know, I could be a real friend to you." Her hand slid down his chest, working its way down his stomach. She purred and looked at the restroom door longingly. "We could . . . play. Right now."

She moved as though to go inside with him, but he stopped her. "I don't think so. I don't wanna play. I wanna pee."

"You're no fun."

The stranger shrugged. "Sometimes I am."

Her smile went serious, and she stepped back. "I think I know who you are."

"Really?"

"Yes. And if you are who I *think* you are, we could help each other out."

"How so?"

She nodded to the bar, to the man in white sitting patiently at the table. "If he were out of the way, a lot of wrongs could be made right. We could *all* be free."

"But that would lead to anarchy."

"Not if someone more . . . balanced . . . were in charge."

"Someone like you?"

She smiled and her green cat's eyes narrowed. "Would that be so bad?"

"Yes." He pushed passed her and into the men's room.

God walked in as he zipped up. The stranger moved aside of the urinal but God shook his head. "I'm not here for that. Let's be direct, you and I. I know who you are."

"Omniscience, right?"

"Right."

"Then you know what I'm here for?"

"Reconciliation. A bringing together of good and evil. An end to the Eternal Conflict."

"Yes."

"It won't work."

"Why not?" The stranger washed up, watching God in the mirror. "She'll never buy into it. I tried. Don't you think I've tried?" The stranger turned. "No, actually. I don't." God blushed. "It won't work."

"It has to. We're done. We're tired of the bullshit. You know us; you know everything about us. You know how fragile we are. Like lost little children in a dark wood that you've helped create. And every bread crumb we drop to find our way Home is gobbled up before it hits the ground."

The stranger held the door, beckoned God with a nod to pass through. The Almighty paused before stepping outside, his face collapsing in thought. "You know . . . Well, never mind."

"What?"

He looked at the woman sitting alone at the table. "You could take care of *that* for me. Then there would just be Good."

"I don't want good and evil abolished. I just want them balanced out. I want fairness. I want justice."

"*I* now?" God said. "Be careful. You were on firmer ground with 'we' than you could ever be with 'I,' you know."

They returned to the table. The stranger drained his glass. "So . . . do we have a deal?"

God laughed. Satan joined in. The stranger found it pleasant to hear . . . like harmony . . . but he knew it could never last.

"Absolutely not," God said through his laughter.

"Hysterical," Satan said as she giggled.

The stranger drew his revolver and it barked twice in the noisy room. Satan slumped over, a shiny patch glistening over her heart. God rocked back, a red flower blossoming over his breast pocket. Their eyes glassed over quickly, their jaws went slack. Outside, the wind howled and the bar became strangely silent.

The pretty bartender spoke first. "Why the fuck did you do that? And who's going to clean it up?"

"We all are," the stranger said. "All of us. In time."

"Who the hell do you think you are," an angry biker shouted, throwing down his pool cue. It clattered on the floor.

The stranger stood, pocketed the pistol, and moved for the door. "I am Everyman."

IN TIME OF DESPAIR
AND GREAT DARKNESS

My uncle, Mordecai Bach, found an old sword in the watery mud of a trench near Ypres at the end of the war. Of course, I never heard him tell of it himself. He was a taciturn, quiet man, rarely speaking outside the walls of the little First Baptist church he deaconed at about a hundred miles outside Boise City, Oklahoma.

Way my father told it, Uncle Mordecai smuggled it home and hung it on the wall of his barn with the rest of his tools until the day he converted.

Reverend Archer was a revivalist in those days and he'd pitched a mighty tent over a sawdust floor, giving testament unto the power of the Lord to save and forgive the sins of men. One particular night, sweat flying from his hair and jowls, he'd pointed a crooked finger at my uncle and cut loose with a stream of Bible like as to make your hair stand up. Something from the second chapter of Isaiah stuck true and my father's brother went down on his knees to take the Christ into his heart and vowed to give over his life unto the cross.

Proud of shoeing his own mules and doing his own ironmongery, he went home straightaway and banged that sword into what the Good Book called a plowshare, following the word of the Lord as best he knew how.

My father always told the next bit with a chuckle despite my uncle's sullen glare.

First time out to field, he ran it into a buried mountain of granite and it stuck fast, breaking the leg of his best pulling mule and becoming somewhat of a local curiosity quickly forgotten.

Every day for well on a year, he hitched mule and snapped reins with nary a budge before he gave up.

My father, less patient I reckon, only tried twice that I know of.

Of course, by the time I was old enough to cotton to those yarns, I was more interested in Amy Sue Peller and how soft her skin felt under my clumsy hands. And not long after that, the world went to hell again despite the jam-packed little church my uncle helped to build amid the corn.

Truth is, I didn't care much about that old plow until the strangers showed up asking after it.

I was walking home from Piker's Creek when the fancy car pulled up alongside. I was whistling and walking slow, thinking about how warm a breast can be beneath the fingers and how a girl's hair could smell like apples and summer, when the man called out to me.

I looked to him. He was older than my uncle by a long shot, his beard white and trimmed close and his spectacles shining bright in the afternoon sun. It was the deep blue turban that assured me he had to be from back East.

"Pardon me, lad," he called out. "I'm looking for a farm."

I blinked, looked around me at the barren fields and nodded. "There are a lot of farms around here, Mister," I told him. I didn't bother to tell him that in these dark times, most were closing down and packing up.

He smiled at me and I saw that one of his teeth was bright polished gold. "Actually," he said, "I'm looking for a particular farm."

Now I noticed he had three friends with him, all old, bearded men in hats to match his own.

He leaned his head further out the window. "I'm looking for the Mordecai Bach farm, but I appear to have missed a turn."

I pushed my hat up on my head. "No, Sir, you ain't." I pointed my fishing rod further on down the road. "It's ahead yonder. Look for the yellow barn."

He smiled again and tossed me a silver coin that I caught from the air. "Thank you, lad. You've done us a great service."

And before I could say another word, the dust from his Ford was in my eyes and mouth and he and his friends were sputtering off down the road towards home.

When I could see again, I looked at the coin but couldn't for the life of me make heads or tails of it. I slipped it into my right pocket, the one without a hole in it, and stretched into an easy jog.

*

When I approached the house, my father and the men were on the porch talking. My uncle was nowhere to be seen but my mother was bustling about with a pitcher of lemonade and a plateful of her blue-ribbon gingersnaps.

When my father saw me coming he waved me over. "Where you been, boy?"

"Fishing," I lied, wondering what excuse Amy Sue would offer up to her own father, another of Reverend Archer's hard-handed deacons. The look on my father's face told me he knew Piker's Creek was nothing but a trickle with the drought on.

"This here's my boy, Arthur Lee."

"Yes," the blue turbaned man said, nodding. "He was kind enough to direct us to you." He nibbled politely at a cookie; I could tell his heart wasn't in it. "A very polite young man. And well-named." His companions nodded their agreement.

My father grunted; it was the closest thing to pride a hard man like Enoch Bach could offer. He looked to me. "These here Englishmen want to see Mordecai's Folly. Why don't you show them?"

"But don't be long," my mother added. "Supper's nearly on."

I don't know if it was curiosity or the potential for another fancy coin but I didn't mind the notion at all. I'd never met Englishmen before but should've guessed it by their dapper dress. I wondered if that meant the coin in my pocket — and the others I was sure to earn shortly — were from that far off place. "I'd be happy to show you," I said.

They put down their half-eaten cookies and quarter-drank glasses as if of one mind and stood. "We'd be grateful for your help, young Arthur."

So we crowded into their car and rumbled off into the field, out towards Piker's Creek.

The sun was low and the sky was red running to brown when we approached the abandoned plough. It stood solitary in a wide open space. The driver set the handbrake and we climbed out.

The leader looked excited. "How long has it been in the stone?" he asked.

I scratched my head. "I was little. Maybe twelve years?"

But he was already crouching beside it, bending over to look beneath the wood frame. He brushed dangling leather aside and gasped.

The others gasped, too.

"Behold," the man with the golden tooth said in a quiet voice.

But the word he said next wasn't one I'd heard before.

They gathered around the plow, testing the wheels with their shiny shoes and gently lifting at the handlebars. Their leader was mumbling to them and I leaned forward to hear him. I only caught every other sentence.

"We'll have to buy the farm," he said at one point. And at another: "We can bring the children over one at a time until the right one is found."

Then, they started speaking quickly among themselves in a language I didn't recognize at all.

Of course, none of this really registered with me. Something else had caught my eye when the wind had whipped up the jacket on one of the men who bent to examine the blade.

It sure looked like a shoulder holster.

Later, we all gathered around the dining room table.

When the old man smiled, his tooth glowed yellow in the lamplight. "How is the farm doing?" he asked.

My father shrugged and looked to my mother. "Not well."

My uncle Mordecai was still hidden away in his room. I could hear the canned sound of old time gospel music trickling out from under his door.

"Yes." The old man reached into his pocket, "I might have a bit of welcome news for you, Mr. Bach."

He drew out a blue gem nearly the color of his hat. He held it up to the lamplight and for just a moment, I thought I saw something bright sparking at the heart of it.

The old man waited until all eyes were on the stone. Then, he started speaking slowly.

"When I put this stone away you will recall that we reached agreement on a more-than-fair price for your land, outbuildings and —" here he paused and cleared his throat, " — any and *all* farm equipment remaining on the premises." I glanced around the room quickly, took in my father's nod and the sudden hope on my mother's face. He saw me looking and frowned. "Tomorrow, you will receive a telegram from the Merlin Trust with the full and final terms of our offer. The day after that, my colleagues and I will return with papers to sign." He leaned in. "You will take the offer, of course, and leave for greener fields once you've packed." Then his voice dropped and sounded near to menacing. "And selling us this farm is the most important and meaningful thing you will ever do. Nothing can get in the way of it."

Out of the corner of my eye, I saw my father's smile break open as he nodded more vigorously. I'd not seen a smile like that on him in more years than I could count. In the back of the house, I heard four voices converging in harmony against a backdrop of guitar and fiddle, and I wondered how my Uncle Mordecai would feel about this sudden development considering half the farm was his, including the sword these men seemed so keen to possess.

Still, they had to know he was back there and not one of them moved to fetch him.

He put the stone away and my parents blinked.

My father spoke first. "That's an extremely generous offer given the drought that's on," he said. "What does this here Merlin Trust want with a failing corn farm?" His eyes turned hungry. "Is it oil?"

"Ah," the leader said. "No. Not oil." He looked to his friends for a silent consensus. "We believe your land may have, buried in its soil, certain historical artifacts of particular interest to the Board of Trustees."

Mother spoke up though her voice sounded far away. "Arrowheads and such?" She looked to me. "You found that arrowhead down near Piker's Creek that time, Artie."

I nodded.

The men stood up now, smoothing their jackets and slacks with their hands. Any excitement I'd seen in them out at the plough was now quietly put away, hidden behind the curtain of official business.

We walked them to the porch and we all shook hands.

After they climbed into their car and rolled out of the yard, they honked three times, and their leader waved to us from the window.

I waved back but suddenly, the reality of it all was settling in. "Where will we go?" I asked.

"California," my father said without hesitation.

And all I saw when he said it was Amy Sue Peller's face, framed in her long blonde hair.

I wondered if she would write to me when I was gone.

*

I tossed and turned that night and didn't find sleep until the wee hours. The look on the old men's faces as they examined the plough and its blade, buried in the rock, kept coming back to me. And the empty-eyed stare of my parents as they watched the blue stone. And how easily they seemed to remember a negotiation that hadn't happened. And last, Amy Sue and her bright blue eyes rimmed with tears at the news that I was moving away.

My mind spun with questions I wasn't sure how or who to ask. When the rooster crowed, I was up and getting dressed. My father was on the porch drinking coffee that steamed into the gray morning air. He looked at me when I came out. "We've got a lot of work ahead of us," he said.

I looked at him and noticed he seemed different. The lines in his face had vanished and he smiled easily now. I wanted to sniff his coffee for whiskey but knew better than that. "Are you okay, Pa?" I asked him.

He nodded. "Never better."

"Have you talked to Uncle Mordecai yet?"

He shook his head. "I'll talk to him later. I want the telegram in my hands first."

I wanted to ask my father about the blue stone. I wanted to tell him about the shoulder holsters and the strange language they spoke. More than anything else, I wanted to tell him that I couldn't bear the notion of leaving Amy Sue in Oklahoma.

But in the end, I couldn't find any of those words. I banked them like a campfire.

Instead, I just sat with him and watched the sun come up over our barren land.

Later that morning, we drove into town for crates and groceries. We rode in silence, my brain wrapped around yesterday and everything that followed. When we rolled past the new library an idea struck me. "Can we stop here?"

My father slowed down but didn't stop. "We're moving in less than a week," he said. "I don't think —"

I learned a long time ago not to interrupt my parents, but now I did it anyway. "Just while you're shopping, Pa. I've never been inside. I'd like to see it before we leave."

He scowled for a moment, shrugged, and pulled the truck to the side of the street. "One hour," he said.

I nodded and scrambled out onto the sidewalk.

The library was quiet and Mrs. Derkins sat alone at her massive, ship-sized desk surrounded in paper and rubber stamps. She looked up when I walked in.

"Arthur Lee Bach," she said with a frown. "Why, I *never*." She'd been my Sunday School teacher out at the Baptist church for years and knew that Amy Sue Peller, there next to me in class, was the only studying I was interested in. Twice she'd taken away the notes we passed during the boring bits of Old Testament begats.

"Morning, Ma'am," I said, removing my hat. I'd heard tell of much bigger libraries in the big cities and universities but this large room was filled with more books than I'd ever seen in one place. "Is this a good place to find stuff out?" I figured it was.

She surprised me with a smile. "It's a great place to find stuff out," she said. "Well, *some* stuff. The Good Lord didn't intend us to know *everything*."

I got straight to the point. "I need to know about the Merlin Trust."

Her brows furrowed. "Merlin . . . like the magician?"

I'd seen a magician once, though afterwards my folks had been fairly upset, considering such to be contrary unto the Lord. But I'd watched him make flowers appear and disappear for the ladies, watched him cut his assistant in half, watched him make Gus Holler bark like a dog when he heard Dixie whistled. And of course, at the end of his show he'd pulled a rabbit from a black hat. "Merlin the magician?"

She shook her head slowly and clucked. Then, she stood and took me back into the shadowy, narrow aisles amid the smell of books and new paint.

She walked the rows methodically, pulling down a book here and there. Then, she took me to small table in the corner and placed the goodly pile on its plain wood surface.

Some of the words were hard, but most weren't beyond figuring out. I sat there and turned the pages, looking for one thing and finding another.

I read about another boy named Arthur and a sword stuck in a stone. I read about a Lady in a lake and a wizard named Merlin and a host of others that made the apostles' names look easy to pronounce. I'd never been much of a reader but those stories birthed something in me that was almost as urgent and mighty as the hope I felt every time I heard Amy Sue's voice or touched her soft skin or kissed her wet mouth.

And along with whatever that strange, brain-opening sensation was, I also started to wonder if maybe, just maybe, these stories might have as much truth in them as Joshua and Jericho and Jesus and Jonah.

I heard my father's horn outside the library and looked up at the clock on the wall. An hour had slipped past.

When I went out to the truck, two men in suits were standing by it and Pa was talking to them through the open window. Sheriff Radke stood there with them, looking disinterested in the conversation. The men looked like big city folk, uncomfortable with the notion of dusty streets and hot wind.

"We know," one of them was saying, "that some folks have been asking after you and your brother's farm. We'd like you to get in touch if they contact you."

I couldn't see my father's face, but I heard his voice. "Why would anyone ask after our farm?"

I stopped a few steps from the truck.

One of the men pushed back his hat and scratched his head. There, clear as day, beneath his armpit hung a holstered revolver. "We're not rightly sure, but we'd like to ask them some questions and find out."

"Have these folks broken the law?"

"Not that we know of, Mr. Bach."

My father nodded, then glanced over and saw me standing on the sidewalk. "There's my boy now," he said. He looked back to the men. "I'll surely call if anyone turns up," he said, "but I can't imagine why they'd care about an old, dead farm."

"Much obliged," the other man said. Then they looked to the Sheriff. "Thank you for introducing us."

The Sheriff looked pleased with himself. "Happy to." He smiled at my father. "See you in church, Enoch."

My father smiled back. "See you there." Then, he looked back to me. "Come on then, Artie. We've work to do while the day's still young."

I opened the door and climbed in, moving a stack of legal-looking papers from the passenger seat into the glove compartment. As we rumbled off homeward I stared at my dad. I wanted to ask him why he'd just lied to those men in front of Deacon Radke, but I didn't know how. Instead, I asked him who they were.

"Federal men out of Oklahoma City," he told me. "But don't concern yourself with them."

I didn't know how to tell him that they concerned me far less than his sudden, easy smile and the sudden, easy lies that hid behind it.

That night, Amy Sue Peller met me down at Piker's Creek. We sat on a rock there and watched the trickling water go silver as the moon rose over it.

She shifted beneath my arm and pressed herself closer to me. "I can't believe you're moving," she finally said. She hadn't cried yet, but I thought I heard her voice catch.

I squeezed her shoulders. "I surely don't want to."

"When do you leave?" I felt her hand on my thigh, her fingers picking at the denim nervously.

"Saturday," I told her. "I spent all day packing."

She sighed. "My folks have been talking about selling, too. Pa says it's going to get worse before it gets better. My uncle has an orchard up in Washington and could use the help." She pulled away and turned to face me. "What's happening to the world, Arthur Lee? It wasn't supposed to be like this."

Her eyes held me until I saw her lower lip quivering. Leaning in, I kissed her slow and long. When we finished, I held her for a minute or two until our breathing came back to normal. After that, we worked ourselves up a few more times before she disentangled herself and stood up, brushing the dust from her dress. Even in the dim light, I could see her face was flushed. "I have to get back," she said.

We walked together, holding hands, until we got to the plow there on the back of our farm. Then we kissed and she slipped away.

I wasn't ready to sneak in yet. The events of the last two days and the aching bits of me that Amy Sue brought to life had my brain stirred up, and I knew my bedroom, strewn with crates, would stifle me.

The plowshare lay like an awkward skeleton in the moonlight but I approached it as if it were a living thing. All of the words I'd read that morning came back to me and I thought about that other boy with my name and the man he became in that far off place. I put my hand to the handle and wondered about the blade that this so-called Merlin Trust thought was so all-fired important.

Then I wondered something else and gripped the wind-worn wood more firmly. Sucking in my breath, I tugged at the plowshare. When it moved beneath my touch, I nearly fell over.

Clouds blocked the moon for me as I approached the house. A warm wind rose and licked the hairs that still stood up on my neck and arms.

I'd sat by the plow for a goodly time thinking about it all and wondering what it might mean. Now, as I slipped through the yard, I still wasn't sure. But I'd moved it — three times to be sure — and each time butter and hot knives came to mind. And wizards and kings.

I was nearly to the trellis leading to my window when I heard the voice.

"They're not who they seem to be," she said. The voice was thick as honey and prettier than a hymn.

I looked around and saw no one.

She spoke again. "It's not theirs to take."

I looked around again, my eyes settling on the well and the pump that squatted over it. My whisper sounded more scared than I wanted it to. "Hello?"

"Over here." Definitely the well. I walked over, my feet feeling suddenly heavy.

"Who's there?"

Her chuckle was warm along my spine. "You know who I am, Arthur."

And I was afraid I did. I said nothing.

"A time of despair and great darkness brews," she said. "Another war is coming and would-be kings are lining up upon the stage." She sighed and I heard sorrow in it. "How long will your kind glory in blood?"

But I didn't answer. The fear overtook me, and praying under my breath, I sprinted the dozen yards or so to the house and scrambled silently up the trellis into my waiting room.

*

Angry voices woke me from the troubled sleep I finally found. I'd been dreaming about the woman in our well, only she looked a great deal like Amy Sue Peller, naked and shimmering in the dark water, pulling me down beneath the surface as hungry hands moved over me.

But now, I heard my father shouting in the yard, and I climbed into my jeans and boots, grabbing up my shirt. It was early yet — the sky still pink — and my mother watched nervously from the porch. My father had a sheath of papers in one hand and a yellow telegram in the other. He was waving them at my uncle.

"I don't give a good goddamn," my father said. "We need this, Mordecai. And by hell, you'll sign. It's a good price — more than fair." My father's face was red. He was more angry than I'd seen him since he caught me painting the horse yellow eight years back.

"Mind your tongue, Enoch," Mordecai said in a quiet voice. "I'll not hear blasphemy from you. And I'll not sell my farm to these ravening wolves."

I leaned close to my mother. "How long have they been fighting?"

She shrugged. "They woke me up a bit ago. I'm not sure why your uncle is being so difficult about this. It makes perfect sense to —"

But she stopped in mid sentence when my father flung the papers — and then himself — at my uncle. I moved toward them but she caught my shirt sleeve. "Let them sort this out, Arthur. If your father can't *talk* any sense into him, maybe he can beat it into him instead."

But I think my folks underestimated the wiry, quiet man the war and Jesus had shaped my uncle into. He moved fast, taking a fist on the jaw but easily spinning my father and dropping him with a well-placed boot behind the leg. He pushed him down into the dirt and pinned him there with a knee in his back. I could hear the snarl on the edges of his voice. "The devil's gotten into you, Enoch. You know from the Good Book that the Lord don't look kindly on brothers raising fists to each other."

My father struggled and sputtered in the dust, and I knew then that I had to do something.

Setting off at a run, I flew past them and into the barren field. I took no notice of my mother shouting behind me.

"It's not theirs to take," the woman in the well had told me the night before, and what I'd seen that morning told me why. When I got to the plowshare, I went around to the front of it and lifted the harness, winding it around my shoulders and torso.

I tugged at it and felt the blade give way. I heard the groan of steel on rock and pulled harder, feeling the plow shift and move beneath my hand.

I broke sweat quickly, grunting with the effort as I dragged that plowshare across the open ground. I wasn't sure exactly where I was taking it, but I'd made nearly a mile before I saw the distant dust cloud rising from a car on the road. I stretched as tall as I could and when I recognized the sedan, I hunkered down and prayed they wouldn't see me.

There, in the shadow of the plow, I looked back over the furrow I'd dug into the earth and gasped.

A trail of rich, red soil — stark as blood on the sun-baked land — stretched back as far as I could see. It had been two years since I'd seen soil like that on our farm and now the line of it ran back behind me like a wound in the earth.

And there on the horizon, I saw a figure moving towards me, moving at an easy pace and following the trail I'd left behind me.

I don't know why I thought I could outrun him, but I tried anyway. I gathered up the harness, mindful of the welts it had raised on my back and shoulders, and planted my feet for the pulling.

I'd only gone a few yards when my uncle caught up to me. I looked up when he approached and saw his bruised jaw. I don't know what I expected him to say, but it surely wasn't what he said. I also didn't expect the low, reverential tone. "They're after the sword, aren't they?"

I tugged at the plow. "Yep," I said. "They took quite a cotton to it."

"It's not theirs to take," he said slowly and I stopped. Our eyes met.

"You've heard her, too?" I asked him.

He nodded. "Yesterday when I was at prayer and chores. Lord knows I'm no Papist but when the Mother of Christ speaks, it's right and proper to listen."

I thought about correcting him, offering up a bit of what I'd read at the library, but thought better of it. He'd think such to be nonsense at best or Satan's handiwork at worst. "What should I do?"

He scratched his head, looked at the swath of fresh, dark soil. I followed his gaze to the plow. The blade shone fiercely, contrasting nearly white against the red soil. "Years and years of trying with the mule and a boy breaks it loose all on his own. I reckon you're the one to decide what to do." He chuckled and glanced back to the furrow. "I also reckon you've already decided."

The truth is, I hadn't — at least not that I was aware of. But as I looked around me, I realized the direction I'd chosen to pull in and could see the last bits of green scrub on the banks of Piker's Creek a half mile off, shimmering in the sun.

I remembered the books, remembered the pictures of the graceful hand and the shining sword, thrust up from the calm surface of that long ago lake. Then, the full weight of it all settled onto me when I considered the freshly healed land.

Until now, the blade had seemed a thorn in our otherwise peaceable lives, bringing my father and uncle to blows, threatening to separate me from my girl, even bringing down the G-men from Oklahoma City with their big city shoes and their discomfort with the dust that dominated our lives these last few years. Suddenly, possibilities stretched before me, and I saw the land healed, Amy Sue Peller smiling with pride and love, cheering me on with my folks and the teeming crowd as I pulled at the plow and brought back the corn.

It's not theirs to take.

Maybe, I realized, it wasn't mine to take either. And maybe, just maybe, a hand waited for us there in the last trickling water of Piker's Creek.

I looked in the direction of the house and saw that the dust cloud was on the move again. Uncle Mordecai saw it, too. He stepped up to the front of the plow. "We'd better pull together," he said.

He wrapped leather around his hands and over his shoulder, digging his own boots into the ground beside mine. For a moment, I thought maybe it wouldn't budge, resisting any hand but my own, but as we both tugged at it, the plow bit into the earth and followed us.

Step by step, we pulled with our eyes down and our backs bent, halving the distance again before we heard the car approaching behind us.

I glanced over my shoulder and then looked at my uncle. "We have to get to the creek," I told him.

"We're not going to make it," he answered. He stood up straight and dropped the harness.

The car rumbled up to us and the doors opened. My father and the four blue-turbaned men stepped out.

"What in the hell are you up to, Arthur Lee Bach?" he said. He glared at his brother, and I saw something in his eyes that frightened me.

"He's doing what needs done," Mordecai said. "If you've any sense left in you, you'll help us."

"I don't think that is advisable." The old, gold-toothed man reached calmly beneath his jacket, and I remembered the shoulder holsters. "I think I can help with this little misunderstanding."

"They have guns," I whispered, and my uncle said nothing. But he moved with that quiet speed I'd seen earlier.

The old man fell beneath him, the blue gem flying up into the air and dropping with a thud near my foot. I stooped to grab it as two of the others lunged at me, and then I tumbled over, tangled up in their arms and legs as they tackled me. I got my fingers around the stone and pulled in close to myself, feeling the fists and feet that pummeled me. We scrambled in the dirt, and I was dimly aware of my father pulling at my uncle where he wrestled with the old man.

When my uncle finally came up, he held a black pistol in his hand, and he pointed it first at my father and then at the old man. "Call off your kraut friends," he said. The anger in his voice was coiled like a sidewinder.

The old man smiled. "I can assure you that we're not —"

The pistol cracked and the front window of the car exploded. Eyes narrow, the old man said something in that language I hadn't recognized before. The men holding me let go suddenly, and I crawled free, the blue gem clenched tight in my fist.

"Danke," my uncle said with a grin.

After stripping them of their pistols, we tied them up — even my father — with the rope we found in the trunk of their car.

"I'll wait with them," my uncle said. "You go on with what you need to do."

Their leader looked to both of us. "You're making a tremendous mistake."

I looked at him. "We already know it's not yours to take. The Lady told us."

Color drained from his face. "What Lady?"

My uncle opened his mouth to speak, but I was faster. "I think you know what Lady."

The man glowered and spat between my feet. "A new Reich arises," he said. "That blade is meant for the chosen among its princes."

"No," I said as I took up the harness again. "It's not yours to take. And it's not ours to give."

If anything further was said, I didn't listen. I put one foot in front of the other and set out for Piker's Creek.

When I reached the bank and dropped the straps, I looked over my shoulder and saw my uncle waving. Then, I looked back to the narrow creek and its wide, stone-strewn bed. I reached for the plow, put my hands upon it and paused.

I thought about the red and ready soil that stretched out behind me and how the blue in the gem in my pocket matched the blue in Amy Sue Peller's eyes. I thought about my father and his curled fists and easy lies, my uncle and his gentle gait and quiet ways. I thought about the four men in their strange hats, their so-called Merlin Trust and rising Reich.

I lifted at the handles and tipped the plow over the bank. It fell end over end, the leather straps slapping at the rocks and brush as it rolled, the wood cracking but not breaking. When it reached the bottom, the plow came to a stop, and the shining white blade buried itself into what remained of the creek.

Even though I expected it, when the hands surged up from the water to break Excalibur loose from its frame, I jumped back. The slender arms were alabaster and strong enough to splinter the hard wood as she tugged the sword free and homeward.

"Thank you, Arthur," she said.

I knew it was the last time I would ever hear that voice, but I didn't mind. And I knew there would be hell to pay back at the farm once my father calmed down and once the federals visiting from Oklahoma City were called to fetch the four strangers.

But I also knew we wouldn't be selling the farm. Ever. And I knew later that night I'd see Amy Sue Peller, and that if I could learn the trick of it, the blue gem in my pocket would make all things right and good for everyone.

And maybe someday, I thought as I turned back to where my uncle and the others hunkered down near the car, instead of pulling plows out of boulders, I'd try my hand at another kind of magic.

Maybe I'd pull rabbits from hats.

OF MISSING KINGS AND BACKWARD DREAMS AND THE HONORING OF LIES

Because Entrolusians despised waiting, Rudolfo took longer than usual with his breakfast. And because they abhorred stillness and heat, he moved the meeting at the last moment to his favorite rooftop garden when the sun stood at its zenith.

Reclined on his cushions, sipping chilled peach wine, Rudolfo watched the ambassador sweat and fidget. After a few moments, he smiled and took in a deep breath. "A fine day as such would be wasted indoors."

The ambassador inclined his head. "Yes, Lord Rudolfo."

"The wine is good?"

The Entrolusian lifted his glass. "The wine is superb."

"We orchard the peaches in Glimmer Glam," Rudolfo said as he also raised his glass. "A father and his son select the best from the harvest each year and barrel the wine for us." His other hand moved in a flourish. "There's an underground river beneath us, cold as the glaciers it springs from —" Rudolfo interrupted himself, grinning even as his eyes narrowed. "But you're not here to talk of such things, are you, Ambassador?"

"No. And yet I find it fascinating." The ambassador's quick smile betrayed his discomfort and Rudolfo leaned forward.

"Do you know what *I* find fascinating?" Rudolfo asked.

The ambassador shifted on the cushions. "What, Lord?"

"That the war's been done for a year, the treaty's been signed for half that and I've yet to see a letter of transfer from the Banks of Delphi Mott."

The fat ambassador's jowls shook. Sweat ran from his wet blond hair onto his wide face. "My apologies, Lord Rudolfo." He fumbled with a leather cord around his neck and three slight men, dressed in the bright colors of Rudolfo's Gypsy Scouts, slipped out of hiding with knives drawn.

Rudolfo lifted his hand and raised his eyebrows. The Scouts each nodded once and stepped back.

The ambassador pulled a sweat-stained leather message tube from beneath his robe and extended it toward Rudolfo. "The new Overseer sends his regrets that he could not present this token in person."

Rudolfo waved the tube away. "The new Overseer was not invited. And the letter of transfer is not a token. It is reparation for ignorance and genocide."

The ambassador knew better than to argue. He set the tube aside; Rudolfo glanced at it, tipped his head slightly and watched slender fingers pluck it from the silk-draped ground.

"You'll find," the ambassador said, "that it is more than the settled amount according to the traditions of kin-clave."

Rudolfo smiled and drained off his wine. "Very good. Tell Erlund I am satisfied for now. But next year's letter had best arrive in a more timely fashion." He looked west at the nearest hill to his manor. He had intended it to someday be cultivated into a Whymer Maze like the ones he'd read about as a boy, but now the high mound stood bare of tree and fern as the foundation and cornerstones of a massive building began to take shape. "The library is ahead of schedule and it is only right that the City States rebuild what they destroyed."

Rudolfo watched his guest force a weak smile. "I toured it yesterday. It is truly fabulous, Lord. It will make your ninth forest manor the center of the world."

Nothing like its original, Rudolfo thought with a twinge. An entire City of magic and machines laid waste, the light of the Androfrancines extinguished by a meaningless act of deception and violence. "It will be a wonder to behold," he said, standing.

The Entrolusian ambassador pushed himself to his feet with a grunt. Both men stood for a moment in silence, then the ambassador coughed. "Have you reconsidered on the matter of Sethbert?" he finally asked.

Ah, Rudolfo thought, this is the real matter at hand. "Tell Erlund that I *have* reconsidered and that his uncle will remain my guest at my leisure." He turned toward the stairs as his Gypsy Scouts moved to his side from their various positions around the garden. Rudolfo paused at the top of the stairs and turned back to the ambassador with a smile. "Tell Erlund that it should be a lesson to him, that he rule wisely and in peace." He inhaled the warm scent of forest roses and brook lavender, drawing the breath deep inside of himself.

"Yes Lord," the ambassador said. But Rudolfo pretended not to hear it as he walked quickly down the stairs.

Sethbert waited on Tormentor's Row, nearly a year now under the tutelage of Rudolfo's Physicians of Penitent Torture.

That former Overseer who had instigated destruction of Windwir was an Entrolusian Rudolfo didn't want to keep waiting.

The sun was a pink memory in the west when Rudolfo slipped into his manor through the Scout's Gate. It was a concealed passage half as wide as a small man, running between the stable and the armory, up narrow stairs and into his private study through a hidden door.

His time with Sethbert had brought him no joy. The Physicians were on the seventh peel of Coomlis Whym and, after weeks of ministration with their salted blades, their patient still was not embracing the depth of the lesson. Rudolfo reclined on the observation deck, listening to the screams while he sipped wine and ate chilled plums.

As he watched and heard the Physicians at their redemptive work, he remembered the first time he'd met the Overseer years ago. Sethbert was eating a raw boar's heart, his foot planted firmly on the animal as it twitched in its own blood. Rudolfo had arrived just after the kill, coming from the deathbed of his youngest aunt — Sethbert's bride.

Rudolfo's father, Jakob, was in his last years then and glowered at the young Entrolusian overlord. "Your wife lays dying, bringing your heir into this world, and you are hunting pigs?"

Sethbert looked at him, eyes narrowing, blood spilling from his open mouth as he spoke. "My reasons are my own, Jakob." Then in afterthought, as if remembering the proper form of the kin-clave his young wife from the Ninefold Forest Houses had brought, he added: "I'm sorry for your loss."

Mother and child were both dead within the hour and perhaps it was fate that Sethbert never fathered another child.

Of course that sin and many others had been cleansed by the Physicians during their time with Sethbert. Only one — his greatest and most grievous, the destruction of the Androfrancines and their city — remained. But try as they might, the Physicians were unable to find the heart of that particular boar with their hunting blades.

Maybe with time, Rudolfo thought. But he realized as he thought it that perhaps he did not wish Sethbert's redemption so very much after all.

Eventually, he found himself swept off on the hundred fool's errands of his station. Now, after a long day's work, he snuck home.

He heard a horse snicker from its stall just on the other side of the wall. Rudolfo suddenly wondered how long it had been since he'd ridden?

Since the end of the war? Surely not, but it made him pause. No, just three months ago they'd ridden to Glimmer Glam. He thought of Jin li Tam, his betrothed, and the week they'd spent at his third manor there. Now she waited for him just two doors ahead, freshly returned from her family and from planning their winter nuptials at the Li Tam palace on the southern tip of the Emerald Coast, twelve days south and west at hard ride. He remembered his first dance with her in the Entrolusian Overseer's banquet tent, and his epiphany about her, the one that had brought about his invitation, just moments before she confirmed his fears about Sethbert. *She was living art and I knew I must have her.* He smiled at the memory of it, working the lever to the study door.

He was halfway through the room when a click and a slight wheeze stopped him. He turned. "Isaak?"

Dull, amber eyes sparked open in the dimly lit room.

"Yes, Lord?" the metal man said, standing and self-consciously smoothing his Androfrancine robes. He limped forward on a damaged leg he refused to repair. He'd lost it in the Desolation of Windwir and Rudolfo's armorer had reattached it as best as he could the day that they found him. And though Isaak could've easily rebuilt the leg entirely at this point, he claimed he bore the limp as a reminder of his part in the city's destruction. It fascinated Rudolfo that a man made of metal could feel responsibility so deeply — despite the clear evidence that Sethbert was the malefactor and Isaak had been a convenient and unwitting pawn.

Rudolfo tried to keep the irritation from his voice. "What are you doing here? It's late."

A clack and a whir. "Apologies, Lord Rudolfo. You had suggested that I meet with you sometime after three, so I came and waited for the most opportune time."

Rudolfo chuckled, the frustration melting away. "Apologies, Isaak. I lost track of the day and the time." He waved to the chair, his glance pausing for a moment on the door to the quarters he shared with Jin. "Please. Sit."

Rudolfo pulled a chair over and sat, too. "How is the restoration going?"

"It's going well, Lord. Construction is so far ahead of schedule that we'll have to start working at night to keep up with them."

During the summer months, the fourteen mechoservitors worked beneath a large silk tent at the base of the hill. They had tables stacked with parchment and quills and bottles of ink and they reproduced from memory what they could. The completed stacks were bundled, tied with twine and hauled by wheelbarrow to the bindery across the river. Originally, they thought it would take three years to restore what remained of the world's largest receptacle of knowledge. A cursory catalog hastily scribbled by each indicated that the fourteen mechoservitors, between them, retained approximately a third the library's holdings in their memory scrolls. If it hadn't been for the Androfrancines's amazing mechanical men, there'd have been nothing to build from.

"That's good news," Rudolfo said. "And I've received the letter of transfer. More good news."

Isaak nodded. "It is."

"Are any other holdings finding their way home?"

Isaak hummed and clicked. "Two hundred twelve volumes have arrived from various sources. And we have letters from two Universities inviting emissaries to review their holdings for items unaccounted for. We may get close to forty percent when we're finished."

Rudolfo smiled a tight smile. "It's better than we hoped, then. But it would be better if the Androfrancine Remnant would cooperate."

Steam whispered out of the metal man's exhaust grate and his eye-shutters flashed. "They're not helpful. They don't recognize our authority. They are gathering what little they have at the Patriarchal Summer Home."

"They're scattered sheep without leadership or vision or hope. How many of them are there?"

"About a thousand," Isaak said. "We're keeping a log of those we learn about. Most were archeologists, scholars and book buyers — out in the world doing their work when the city fell. There are a few abbots, too."

Only a thousand left of a hundred thousand, Rudolfo thought. "I've told my Scouts to pass the word along the borders. I *could* send them to the estate in Hyris Wood and compel their cooperation more persuasively."

"If it pleases my Lord," the metal man said, "I may have a less forceful idea."

Rudolfo leaned forward. "Oh?"

"I think I've found Petronus."

Rudolfo sat back, eyebrows raised. "Really?" He folded his hands beneath his chin. "What makes you think that?"

"Mechoservitor Twelve is restoring archived files from his assignment to the Papal office. He's reproduced three message bird logs to Caldus Bay from Pope Serious XI to *The Fisherman Petro* during the Grundmor Heresy."

"So he is alive?" Pope Petronus had been buried in the Patriarch's Tomb, the supposed victim of an assassin's poison. Rudolfo had attended the funeral with his father when he was a boy.

"Possibly. If so, he could help."

Rudolfo nodded. It was uncommon for leaders to fake their deaths, but not unheard of. "He would still be pope, conceivably, if my memory of Androfrancine Succession is true."

"Correct. He could compel the remnants of the Order to support our work."

Rudolfo's eyes narrowed. "It's been over a year and he's not come forward. By now, news of Windwir's fall has reached every corner of the known world. He may not wish to help."

Isaak shook his head. "He is the pope; he must."

Rudolfo looked at the hill outside his window. The construction site lay shrouded in gray — perhaps his largest and finest undertaking. He felt a twinge of something, remembering again the smell of the stable and the sound of the horses. Before this war, he'd lived between nine scattered houses, spending more nights in a wagon than in a bed. Since the war, with the rebuilding of the library and Jin's arrival, everything had changed. His wandering army wandered no more than necessary and the Gypsy King slept in a bed, albeit beside a formidably lovely woman. "We all do what we must."

Isaak's eye flashed open and shut; his mouth opened and closed. He didn't speak.

Rudolfo stood and clapped him on the shoulder. "I'm sure he will help," he said. "I'll send a bird in the morning."

True to his word, he sent the bird at dawn, tying the blue thread of inquiry to its foot along with a simple question: *Are you truly the lost Androfrancine Pope, the missing King of Windwir?* He whispered a destination to the bird, stroked its small gray head and tossed it out of his study window.

When it returned three days later, the message was gone.

The blue thread was gone, too, replaced with the white thread of kin-clave.

A captain of the Gypsy Scouts slipped into the silk breakfast tent just as Rudolfo speared a sliced apple. Across from him, Jin Li Tam adjusted her riding skirts.

"Apologies for the interruption, General Rudolfo," the young captain said.

Rudolfo placed his fork on the mat beside his plate. "Unnecessary," he said, dabbing his mustache and beard carefully with a silk napkin.

They had ridden a few hours out from the city to breakfast in a meadow near the river and hemmed by an abandoned pear orchard. A welcome break in an otherwise monotonous routine.

"I have word from Gregoric," the captain said. "Your guest will arrive just before sundown."

Ten days after the message bird had returned, an old man riding a mule had crossed the borders from the direction of Caldus Bay. Unseen ghosts in bright colors shadowed him as he made for the ninth manor. One of them was Gregoric, the First Captain of Rudolfo's Gypsy Scouts.

He brushed Jin's leg with his fingers, tapping a message into her soft skin as he did. *A quiet dinner for four?*

Her eyebrows furrowed and her fingers sought his forearm. *Four?*

Isaak, he tapped.

She nodded and smiled.

"Allow him to arrive unescorted and unannounced," Rudolfo told the captain. "Bring him to the western garden after he's refreshed himself."

"I'll instruct the kitchen to prepare something simple and modest for us," Jin said. "You might consider inviting Isaak."

Rudolfo smiled. "An excellent idea, Lady. I will invite him myself."

The captain nodded and slipped back into the late morning sun.

Rudolfo picked up his fork and bit into the apple slice. He chased it with sharp cheese and a sip of the thick, purple wine Jin had brought back from her visit to the coast. "Your family vineyard is excellent."

She nodded and her red hair cascaded down, a copper river contrasting the green of her shirt. "House Li Tam is known for its vineyards."

He grinned at her. "House Li Tam is known for its beautiful women."

She snorted. "I may not be beautiful for so long. You were wrong about your soldiers."

My soldiers? Rudolfo tried to find the reference she was making but couldn't quite reach it. "My soldiers?" he asked out loud.

She leaned into him, her hand finding his leg and traveling up it. She stopped at the place he hoped most she would. "*These* soldiers," she said, giving him a gentle squeeze. "I saw the River Woman last week."

Rudolfo's world stopped. Missing pieces fell into place and emotion rushed him like a Ka'ali windstorm in Low Winter — desert winds raging from all directions at once. He felt his throat clench; he cleared it before speaking. "How did I not know of this until now?"

Her laugh was water over crystal. "As with *all things*, you knew it when I wished you to know it, my Lord." Her smile widened. "The River Woman said it will be a boy."

An heir of my own blood. The weight of it fell on him in an instant and he knew that she looked as alive as he suddenly felt. "Favorable and unexpected news," he told her.

I am to be a father. He nodded at no one and then repeated himself. "This is . . . *highly* favorable news."

Jin Li Tam's voice lowered, her eyes flitting to the silk-curtained doorway. "I concur. Do you think you are up to the task, my Gypsy King?"

Rudolfo realized that her hand had kept up its steady, delicate movement throughout her revelation. His eyes narrowed. "Which task exactly?"

She leaned in and kissed him hard on the mouth. "Both," she said.

Rudolfo smiled and kissed her back.

That night, the three of them dined on simple fare while the sky moved from purple to gray and the moon started its slow, upward crawl.

At Jin's suggestion, the cooks presented grilled venison and forest mushrooms in a garlic sauce, folded into a bed of rice and served with flat, fried bread and steamed vegetables. They drank crisp, cool water and ate creamed berries for dessert.

Isaak sat politely at the table from beginning to end, speaking when spoken to but otherwise just listening. Rudolfo made a point of engaging him in the conversation where appropriate.

Afterwards, they reclined on pillows and listened to the beginning of night.

Isaak stood. "Humble apologies," he said, "but with your leave, I will return to my work." He clicked and clanked, then bowed before Petronus. "It is an honor to meet you, Father."

Petronus chuckled. "It is an honor to meet you, Isaak. Continue your excellent work. I'm sure we'll talk more tomorrow."

Isaak nodded, looked at Rudolfo and Jin Li Tam. "Thank you for your graciousness."

"You are always most welcome," Rudolfo said.

They listened to his pistons clacking as he exited the garden and took the stairs inside.

Jin's left hand moved quickly, her fingers shifting against the backdrop of her gown and table cloth, as her right hand reached for her napkin. *You should dismiss me, love*, she signed.

Rudolfo inclined his head slightly. "Perhaps our guest and I should take our plum brandy privately tonight?"

She smiled at them both. "I think you both have much to discuss." As she stood, her hand moved again, now against her hip and leg. *Be mindful; this old fox is crafty.*

"Not just crafty," Petronus said, "but also fluent in seventeen different non-verbal Court languages." He looked at her, his eyes crinkling with his smile. His own hand moved in the same pattern of language. *You have found a strategic and strong and beautiful woman, Rudolfo.*

Jin Li Tam blushed. "Thank you, Father."

She leaned over Rudolfo briefly, squeezing his shoulder before she left. Two Gypsy Scouts followed her as she left the garden.

Rudolfo clapped and a server appeared with a bottle and two small glasses. He filled their glasses and vanished.

Petronus dug an ivory pipe and a weathered leather pouch from his plain brown robe and held it up. "May I?"

Rudolfo nodded. "Please."

Petronus looked nothing like a king, Rudolfo realized, and certainly acted nothing like any pope he'd seen. He watched the old man pinch dark, sweet-smelling leaves between his thumb and his forefinger, watched him shove the wad down into the pipe's bowl. He struck a match on the table and drew the pipe to life, a cloud of purple smoke collecting and twisting around his head before drifting out over the garden.

Petronus waited until Rudolfo lifted his brandy cup, then raised his own. They held their cups up, saying nothing, and then drank.

Rudolfo tasted the sweet fruit, felt the fire as the brandy burned its way into him.

After a minute passed, Rudolfo cleared his voice. The gardens emptied as his Gypsy Scouts and servers shifted to take up positions nearby but out of earshot. "The time to talk plainly is upon us," he said.

Petronus put down the cup, lay back on the cushions, and smoked his pipe. "You invited the metal man because I invoked kin-clave and you wanted to show me why he had become important to you."

Rudolfo nodded. "Yes."

"You were concerned that I might not see his value and that I might want to hold him accountable for the destruction of Windwir along with the Entrolusian Overlord."

Rudolfo nodded again. "Yes. He was a pawn. As you can see, he mourns his part in it with his every step."

"And he considers himself an Androfrancine now."

Rudolfo sipped his brandy, casually stroking his beard. "He does. But more than that, he considers himself a person."

"Yes," Petronus said.

"And even more importantly," Rudolfo said, his eyes narrowing, "I consider him a person as well." He paused. "And a friend."

Petronus waved a hand through his smoke, chuckling. "We can take Isaak off the table. He is many things — a quandary, a puzzle, a made-thing with a soul perhaps — but he is not a killer. He's an innocent."

Rudolfo smiled. "I think we know what one another wants."

"You want me to call a council and install a new pope, pass the patriarchy on to someone who will pull the remnant together and preserve the work and the lineage of P'andro Whym."

"Yes," Rudolfo said. "Or return to that throne yourself."

"I can't return. Or rather, I won't." He drew on the pipe again. "And you know what I want?"

"I believe so, yes." Rudolfo had guessed it when he first saw that white thread on his message bird's foot.

"I will make it plain." Petronus looked at him, his eyes suddenly hard and bright. "By way of the kin-clave between your houses and mine, as King of Windwir and Holy See of the Androfrancine Patriarchy, I require the extradition of Sethbert, former Overseer of the Entrolusian City States, that he might be tried for the Desolation of Windwir and for the souls lost in his act of unprovoked warfare."

Rudolfo thought of Sethbert now, in his cell on Tormentors Row. At some point, he would've killed him. He'd come close to giving the order on his last visit. And he'd thought a great deal about what he would need to do when Petronus invoked his rights by kin-clave.

"I will extradite him for trial," Rudolfo said. "And you will give me a pope."

Petronus smiled and shook his head. "I will give you what you need; I will hold your council but I do not guarantee you a pope." When Rudolfo opened his mouth to protest, he continued. "The honoring of kin-clave should not be confused with someone else's backward dream."

"Backward dream?"

"The world of P'andro Whym — like the world of Xhum Y'zir and his Age of Laughing Madness — is not the world of today, Rudolfo, and certainly not the world of tomorrow. In the early days, before the Whymer Bible was compiled, before the Androfrancines named themselves and robed themselves and built their Knowledgeable City at the heart of the world, they met a need because it was there at the moment." He held up his empty cup, turning it in the candlelight. "The cornerstone of Androfrancine knowledge is that change is the path life takes and yet we all dream backwards to what has been rather than dreaming forwards to what *can* be . . . or better yet, to dream in the *now*."

Rudolfo sighed. He could feel the truth of the old man's words in the dull ache of his muscles from this morning's ride. "We love the past because it is familiar to us," he said. "Yes," Petronus answered. "And sometimes, we try to carve the future into an image of the past. When we do so, we dishonor past, present *and* future." The words struck Rudolfo and he understood now. "You do not feel the Androfrancines need a pope. It is why you left." Petronus waved his hand. "It was many things. It was also about knowing my own soul. If I had continued, whatever I did would be a lie." Rudolfo leaned forward. "How did you know? What brought you to that place of knowledge?" Petronus shrugged and laughed loudly. "My whole life brought me to that place of knowledge. There was no one thing. I woke up one morning and simply knew." He tapped out his pipe. "You'll understand soon enough." Rudolfo raised his eyebrows. "What makes you say that?" The old man smiled. "I've been absent but not uninformed. Your life has changed, Rudolfo. Your wandering army wanders no more and your Gypsy Scouts run the forests without their Gypsy King. You live in one house with one woman. And soon, your library will be the center of the world. This little city will grow beyond its past just as you have grown beyond yours. Add a few children — an heir to nurture, perhaps . . . ." Petronus let the words die. "I know you know these things. I know you think about them." Rudolfo's guard slipped and his thought slipped with it, coming out in a quiet voice. "What if my life becomes a lie?" "Or what if it's becoming true?" Petronus stood. "The night is late, and I'm weary from the road. Thank you for hosting me." Rudolfo shook the sudden doubt away and stood as well. "My men will give you anything you need, Father." "Will you take Sethbert off Tormentors Row and place him in a simple cell?" Rudolfo felt a twinge. "I will order it so." "I will see him tomorrow." Petronus walked to the stairs, then turned back to Rudolfo. "We should hold the trial and council here, near the library," he said. "It will lend legitimacy to Isaak's work and send a clear message to the Remnant." Rudolfo nodded. "I concur."

"Sleep well," the pope said as he started his descent back into the manor.

"I will," Rudolfo replied. But he knew that he wouldn't.

Petronus, the King of Windwir and the Holy See of the Androfrancine Patriarchy, re-convened the council with upraised hands. Throughout the pavilion, voices went silent. Rudolfo sat aside from the others not just as their host but also as someone who wanted to see as much as he could.

They'd spent three months preparing for the event, pouring tirelessly over books of Androfrancine law — in some cases, smudging ink still wet from a mechoservitor's pen — to prove out the Order's rules of succession in Petronus's case. Scouts and birds had shuttled messages, announcements and legal references to every corner of the world that they could reach. Carpenters had built large frames of staggered benches and raised massive tent poles while seamstresses worked tirelessly to produce an enormous tent that blended the rainbow colors of Rudolfo's houses with the purple and gold of fallen Windwir's crest. In the end, the Androfrancines came.

The first two days of the council had been simple matters of organization. Petronus had first submitted himself for examination — receiving confirmation from at least a dozen gray-headed Androfrancines that they did indeed know him to be who the announcements and letters claimed he was. With that out of the way, he promoted bishops, had a newly crafted papal signet blessed by the new bishopric and had issued encyclicals on everything from property dispersal to the construction and management of the library.

Before adjourning for lunch on the third day, he had elicited gasps of surprise when he gestured to the metal men in their acolyte robes. "These new brethren that we have made will watch over our library."

One of the new bishops stood, angry. "They have no souls and you give them our library?"

Petronus had stared at the man and raised one of the new books into the air. "I give them nothing; they earn this. They work night and day to give back what was taken from you." The pope smiled.

"And you who have souls — how many of you have helped them?" The bishop reseated himself while Rudolfo smiled.

After lunch, after Petronus reconvened them with his silent blessing, he looked at Rudolfo and gave a grim smile. "Soon," he said, "I will close this last council of mine. But first, we have unfortunate business together." He nodded towards the main entrance and six Gypsy Scouts escorted Sethbert into the tent. They walked slowly to accommodate his shackles.

Rudolfo looked at the man who had been his prisoner all this time. Despite being fed well under his care, Sethbert had shed most of his fat. Most of his hair had fallen out and what little that remained had lost its color. His flesh had healed over the last three months, the scars forming the holy lattice of a Whymer Maze upon his skin. Rudolfo felt Jin Li Tam stiffen beside him and wondered how it was she had ever been this man's consort, wondered how it was that she never spoke of him or asked after him.

He also felt a stab of shame but could not fathom why.

The crowd went to their feet; the thousand indrawn breaths were audible. Rudolfo and Jin Li Tam remained seated.

"Sethbert, formerly Overseer of the Entrolusian City States, once kin-clave of the Androfrancine Order, do you understand why you are here today?"

Sethbert's lower lip quivered. "I do, Father."

Petronus looked at Isaak and nodded. The metal man stood.

"Did you, of your own free will and with forethought of malice, order this mechoservitor's script altered in secret?"

Sethbert hung his head. "I did, Father."

"And what was the nature of this alteration?"

Sethbert looked up briefly, his eyes red and hollow. He opened his mouth and closed it. "I . . . I had it altered, yes."

Petronus's jaw went firm. "How did you alter it?"

Rudolfo looked at Isaak and found himself squeezing Jin's hand harder than he realized. The metal man stood alone among his kind, his eye-shutters flickering and his bellows pumping. A low whine came from his exhaust grate.

Sethbert glanced at the metal man. Then he looked around the room for the first time. He saw Rudolfo and their eyes met. He saw Jin Li Tam and she looked away.

His voice shook. "I altered it so that he would recite Xhum Y'zir's Seven Cacophonic Deaths in the central square of Windwir."

Now he collapsed, prostrating himself. The guards pulled him back to his feet. "I didn't mean it," he said. "I had no idea it would do what it did."

Petronus leaned on his podium. "You did this thing?"

"I paid someone to do it," Sethbert said. His eyes lowered again. "I did it. Yes."

"Why?"

Sethbert said nothing.

Petronus scowled. "Surely you had a reason."

Sethbert looked around the room, possibly for a sympathetic face. There were none. And he had no way of knowing, as Rudolfo knew, that his own family had been excluded from the proceedings at Petronus's command. Rudolfo had actually protested this the night before but had left the matter alone when the old pope's voice took on an edge and reminded Rudolfo that though the trial was held on his soil, it was entirely an Androfrancine affair.

Sethbert drew himself up. "My reasons were my own."

At those words, Rudolfo sat forward. For the slightest moment, he saw the young, fat lord with his mouth covered in blood.

Petronus continued. "But you acknowledge guilt?"

"I do."

"Then as Patriarch and King, I find you guilty." Petronus moved around the platform. "Does any one here dispute my finding?"

No one spoke. No one moved.

Petronus continued his slow walk, his eyes narrow and studying the faces around him. He stopped in front of the new bishop who had challenged him on the matter of the mechoservitors. He stared at him and the bishop stared back. "What sentence does this crime merit?"

At first, the bishop didn't answer. Slowly, he worked his mouth open. "He should be put to death, Father."

Petronus nodded. "I agree that he should." He walked slowly to another bishop, one Rudolfo knew to have been an archeologist working in the Churning Waste until recently. "Do you agree?"

The archeologist nodded. "I do, Father."

Petronus whipped a fishing knife from his robes. He held the short blade aloft even as Rudolfo signed and gestured his rushing Gypsy Scouts to stand down.

Rudolfo felt the tickle of something like alarm growing in his stomach. *What do you play at, old man?* he signed quickly.

Petronus saw but turned away. "Sethbert dies today. Who will carry out his sentence?"

Someone nodded to the band of Gypsy Scouts. "Have them do it."

Petronus chuckled. "Too long we've invited others to do our unpleasant tasks. This one we will do ourselves."

Sethbert now was shaking. His bladder cut loose, wetting the front of his tunic and breeches. But he did not speak.

Now Petronus turned to Isaak. "You. What of you?" Isaak took a tentative step forward. "Of all of us here, he wronged you the most. He bent you against your will and turned you into a weapon beyond our wildest imaginings. He gave you the words to level a city and kill every man, woman, child and beast within."

Isaak took another step forward, and Rudolfo remembered his question that night nearly two years ago, after they had interrogated the apprentice Sethbert had hired to alter his script.

"Do you want to kill him yourself," he had asked the metal man.

Isaak had said no and Rudolfo had then given the task to Gregoric.

"I want to," Isaak said now. "I truly do." He hung his head. "I can not."

Petronus nodded and turned away from the metal man, facing Sethbert and the rest of the room. "You have asked me for a new pope. I will give you one. Whichever of you Androfrancines gathered here will come, take this knife and execute this condemned man, may have my Patriarchal blessing and bear the signet of the Gospel of P'andro Whym. Kill this man and be our pope."

"A pope would not do such a thing," one of the bishops said. "The Whymer Bible forbids it."

Petronus waited. A murmur rose beneath the tent and a wind outside whipped through the three entrances, carrying the scent of evergreen and lavender.

"Very well," Petronus said. He walked to Sethbert and stood before him. The Gypsy Scouts looked to Rudolfo and Rudolfo nodded. It was not assent, but something closer to acceptance, and they stood back.

Petronus laid his hand on the side of Sethbert's face, gently as if he were a father comforting a wayward child.

But when the old man brought the knife up with his other hand, he was fast and sure with the precision of a fisherman.

Petronus dropped the blade. He raised his bloody hands above his head.

"This backward dream is over," Petronus said. "I am the last Androfrancine Pope."

Then he tugged off his ring and dropped it, too.

Rudolfo caught up with Petronus on the road to Caldus Bay on the evening of the following day. He'd spent most of a night and a day soothing his shaken guests. When he heard that the old man had slipped quietly out of the city that morning, he called for his fastest stallion. He waved off his Gypsy Scouts and Gregoric didn't balk when he saw the anger in Rudolfo's eyes.

He pushed his stallion hard, riding low and feeling the wind tug at his cloak and hair. He inhaled the smell of the forest, the smell of the horse, and the smell of the plains ahead.

When he spotted the old man and his mule two leagues into the prairie, he felt for the hilt of his narrow sword and clicked his tongue at his steed. He pounded ahead, overtaking Petronus, and spun his horse. He whipped out his blade and pointed its tip at the old man.

Petronus looked up and Rudolfo lowered his sword when he saw the look of devastation on the old man's face. Those blood-stained eyes, he realized, looked too much like the red sky he'd seen over the smoldering ruins and blackened bones of Windwir.

The old man did not speak.

Rudolfo danced the stallion closer to ask a question that he already knew the answer to. "Why?"

"I did what I must." Petronus's jaw clenched firmly. "Because if I didn't, everything else I did would be a lie."

"We all do what we must." Rudolfo sheathed his sword, the anger draining out of him. "When did you know? When did you decide to do this?"

Petronus sighed. "I knew it before your bird arrived."

Rudolfo pondered this and nodded slowly, searching for the right words to say. When he couldn't find them, he spurred his horse forward and left the old man alone with his tears.

Rudolfo raced the plains until the moon raised up and stars scattered the warm, dark night. At some point, everything fell away but a false sense of freedom that Rudolfo embraced for the moment. He sped through the darkness, feeling the stallion move beneath him, hearing its hooves on the ground and the snorting of its breath. It was him and his horse and the wide open prairie, with no library, no Androfrancines, no nuptials and no heir. And though he knew it was false, Rudolfo honored the lie of it until he saw the forest on his right. Then he slowed the stallion and turned for the trees, eventually slipping from the saddle and leading the horse on foot back in the direction of what was true.

He took the less familiar paths and thought about his life. He thought about the days before Windwir fell and the days after. He thought of nights spent in the supply wagon because he preferred it to a bed. He thought of days spent in the saddle instead of his study. Beds shared with more women than he could count and the one woman he knew he must have.

My life has changed, he told himself and he realized that it would not have if he had not wished it so. He had chosen to rebuild the library, to keep something good in the world of its philosophies, art, drama, history, poetry and song. He had also chosen to align himself with Jin Li Tam, a beautiful and formidable woman. And now they would bring forward a life between them who would also, if Rudolfo had his way, be formidable.

He thought of these things, and he thought of the old man making his way towards the coast, tears wetting his white beard. He thought of his friend Isaak limping about on his mangled leg and wearing his Androfrancine robes. He thought of Jin Li Tam and the calm, reserved look on her face throughout Sethbert's trial and execution.

The Desolation of Windwir has reached us all, he thought.

The less familiar paths fell away, spilling him onto the road. He crossed it, still leading his horse, and stayed to the forest though he could see the lights of his sleeping city now. He continued on, approaching the library hill from the southern side.

Ahead, he heard soft voices, a low humming, and a whispering sound he could not quite place. Leaving the horse, he stepped forward, silent as one of his own Gypsy Scouts, to pull aside the foliage that blocked his view.

The book-makers tent lay open before him, its silk walls rolled up to let in the night. The soft voices were those few of the remnant who had stayed behind to help, moving from table to table, laying out parchment and fresh quills. The metal men worked at those tables, their gears and bellows humming and their jeweled eyes throwing back the lamplight.

Rudolfo stayed for an hour, sitting in grass that grew damp with dew, soothed by the sound he couldn't place before.

It was the sound of their pens whispering across the pages.

GRIEF-STEPPING
TO THE WIDOWER'S WALTZ

Martin was finishing up the first stage of his grief when his dead wife, Julie, knocked on the door. He *knew* he was done with denial because just that morning, he'd stopped working on her dollhouse and decided that later he would pack it away in the garage. And he knew it was his wife at the door because eleven years with someone and you just know their knock, their tentative steps on the porch, the shifting weight of them as they wait patiently for an answer.

He swallowed, put down the book by Kubler-Ross, and went to the door. Her cat, Freckles, rubbed against his legs and meowed plaintively. It was the first time he'd seen Freckles since the accident.

He opened the door quickly, a hundred things to say rattling the cage of his stunned brain. One of the hundred slipped past before his eyes registered the sight of her. "I knew you weren't dead. I just knew it."

Julie stood there in her muddy dress with her broken nails and her torn stockings. For the funeral, her hair, makeup, collar, sleeves had all been in on the cover-up — the undertaker's best work if he did say so himself — to make her look asleep rather than battered unrecognizable by gravity working so goddamn well.

Now though, instead of looking asleep, she looked sad and perplexed. "Marty. I *am* dead."

Martin blinked three times and shook his head. More words elbowing the soft spaces between his ears, jockeying for position in his throat. She moved towards him. He nearly threw his arms around her, nearly dragged her to him, nearly covered her white cheeks and blue lips with kisses that had wandered about homeless since she'd left six weeks ago. Instead, he stepped back. She shot him a puzzled look, then crouched to pet Freckles.

"You missed me. I missed you, too," she told the cat. Freckles purred and she scooped him up.

"I missed you, too," Martin said.

She stood. "Really?"

He swallowed again and nodded. "I'm just glad you're finally home." He turned to face the dining room and the massive dollhouse that dominated it. His eyes settled beyond that on the kitchen where dirty dishes overflowed the sink and counters. "Do you want some tea?"

"I can't drink tea, Martin." She sighed. "I'm dead, remember?"

"I'll just put the water on," he said. "Don't take off again." He turned, started for the kitchen, then came back to kiss her quickly on the mouth. "I've been worried sick. I want to hear all about it."

He shoved the dishes aside to reach the faucet, realized he'd misplaced the kettle, and dug a sauce pan he'd used for Ramen water out of the pile. He rinsed it quickly, filled it, moved more dishes away from the front burner, and put the water on to boil. He did the same thing with his favorite tea cup — a chipped white mug with the words "My Favorite Husband" brightly emblazoned on the side. Her mug, of course, was clean. It might actually have been the only clean dish in the house, he thought.

Martin moved to the doorway, opening his mouth to shout to her. She wasn't in the entryway anymore. Now she stood in the dining room, holding the cat and stooping to look into the various cut-aways of her dollhouse.

"I can't believe you drug this old thing out," she said. "What's got into you?"

He shrugged. "I never finished it. I wanted to finish it for you."

Julie picked up the one doll he'd dared take from its shelf to use for scale. She brushed its long golden hair absently with her thumb. "I thought you'd be mad," she said.

"I was at first," he said. "At first, I was going to sue their sorry asses back into the stone age. But then the investigators said it wasn't faulty equipment."

"Not mad at them. Mad at me."

He blinked again. "Why would I be mad at you?" He shifted uncomfortably, then offered a wry grin. "I mean, I *have* always said it was a dangerous hobby, that it was an accident waiting to happen —"

"You didn't get my note."

"Note?" Of course he had gotten it. She'd left before dawn that morning. She'd put the note on the tea kettle, the same place she always put them. "I did. On the tea kettle. That's how I knew where to tell them you were when you didn't turn up."

She pursed her lips. "The *other* note, Martin."

He could feel the blankness of his own stare. "What other note, Julie?"

Sadness washed her face. "Oh Martin." Freckles, suddenly uncomfortable with the arrangement, struggled free and landed lightly on the floor. "It's in the book. Our book."

The book from the marriage counselor. The book they'd been taking turns reading. Martin felt a sinking feeling. "There's another note?"

But it made sense now to him. Of course. She hadn't really gone rock-climbing that Saturday morning. No. She'd left him. She'd thrown in the towel and after only three sessions. Eleven years gone.

He didn't speak. He moved past her, up the stairs and into the bedroom. He went to his nightstand and stared at the book there. Its title was a pithy promise about the contents, pretentious to him now in the face of this new revelation. With a shaking hand, he reached out and picked it up. His fingers smudged the dust that had settled onto its cover.

Who was he? Who was Julie leaving him for? Would she have said in the note? Or would he have to ask her after he read it. He opened the book to the place where he *should* have started reading all those weeks ago. Waiting there lay an envelope with his name printed on it carefully.

He picked it up and went back down the stairs.

She stood in the kitchen, pouring tea. He realized as he entered the room that it smelled faintly of chemicals and dirt. She bit her lip as she handed him the steaming mug.

"Have you read it?"

He held the tea in one hand and the envelope in the other. "Not yet."

She walked into the living room and sat on the couch. He followed her and sat in the armchair. Setting down the tea, he flipped the envelope over in his hands and opened it.

Martin looked up at her. "Do I want to read this?"

She shook her head. "You don't. But you should read it anyway."

He pulled out the sheath of paper. Two or three pages, front and back, all in that same, careful script.

Dear Martin, he read. His eyes moved forward, stumbled against something he did not expect and pressed on ahead. They moved faster, a jog and then a run and then a gallop. He went through the first page, then stopped. "It was an accident," he said.

"No," Julie said. "No. It wasn't."

He stared at the letter. "You're wrong."

"I'm sorry, Martin," she said. He studied her. Her eyes were hollow and dry. Her lip trembled and she blinked a lot, though she didn't need to.

Martin leaned forward, dropped the letter on the table, and lifted his mug. Peppermint. She always liked it because it made her sleepy at night. He liked it because it was supposedly good for clearing and sharpening the mind. He sipped, then risked another look at her.

She still watched him. "Well?"

He chose his words very carefully. "It doesn't matter," he said. "What matters is that you didn't go through with it."

Without a word, she stood up. Without a glance over her shoulder, she left the house.

And without finishing his tea, Martin went back to working on her dollhouse.

Rage came upon him like a rising squall.

It rode Martin all day long into the ground, then chewed at him in his dreams. The first day, he contained it. On the second day, he changed the cat's brand of food. Freckles didn't care, but Martin knew that sort of thing would drive Julie bat-shit. On the third day, he threw the marriage counselor's book into the fireplace they never used because she didn't like the mess it made. The day after *that*, he lit the fireplace.

At the end of a week, he put his foot through the kitchen of her dollhouse — no small accomplishment given that it was up on the dining room table at the time. It made a terrible mess and scared the cat. After *that* boost of confidence, he put his foot through the den and little books that he'd carefully made with glue and construction paper and the little bookcases he'd made with popsicle sticks and wood-colored contact paper shattered and scattered.

At the end of two weeks, his dead wife knocked on the door just as he hurled her favorite tea mug at the wall. It flew apart in a rain of ceramic shrapnel. Ignoring her knock, he threw the "My Favorite Husband" mug, too.

He was reaching for her grandmother's china on the little shelves in the breakfast nook when Julie's face appeared in the window. She didn't look sad this time; she looked bemused.

"What are you doing, Martin?" she asked through the glass. "Open the door."

"Fuck you, Julie," he said. It didn't come out quite as loud and angry as he wanted it to. He reached around in his brain for something with a bit more clout. "Better yet, fuck off and *die*." He paused, forced an Aspartame smile and stared at her. "Oh wait. You already did."

He dropped the plate. The noise of it satisfied him. It satisfied him greatly.

She disappeared from the window, but Martin didn't care. He reached for a china saucer and laughed as it joined its cousin on the floor.

Suddenly, the weight of the anger struck him and he sat down heavily on the kitchen floor in the midst of the porcelain shards. He felt tears pushing at his eyes, sadness bigger than his rage pulling at his heart. He ran his hands through his hair and sat there, his back resting against the cupboard.

For a moment he thought he was finished. Then he heard the key in the lock and remembered the red-hooded gnome. She'd locked herself out too many times. She'd tried everything from sticky notes to duct-tape and when Julie realized there wasn't anything she could do to remember her keys, she'd brought home the red-hooded gnome.

"See," she'd said like a little girl at Christmas. "He has a secret compartment in his left foot."

The front door pushed open slowly. "Martin?"

All the rage came back and he stood. "Get out."

"Martin, this isn't like you."

It wasn't, some part of him realized. He didn't access anger well, the counselor had said. Because his parents had always told him it was wrong. That, the pretentious man with his pretentious book had said, may be at least some of the problems in your marriage.

Julie was stepping through the door now. She saw the dollhouse, saw Martin shaking on his feet, and her eyes went wide for a moment. If she'd been breathing, Martin knew, her nostrils would've flared in that surprised way they did when she was scared. But she didn't breathe now. Because she was dead. And that knowledge twisted him into more rage.

"Consider it a breakthrough," he finally said.

"Martin, it's normal to be angry under the circumstances."

"Which circumstance?" He waited and when she didn't answer, he continued. "The one where I'm your normal thirty-eight year old widower just processing his grief or the one where my goddamn wife chicken-shitted her way off a big fucking rock because she was —" he paused, dug around in his pocket, found the letter, pulled it out and un-crumpled it before continuing " — *too tired to keep doing this, too tired to keep pretending life can ever be any more than what it is?*" He looked up, watching her face.

"I didn't do it to hurt you."

"That hardly matters, doesn't it? You *knew* it would. Or else why would you leave the letter?" He waited again. "Maybe I should read you some more?" He scanned the letter again. "Here we go: *I already feel dead, buried in sadness that I can't dig out of. I've done the math and, darling, it's better this way.* So I have a question for you, sugar-lips." He worked himself up into his best sneer. "How is it? Being dead? Is it really that much better?"

Now she looked sad. Now she looked lost. Now she looked crushed and something like pride swelled in him for finally, finally finding something that scratched his itch to punish.

Her words came slowly. "Martin, that's not fair."

"No," he said. "You're exactly right. It's *not* fair. Do you want to know why?"

She didn't speak, but she did nod. Slightly, though, as if she really didn't mean it.

"Because in your brilliant plan to unload *your* life, you've *completely* ruined mine." He stepped forward quicker than he knew he could, snatched the dangling key from her cold, dead fingers and slipped it into his pocket. "Now get out of my house. Don't come back."

She left the door open when she did.

First, he switched the cat back to the old brand of food though by this time, the cat was quite content with the new arrangement.

Then, Martin spent half a night scouring the internet for exactly the right pieces of china. The mugs were a loss, the ashes in the fireplace were easy to clean up, and he really saw no need to replace the book. He spent part of a weekend repairing the broken bits of the dollhouse before moving it all back into the garage along with the tools.

Gradually, a prayer formed in his mind. *Please come home.* He didn't need to pray it; it prayed itself. It uttered itself out in his actions, and when it did not answer itself after a few weeks, he bought her favorite flowers and went to her grave for the first time.

He knelt there, even though it had been raining for months and the ground was wet and spongy. He felt the water soaking through his cotton slacks. "Please come home," he said.

He wanted to say more. And maybe, deep down inside where there were no words, a litany spilled out: I didn't mean it, Julie. I know you didn't mean it, either. I know how hard you tried. I know how hard you worked to get beyond what he did to you. And in the end, you did the best you could. But it can be different. Somehow, I know it can. I can change. You can change. I'll do anything. I'll do anything.

And up near the surface, where there *were* words: "Please come home."

He set the flowers on her stone. He set the key he'd taken from her beside them.

Then, with bargains made, Martin went home to cry.

Sadness moved in and set up its shadowed house. Martin worked around it, through it, for as long as he could before he gave up. The leave of absence from his work ran out. So did his boss's sympathy. Martin didn't even go in to be fired in person. He bought three months of Ramen noodles and frozen dinners. He lived on the life insurance and didn't worry what would happen when it ran out. Because by then, he thought, he'd run out, too. Surely he'd run out.

Of course, he thought about pulling a Julie. He thought about it, but not for long.

He stayed in the bedroom, stayed in the bed mostly. He'd read somewhere about a famous comedian whose wife had died. Someone asked that comedian what bothered him the most and he said it was the emptiness on his wife's side of the bed. Then they asked him what he did about it.

"I sleep on her side of the bed," the comedian answered.

Martin did the same. And he cried into her pillow until his eyes went dry and his voice went hoarse.

And then he cried some more.

Martin woke up in the middle of the night. He went into the bathroom, lathered up, shaved off his two-month beard and ran his first shower in weeks.

Tomorrow, he thought, he'd get a haircut, pick up some *real* groceries, maybe catch a movie. Sunday, he'd pick up the classifieds. Maybe Monday, he'd call his ex-boss.

Pulling on his robe, he went downstairs to make some tea.

Picking up the Kubler-Ross book, he started reading where he'd left off so long ago. He sipped his tea. Eventually, he went back to bed.

When he heard scratching at the window an hour later, he wondered if maybe Freckles had gotten outside. Julie had always kept the bedroom window open just enough for her cat to get in. He'd become pretty adept over the years at scaling the tree and dropping to the top of the porch.

Of course, he'd curtailed Freckles's outdoor trips after Julie died. He didn't like the fleas or the dead rodents. And he didn't like sleeping with the window open.

He moved the curtains aside and saw Julie crouching there, her small hands straining at the window. Her eyes were big when they met his and her mouth formed a little 'o' of surprise. She looked sad again.

He unlocked the window and helped her push it up. It was snowing now, he realized, and broken ice scattered on the hardwood floor. How many seasons had he missed?

Stretching out his arms, he lifted his dead wife inside. She looked better now than the last time he saw her. The winter suited her. And she was light as leaves in autumn.

"Martin," she started to say, but he kissed her. Her lips were blue frost.

"It's cold out tonight," he said when he finished the kiss. "Come to bed."

"Martin," she said again, but he shook his head.

"You're frozen, Julie. Come to bed and I'll warm you up."

The sadness on her face shifted. A half smile pulled at her mouth. "It won't change anything. I'm dead."

Here is where you choose your words most carefully, he told himself.

Do you make promises, Martin? We can go back to counseling. We can get another book. I'll try harder.

Do you ask questions? Why are you back? How long will you stay? Will we need central air for the summers now?

Or do you rattle off solutions to all of the obvious problems? They could move away. They could change their names. And the insurance company could inquire after their money but dead is dead, after all, and a well-placed stethoscope or maybe one of those little mirrors under the nose could settle that for good.

But his questions, answers and promises really didn't measure up to the sight of her before him in her torn dress and matted hair and hollow eyes and woeful look.

As if she weren't sure he'd really heard her, Julie repeated herself as she often had in life: "It won't change anything, Martin. I'm still dead."

"I know," Martin said. "But I'm prepared to live with that now."

And whistling softly, he waltzed her to the side of their bed. And lifting her easily, he laid her on his side of it.

LOVE IN THE TIME OF CAR ALARMS

ook, Bob," I told the empty chair, "I've been thinking a lot about it and I'm not sure we're right for each other."

The empty chair remained silent.

I sighed.

I'd met Bob Reynolds at a fire scene on the day after. I was helping the captain with his investigation and Bob was there from CARECO insurance. We'd struck up a conversation and I'd asked him out. He blushed, said yes, and here I was for Date Number Four.

Well, not a date exactly.

The trouble with insurance agents is: They take their jobs far too seriously. I put out fires. I face danger every day. But I still make time for my life.

Not Bob.

My cell phone rang and I dug it out of my pocket. I hated purses and refused to carry one. I looked at the caller ID — it was my old college roommate, Sarah.

She didn't bother with pleasantries. "So," she said in a cheerful voice, "did you pull the trigger on Bob yet?"

"He didn't show up."

Sarah groaned. "Yikes. He's even late for the Break Up Coffee?"

"It's not a break up," I said. "We haven't technically started dating yet."

Sarah laughed, then coughed. "Sorry, Rachel."

I sighed again. "It's okay. He's a sweet guy. He just loves his work too much."

"Probably has deep-seated, intimacy issues," Sarah said. "And a wee little —"

There was a loud boom outside and the windows vibrated. Every car alarm in a five block radius went off as paper from the trash cans and from the street were stirred up into a brief tornado.

"What was that?" Sarah asked.

"One of *them*," I said. Then, I looked up as Bob rushed in through the back door, fumbling with his briefcase and, of course, the roses. "Look, Sarah, he just showed up. I gotta go."

"Call me when you're done," she said. "I want details."

I hung up and put the phone back in my pocket.

Bob saw me and walked over quickly. He looked rumpled and worried but wasn't out of breath. "I'm so, *so* sorry," he said. "The bus and then the taxi and then there was this bicycle and —"

I raised my hand. "Don't worry about it, Bob. Sit down."

"These are for you." He extended the roses.

I shook my head. "I only have three vases," I told him.

Bob blushed as he sat. "I could get you another vase."

"I'm a three vase girl, Bob. Four is too many." And then I pulled the trigger. "Look, Bob, you're a sweet guy. But this just isn't working."

"What's not working?" he asked. But the look in his eyes told me he'd heard this before. His shoulders slouched and his face took on that kicked puppy look.

When his cell phone started to ring I felt my blood pressure rising. "This —" I waved my hands in the air. "This *whatever* it is. I can't really call it dating because you're late every time and leave in the middle."

He nodded. His voice was heavy. "I know. It will slow down, I promise. Things are just really busy right now."

His phone continued to ring, then stopped abruptly.

I sipped my latte. "Things have been busy for the last three weeks, Bob."

He sighed. His phone started ringing again and his eyes went guiltily to his suit jacket pocket. "I'm sorry, Rachel," he said.

Then he answered it. "What is it?" He waited, turning away and cupping his hand over his mouth. "Can't you get NM on it?" He nodded while listening. "Okay."

I opened my mouth to speak and closed it when my own cell phone started to ring.

Bob was already standing. "Rachel," he said, "I am so, *so* sorry. Can we finish this later on? I'd really like to try again."

I looked at the caller ID; it was the fire station. "I don't think that's —"

But when I looked up from my phone, Bob was already gone. "It's a big one," the chief said. "You'd better get down here."

Outside, the car alarms that were so recently silenced suddenly went off again and the windows rattled.

"I'm on my way," I said.

It was a high rise with a daycare and lots of families. The good news was that most people were at work. The bad news was that the traffic was even worse than usual.

I suited up and checked the flow to my OBA. "What's the situation?"

"Boy America is here. He's getting people out through the top."

"Great. Colonel Patriot." He was one of the oldest and probably the same one who kept setting off the car alarms and scattering trash all over the city in his mad hurry to interfere somewhere else. I rolled my eyes. "These guys just can't let us do our job, Chief."

His face was drawn. "We need it on this one, Tenner."

I looked at the building, flames rising from the middle section and licking the walls and windows, at least six stories and climbing. Maybe he was right, a voice inside nagged me.

"He's getting the upper stories. We're taking the ones beneath the fire." The chief pointed. "Take a crew in."

I looked and saw a blur of red, white and blue and an old woman materialized on a gurney near the ambulances. A crowd of reporters shouted questions from a police line.

"I'm on it," I told him.

We worked our way in and I lost track of time. My life was reduced to the sound of my heart in my ears and the sound of my breath in the regulator louder even than the roar of the fire or the rush of the water. My eyes on the ground before me, my feet careful to find their way.

We'd finally gotten everyone out and were doing what we could to fight the fire.

We weren't winning.

An explosion above pushed us to the floor under a hot fist of wind and a cascade of burning debris.

"We need out," I yelled. "The building is going to come down on us." I looked around, saw a window down the smoky corridor and made for it.

Suddenly, the window was filled with a broad chest and an American flag. Colonel Patriot hovered outside, pulling the window frame out of the wall and tossing it into the river. "This way, ma'am," he said.

"Don't ma'am me, Freak Boy," I said. I turned to my men. "Go on," I shouted at them. "Get out of here."

He grabbed a man under each of his beefy arms and turned around so another could climb onto his back. "I'll be right back," he said to me over his shoulder.

Then he was gone.

That's when I heard the baby crying.

It was above me one floor, drifting down from a window. I saw the green light of an Exit sign nearby and walked quickly towards it. Dodging flames, I ducked inside the doorway and tried to control my breathing. My heart raced and I felt my sweat drying from the heat.

I took the stairs two at a time, my ears pulling down the baby's cry. There, in the middle of the hallway, lay a basinet, and within it, a baby.

I bent over to scoop it up and the baby stopped crying. Its eyes opened and something shot out of its mouth — something like taffy — and it wrapped itself around my hands and torso. Then, baby, basinet and I were all tugged back down the hall, around a corner and up an empty elevator shaft at a speed that made me see stars.

When we popped out onto the ceiling an armored man awaited us with a something like a fishing rod in his hands. I'd seen him in the papers before. Professor Something.

"Ah," he said. "Not what I was fishing for, but still . . ."

He had an enormous revolver in one hand. The bullets in the cylinder glowed purple. While I lay panting on the rooftop, he took the baby from me and fiddled with it.

"Put down the baby, Professor Destructo," a new voice said.

I looked over and saw Colonel Patriot hovering at the roof's edge, his arms folded across his chest.

I crawled to my feet and forced myself to straighten. "Colonel Patriot, it's a trap. The baby is —"

But in that moment, Destructo hurled the baby at Colonel Patriot and raised his pistol. "Time," he chortled, "to test drive my Freakonium bullets. I named them after you."

I didn't even think about it and it didn't matter that I didn't like him or his kind and their interfering ways. I threw myself between them like it was any other citizen.

"Rachel," Colonel Patriot yelled, "don't!"

But it was too late. The power of the bullet caught my shoulder and tossed me back and over the edge. Above me, a pillar of smoke blotted out the sun.

I felt the hot wind rushing at me and felt my heart rate rising faster as adrenalin drowned my system.

I heard a boom. I heard car alarms going off and saw flaming debris stir up from the burning high-rise. Rocketing toward me, I saw Colonel Patriot with a look of terror and determination on his face like I have never seen, his hands outstretched and clutching for me. He caught me and I felt him shaking. "Are you okay?"

He slowed then hovered, holding me to his chest. "I'm bleeding, Cub Scout."

Then I slipped away into fog.

I woke up in the hospital, arm bandaged and in a sling.

I listened to the doctor drone on about keeping me under observation for a night, listened to the good news that in six to nine weeks I'd most likely be back to work. Then he left and they brought me what was supposed to be food. I picked at it and watched television. The news was all that was on. Ann Marigold at Channel Three was reporting live outside the Medina Institute for the Criminally Gifted. I caught bits of it but the pain medication kept me fuzzyheaded. The gist of it was that Professor Destructo was behind bars again.

Then my picture came up — the old one on file from the last time I somehow managed to distinguish myself in the line of duty. It always felt awkward to hear them recite my record.

There was a knock but I realized it was on the other side of the room, not at the door. I looked and saw a familiar face outside the window. I started to motion at him with my right hand but winced and raised my left.

He opened the window with one hand and poked his head in.

He kept one hand behind his back. "How are you doing?" he asked.

"I'm fine," I said. "I'm going home tomorrow." I nodded to the television. "So it looks like you got him."

He nodded. "I did." He looked uncomfortable. "That bullet would've killed me," he added. "You saved my life."

I smiled. "You sorta returned the favor. And I'm not used to being rescued. I'm usually on the other side of the fence."

"Me too," he said and we both laughed.

"Well, thanks," I said. "But I have a question." It had been bothering me for a while. Well, once I'd had time to process it. "Back on the roof," I said, "you called me by my name. How do you know my name?"

He shifted uncomfortably. "Uh," he said. "I've been keeping my eye on you."

I raised my eyebrows. "Oh really?"

He nodded. "I have.

I chuckled. "So when you're not fighting crime and fires you're a stalker? Or do you have some kind of firefighter fetish?"

He blushed and laughed at the same time. "Can I come in?"

There was something familiar about him but I couldn't place it. Maybe it was the morphine but the way he looked at me made me feel warm and protected. *I've been keeping my eye on you.* I was so busy protecting other people all the time that I'd forgotten what that felt like to be on the other side of the curtain.

"Why are you keeping your eye on me?"

"It's complicated but I was hoping we could talk about that. Especially after today."

"Okay," I said. "Come in."

When he came in, he smiled. "I was hoping for another chance."

"Another chance at what?"

He pulled the roses from behind his back. They were in a vase — a nice one made of crystal — decorated with satin ribbons and a bow. The card read, "I'm so, *so* sorry."

I just stared at them.

He set them on the nightstand beside the bed and stepped back. "You did good work today, Rachel. You saved a lot of lives."

"So did you, Bob."

"You should call me Colonel Patriot in public."

I felt the drugs settling in, swallowing the pain that radiated out from my shoulder. "Okay, Colonel Patriot."

He leaned over and kissed my forehead. His mouth was cool against my skin.

Then I heard his cell phone ringing. "You going to get that?" I asked him.

He shook his head. "I have the night off."

"No," I said. "Save that for later, when I'm out of here and a bit more mobile."

He blinked at me. "Really?"

"Really," I said. "We have a date to finish." I was suddenly liking the way this one made me feel. Of course, it might've been the morphine.

He answered the phone. "Yes, NM?" He nodded. "I see." He nodded more. "Yes. I'll be right there."

He hung up and looked at me. "Lunatic the Clown has taken the President hostage."

"Go get him, Cub Scout," I said, yawning. "I'm sleepy. Taking bullets is hard work."

He kissed me again, this time on my mouth, and I felt it all the day down to my toes. "Okay. I'll be back soon."

"Shoo," I said.

He grinned. Then he was gone. A moment later, there was a boom and the car alarms went off again. The news had changed to a live feed from Washington DC where Terry Barker reported that the President's kidnapper was now demanding fifteen truckloads of Twinkies, air-dropped over West Africa.

I looked back to the window and smiled. Soon, the world would return to normal for a bit. Chaos and pandemonium would bend to the red, white and blue blur that streaked towards them.

As I absently listened to the news, I wondered what we'd do on Bob's next night off. I had at least a few things in mind.

"Maybe," I mumbled to the empty room, "he'll even wear his cape."

I sighed and looked back to the news. The camera had shakily panned the sky, following a streak that impacted solidly in the yard outside the White House. I wanted to stay awake until he wrapped this one up.

Then I was sure he'd be back to check on me before he was off again to the next disaster.

The trouble with heroes is: There's never enough of them to go around. The world needs them and what they want doesn't really enter into it. They do what they have to, without thinking about it and they do it for anyone who needs to be saved.

The trouble with heroes is they belong to us all.

So I guess I'll have to learn how to share.

There's another boom outside and my heart skips. But this time it's just thunder, and as the rain begins to slice downward across the night sky, I let myself drift into a light sleep.

Bob will come back soon, I tell myself, but the car alarms will wake me when he does.

WHAT CHILD IS THIS
I ASK THE MIDNIGHT CLEAR

It could have been snow, gently drifting down. It could have been virgin white and cold as cold. But it wasn't.

It was ash and the night wind was hot upon me.

That's what I remember now when I go out.

That first year when the world was on fire and we slipped over the broiling skin of it, we brave nine. We ran the course all night but found nowhere to land. For the first time ever I did not stop. Not one place. And all the while, as we slid through that broiling night, I kept humming that song. The one about the star, the star. Dancing in the night.

Tail big as a kite.

The end had come suddenly and they'd managed to do it to themselves. I'd always known they would.

I'm airborne now and the past falls away. The ash has long settled and it's really snowing again. We're not as loaded down as we've been in the past but that will come in handy later. Times have changed. The list has changed, too. And so has my work. Naughty and nice are blurrier now so I'm less meticulous in checking. I do the right thing, instead.

I don't have to crack any whips or give any whistles. We build speed to bend time around us. We'll do a year's work this night and then we'll sleep a while. I check the ammunition in my assault rifle and loosen the strings on my sack.

Then we start landing here and there and I'm out doing the right thing. Books for a library in Vancouver. Needles and a whetstone for a circuit rider in Laramie. We haul a starving family out of a dead mountain town in Oregon and assassinate a white supremacist who was building a skinhead army in Maine. A handful of twelve-gauge shells for Leonard in Saskatoon. A bottle of aspirin in Bo Phut, Thailand. And so on.

We're just turning north for home when we see the light.

A star, a star, dancing in the night. Tail as big as a kite.

It builds and then blooms, a piercing white over the horizon to the east. I shield my eyes and look homeward, then back into the light. Is it a bomb? Another crazy moving the world deeper into the hole it has fallen in? Or a satellite falling from orbit? Either way, it's worth looking into.

I steer east and take us low. As I draw closer, the light shrinks to a concentrated point of brilliance and I aim for it. We pick up speed and rip open space-time for a split second. Then, we bear down upon the town that sleeps beneath that unexplainable, spontaneous star.

There in the glory of that bright light, a child screams.

She is not on my list. I've made no stops in this feral country in over a decade. But I hear her screaming and it is as piercing as the star above. I unsling my rifle and we drop right there to hover over what used to be a schoolyard. I don't know what I was expecting. Someone being harmed. Someone being carved up into pieces by primates gone horribly wrong. I work the lever and feel the solid clunk of a chambered round. Slipping my gloved finger around the trigger, I use my thumb to move the switch to three-round-burst, and then I hit ground with a thud. I race across the open concrete, stepping over the frozen clumps of gray weed and watching my breath billow into the cold night air. The screaming stops. I hear heavy breathing instead now. Panting.

What are they doing to her? I feel a rage coming on as the screams start again. I push it down and use it to feed my focus.

Do you hear what I hear, the song asks.

I hear it, I answer.

They rape the world the same way they rape each other.

They kill the world the same way they kill each other.

No list to make or check here. I am bent on violent righteousness when I kick down the makeshift plywood door propped up to keep the wind out.

Someone has turned the old lavatory into shelter but it has gone badly for them. The boy lies cold and still and bloody. The girl's screams change from pain to terror when I storm into the cluttered room and I suddenly know that things were not what they seem. I see her, in the corner, squatting in a nest of blankets. Her brown hair is long and dirty. Her brown eyes are wild and frantic. The blankets are stained with blood and I understand why. Pale and shaking, her eyes go wide as she sees me standing over the cold body of her dead mate, light spilling around me into the room.

Another contraction and she screams again. I turn, run for the medical kit beneath the driver's bench. When I return, I go in slowly with my rifle slung and my hands up showing the kit. "I can help you," I tell the girl.

Her eyes roll and she tries backing away from me but falls back into the corner. Her breath heaves out in ragged gasps.

"I'm a friend." I keep my voice low and assuring, just like in the old days. Only this time, it's not a frightened child approaching me from a long line in the mall, nervous at the presence the myth of me has become. This frightened child huddles in a frozen elementary restroom at the end of her tether, trying to shove life into a dead, cold place. "I can help you," I say again but this time I hear the doubt in my own voice. There is too much blood.

I crouch and move closer, opening the kit and finding nothing at all that I can use.

Then behind me, in the schoolyard, a clatter arises.

The eight snort and stomp, and when the howling starts outside, the light winks out. The moon, hidden behind a layer of clouds, offers little visibility.

Pushing the first aid kit towards the girl, I draw my rifle again, thumb off the safety once more. I never unchambered the round. Too smart for that.

More stamping and snorting but no ringing. I took the bells off their harnesses a long time ago.

"Dashing through the snow," a voice whispers from the edge of the schoolyard.

"O come all ye faithful," another says.

"We wish you a merry Christmas," sings a third.

I look over my shoulder at the girl panting in the corner. "Just stay put and keep quiet."

Donner screams and bucks. Dasher bleats and kicks. I hear the whir of stones in slings, the distant clatters of shots gone wide.

Then, I'm outside and running at a low crouch. I'm fast for a big man, even without laying my finger to the side of my nose. I whistle and I hear the eight lifting off; I hear the labored breathing of the two who've been hurt. I hear the disappointed grunts and hungry sighs. I don't wait; when one of them takes shape in the darkness, large and wide, I put a three-round burst into the center of its mass and listen to the rush of escaping air as that rush twists itself into a shriek of surprise.

Another shape forms beside it, this one bending to see to its friend. I put another burst there. I've done this before. I do the right thing.

Then I stop. I smell the burning powder on the midnight air. I listen for my eight, moving in a slow, widening circle above me.

A third takes shape near the others. I move closer, rifle raised. It moves to the left and I tap the concrete with bullets near his foot. "Hold," I tell him.

I can see him now and he might've been human once but the traces of it have left his face and eyes. He's wearing a red hat like mine, only tattered and dirty. He's dropped his sling and one of his suspenders is loose and dangling. Barefoot with wet trousers, he trembles before a vision he may have dim memory of, from a childhood spent before the world heaved its last sigh.

"Remove the hat," I say, "and look to me."

He pulls it off slowly. Our eyes meet and I'm pleased at the fear I see there. "Life is your gift this year," I tell him through gritted teeth, "but it comes with a string. Tell the others what you have seen and tell them to be afraid. Every other night belongs to you but this one. I ride on this night with justice and grace." I raise myself to full height. I fire the rifle over his head. "Now, run like a rabbit."

He does and as he fades, the night becomes silent and holy for a heartbeat before a new cry, muffled and straining, greets its new home in a broken world.

I turn back and enter the lavatory, and in that I am both too late and just in time. The girl is fading fast and in her arms she holds a sticky, bloody bundle packed into dirty cloth pulled from her makeshift nest. I see the cord that still connects them. Her eyes are wide and her nostrils flare when I draw closer but she doesn't flinch.

She points to me. "Ho, ho, ho," she says in a quiet voice before making the sign of the cross. She passes the squirming bundle to me and says one final word: "Charis."

Slinging my rifle, I take the baby. I do the best I can with the tools I have, cutting the cord, closing the mother's glassy eyes. I remove my jacket. Then I clean the baby and wrap her carefully in it.

I want to stay and bury my dead but I know better. I have not prayed in years but I manage one there beside the fallen mother and father, victims of a nativity gone wrong in a world that struggles between death and birth.

Then, I whistle for my eight. We lift off into the night and I hold Charis close to me, giving the reindeer their heads to take us north and home.

As we fly, I ponder — I wonder as I wander — and I call up my list to see who on this night had wanted the gift of a child. I weep at what I find.

"It's no place for a child," I tell the eight as we soar.

"I'm far too old for this work," I say to them again.

"I am afraid," I finally admit.

But a vision unfolds to me of a tiny girl in red with elves for her friends and family, raised up with the deer and the sleigh as humanity's orphan, taught from their books and their art and the better parts of a species tremendously blessed and terribly flawed, trained to go out into that broken world and do the right thing.

And in that moment, the light returns, but it is inside me and inside of the baby in my arms, and that light threatens to swallow me whole and I beg it to because within that light is hope and promise and I recognize that tonight was the night upon which the universe — or whomever ran it — gave back to me and did so with a holy charge.

Home arises to the north and we pound sky for it. As we fly, the clouds lift and the starshine falls like a mantle of jewels over the crown of the world.

I feel the peace on earth within my chest.

Goodwill towards men lay sleeping in my arms.

"What child is this?" I ask the midnight clear.

"Yours," it says, and weeping, we fly home.

GRAIL-DIVING IN SHANGRILLA
WITH THE WORLD'S LAST MIME

They buried Little Elvis Sanchez in a burned out Volkswagen just outside the smoldering remains of Denver. Reverend Sparkle Jones said a few words. Sister Mika and Aunty Ann sang "Memories" or a near approximation thereof while the Last Mime LeFoie did a nice bit of performance art for dramatic effect.

Then, the Good Reverend urinated on the hobgoblin corpses to keep them from coming back from the dead. He pulled up his dress and squatted like a girl but by now this didn't surprise anyone at all.

Timmy Gallahad watched all of this and wondered if they would succeed in their quest.

When Reverend Sparkle was finished, the troupe, the company, the band, the chosen — whatever you wish to call them — pressed on for Shangrilla.

The world was in a bad way.

You've read all about it by now.

That fateful spring morning a thousand, thousand alarms jangled armies and navies, fire departments and police stations, air forces and astronomers to life. Look! Up in the sky! Exactly what they'd looked for, planned for and maybe even hoped for. Until the flying saucers dropped the bombs. Until their drop-pods spilled slathering monsters on the world.

The Great One-Sided War lasted three days, and at the end of it, hobgoblin hordes, electric harnesses humming a cheerful hum, ran mop-up on the scant leftovers of the human race.

Reverend Sparkle Jones was one such leftover. And he bumped into another, Little Elvis, on his way out of Portland, Oregon.

"Howdy, Ma'am," Little Elvis Sanchez said, tipping the cowboy hat he'd looted from a Western outfitters shop. He blushed when the Reverend turned to face him. "I mean Sir."

"Ma'am is fine." Reverend Sparkle's make-up had smeared all to hell and he'd broken a heel navigating rubble. "Or Reverend."

Little Elvis crossed himself. He'd been contemplating an oversized RV that he didn't think he could drive. He stood from his seat on the curb and stretched out a hand. "Little Elvis Sanchez," he said, "retired amateur wrestler."

The Reverend took the hand, squeezed it lightly. "Enchanted," he said. "Sparkle Jones. Minister of the Lord and Cabaret Performer Extraordinaire."

Little Elvis sat back down.

Sparkle joined him on the curb, careful to cross his legs. "Got a plan?"

Little Elvis shrugged. "Not really."

"Well. *I* do."

Little Elvis grinned. "Well, let's go then."

"Don't you want to hear it?"

The wrestler shook his head. "Nope. Let's just do it. It's got to be better than just sitting around waiting for the world to end."

The Reverend opened his mouth to reply when ululating hobgoblins rounded a street corner ahead. He closed his mouth and drew the twin 1911 Colt .45 automatics he'd been saving for a special occasion. Little Elvis hefted an M60 he'd borrowed from an overturned Humvee. Shell casings flew. Guns roared. Hobgoblins fell in piles of bloody meat, sparks popping from their wire harnesses and metal helmets.

Afterwards, Reverend Sparkle holstered his pistols and walked to the RV. Little Elvis moved away towards the corpses, unzipping his trousers as he went.

Sparkle paused at the door. "What are you *doing?*"

"Can't go yet," Sanchez said over his shoulder. "Have to pee on them first."

"I don't think I want to know," the Reverend said.

Little Elvis smiled and got to it, splashing his name onto the fallen with practiced glee.

Sparkle Jones and Little Elvis Sanchez met Sister Mika and Aunty Ann outside Medford. Sister Mika the Singing Nun and

Aunty Ann of Aunty Ann's Jellies and Jams had already joined forces, piling their Ford Ranger's bed high with supplies, weapons and ammunition. They sat on the roof of a freeway rest-stop, roasting hotdogs on a hibachi and keeping watch for hobgoblin patrols.

The Reverend saw the line of smoke, pulled in, jumped the curb and drew up close to the side of the building. Rolling down his window, he stood up and twisted.

Sister Mika held an untwisted coat-hanger heavy with the weight of a ballpark frank in one hand and a magnum in the other. "May I help you?"

Jones nodded at her torn and dirty habit. "Sister." He also nodded to Aunty Ann, an older woman in a calico dress. "Nice dress, ma'am."

Both women smiled at him.

"Saw your smoke. They probably can, too."

Sister Mika set down the hotdog and waved her hand across the sky. "Lots of smoke these days."

He looked. Everywhere on the horizon, smudges of gray, columns of darker gray, trickles of lighter gray.

"Do you have a plan?" Reverend Sparkle Jones asked.

Sister Mika nodded. "Hole up in the mountains and wait for God's Deliverance."

He grinned. "Your deliverance has arrived. If you have a few extra dogs to spare, why don't me and my traveling companion here, Little Elvis Sanchez, join you for a bite and explain."

Aunty Ann scowled and leaned over. She and Sister Mika whispered for a bit back and forth. Finally, they looked up at him.

"Two questions first," Sister Mika said.

"Yes?"

"First . . . you packing heat?"

Sparkle nodded. "We'll leave the guns in the rig. Second?"

"Second." She pointed her magnum at the RV. "Do you have any mustard in that thing?"

"Mustard?" he asked. "What brand?"

"Why," she said, smiling, "the gray stuff, of course."

And naturally, being that it was the edge of the end of the world and price was suddenly no object, and possibly because he and Little Elvis Sanchez were hungry when they raided those six grocery stores to pack out the Winnebago Roadwarrior, they *did* have the gray stuff, along with every other type, color, texture, flavor, brand and off-brand of mustard available on the market.

They found the World's Last Mime, LeFoie, sitting beneath a casino billboard sign near Reno. He sat in a pile of plastic letters from an overturned box near the ladder he had used to change his billing on the sign. His black beret tilted askew, one suspender dangled loose, his greasepaint showed tear streaks. He leaped to his feet as the RV and pickup approached and pantomimed pulling them towards him on an imaginary rope.

Little Elvis rolled down the window, smiled and nodded to the sign. "You really the world's last mime?"

He nodded, wiping away imaginary tears with an exaggerated gesture.

The Reverend Sparkle Jones scowled. "Be careful, Little Elvis," he said. "Mimes are a dangerous lot, are decidedly French and are an abomination unto the Lord."

Little Elvis looked at the Reverend. "This one seems harmless, Padre."

"You can never be too sure."

By now, Aunty Ann and Sister Mika had climbed out of their truck and approached.

"You all alone here?" Little Elvis asked.

LeFoie nodded.

"Ask him how he's escaped the hobgoblins," the Reverend said.

"I think mimes can hear just fine," Little Elvis said. "They just can't talk."

"Well, not all of us speak French."

Sister Mika and Aunty Ann rolled their eyes. Little Elvis gave the Last Mime an apologetic shrug. "Well?"

LeFoie turned his fingers into pistols, firing one and then the other in an over-the-top cowboy imitation. Then he worked through a half dozen or so exaggerated death scenes.

"Really?" Sister Mika asked.

He shook his head. He pointed to an open root cellar door on the side of the casino.

The Reverend sneered. "As I was saying. French."

*

Timmy Gallahad fired three rounds into the Winnebago Roadwarrior before he realized the hard way it wasn't a saucer after all. Fortunately, he was a piss-poor shot under pressure, completely missing the windshield in his sights. Equally fortunate, the Red Rider BBs pinged off the aluminum siding, leaving only tiny dimples in the paint.

"What the hell are you doing, kid?" Sparkle Jones shouted from the driver's side window.

Little Elvis hustled out of the cab and sprinted for the kid. Zip. A BB stung his thigh. Spang. Another whizzed past his head. Waving his hands and screaming, he fell onto the gangly teenager. Also waving his arms and screaming, the gangly teenager collapsed under three hundred and thirty pounds of angry Mexican.

"Hey, you alien bastards look just like us," Timmy Gallahad said. "Sorta."

Little Elvis pinned him, kicking the BB gun away. "Don't make it harder on yourself, white-boy."

"No," Reverend Sparkle Jones said, smoothing out his dress. "He's the last of the company. I'm sure on that."

"How do you know?" Aunty Ann asked.

He shrugged. "The Lord told me."

"He didn't tell *me*," Sister Mika said.

He shrugged again. "That's because your faith is rooted in a Lie of Satan. And you have poor fashion sense."

Aunty Ann pointed at the Last Mime LeFoie. "Didn't you say *he* was the last?"

"I was wrong. His Frenchness confused me momentarily."

"Abominations can do that," Little Elvis offered. He looked at LeFoie. "No offense."

LeFoie crossed his arms and scowled.

"What's an abomination?" Timmy Gallahad asked.

The group ignored him. They'd pretty much done so since the BB rifle incident the day before. Sparkle continued. "Besides, the name's a dead giveaway, isn't it?"

"Who's name?" Timmy Gallahad asked. No one noticed.

Sister Mika fidgeted with her crucifix. "So you think it's a sign?"

"Of course it's a Goddamn sign," the Reverend said.

"A sign of what?" Timmy Gallahad asked, leaning forward in his lawn chair.

Little Elvis went to the hibachi and flipped the burgers. "I'd have to agree."

Sister Mika slathered mustard onto her bun. "I can't imagine we won't meet more along the way."

"Along the way where?" Timmy Gallahad asked.

"But we shall not break bread with them nor invite them into our Winnebago," Reverend Sparkle said.

"It seems to me," Timmy Gallahad said slowly, "that with the world in such a bad way," he gritted his teeth, "someone around here," he looked at Reverend Sparkle Jones, raising his voice to a full volume, *"should have a fucking plan!"*

"Watch your Goddamn mouth kid," Reverend Sparkle said. Then dinner was served.

After dinner, and after dispatching an unexpected pack of hob-goblins that rushed them from the shadows of an overpass, they went over the plan again.

The Holy Grail, Reverend Sparkle Jones reported, was humanity's last hope. It was also hidden in a faraway mystical place known only by the name —

"Shangrilla?" Timmy Gallahad asked, interrupting. "Don't you mean Shangri-La?"

"I already asked that," Aunty Ann said.

"Rhymes with gorilla," Little Elvis said.

"Or Godzilla," Sister Mika said.

The Reverend Sparkle Jones pushed his wig up and scratched his thin gray hair. "At least the boy reads."

"It's from a book, too?"

They all looked at the kid. Except for Little Elvis, who also hadn't known that fact.

Timmy Gallahad shrugged. *"Treasure Hunter 3: Blood Bath in Shangri-La.* It's a video game."

And with that the Reverend went back to his story.

"— just off the coast of Florida. The grail had lain there, the Reverend Sparkle Jones continued, waiting for humanity's darkest hour to come 'round at last that it might shine its light into —"

"What's a grail?"

The Reverend sighed. "What? No King Arthur video game?"
Timmy Gallahad kept quiet for the rest of the story.

So Reverend Sparkle Jones told his Knights of the Picnic Table the rest of the story and the plan. First, the grail, the cup of Christ, Jesus's Juice Cup, was real. Second, it was in the vicinity of a tropical island off the coast of Florida. (Here, he produced a map with a red magic marker circle and the words SHANGRILLA HERE at the end of a red magic marker arrow and a series of coordinates.) Third, the Lord Himself had told Sparkle the location and the route he must take to bring together the band, the company, the troupe — his grail-seekers.

"And that," closed Reverend Sparkle Jones, "is the plan."

The Last Mime LeFoie danced a jig.

Sister Mika strapped on her guitar to lead them in a song.

Aunty Ann belched loudly, blushed furiously and apologized.

Little Elvis Sanchez folded his arms and leaned back in his chair to watch his last sunset. Of course he had no idea.

Timmy Gallahad yawned. "It's a stupid plan," he said.

Everyone looked at him.

He looked back at everyone. "It's almost as stupid as peeing on the hobgoblins to keep them from coming back from the dead."

"That is all Little Elvis," Sparkle said. "I had nothing to do with that bit."

Little Elvis scowled. "It works doesn't it?"

"How many hobgoblins have you ever seen come back from the dead?" Timmy Gallahad asked.

"None," Little Elvis said, the white teeth of his proud smile gleaming in the twilight. "I peed on every damned one of them."

Timmy Gallahad rolled his eyes.

After a bit of "Michael Row the Boat Ashore" and timeless television theme songs, they took up their various places inside and on top of the Winnebago Roadwarrior, crawled into their sleeping bags and went to sleep.

Little Elvis took the first watch. He sat on the roof, a scoped Winchester cradled in his hands, and watched the stars, inhaled the smells, listened to the mumbles and snores of his newfound friends. When it came time to wake his replacement, he just didn't have the heart. Somehow he knew that tomorrow everything was going to be very different.

Timmy Gallahad dreamed happy dreams about being ship-wrecked on a tropical island with a stranded batch of lonely cheer-leaders.

The Last Mime LeFoie dreamed nostalgic dreams about the old days, the blazing sun, the hot sand, the sting of saltwater in bullet holes and gashes.

Aunty Ann dreamed exotic dreams about an unremembered past life she'd had full of camels, magic lamps, flying carpets, wily thieves, all powerful Djinn and strawberry jam.

Sister Mika dreamed big-haired dreams about her high school days in the eighties and the song on the radio when Jimmy Lance took her virginity, thereby convincing her first, that a vow of celibacy might not be all bad and second, that Latin was really a lovely language when blended with pop music.

Reverend Sparkle Jones usually dreamed of sensible pumps, conservative make-up, Liza Minelli and the Book of Revelations. But tonight he didn't dream at all. He heard no voices, saw no visions and woke up in the morning with a sense of doom far stronger than what he'd felt regarding the recent (and now irrelevant) political elections of his day.

The next day, everything became very different.

They awoke to ululating hobgoblins, the crack of rifle shots, the roar of motorcycle engines, the repetitious thud thud thud of heavy machinery, exploding concrete, and the spang-a-lang of bullets striking metal.

Reverend Sparkle Jones joined Little Elvis on the roof. Little Elvis passed the Winchester to him. "They just showed up . . . came from the northeast."

The Reverend sighted in. "Hell's Angels?" he asked. "Sporting American Flags?"

"And those there look like Reservists or Regular Army. Looks like they're all working together."

"Glory be." He panned the scope over the moving battle. Bodies on both sides were already piling up. "What the hell is *that?*"

Little Elvis squinted. "Some kind of machine. It's not one of ours." Large as a building, tottering on four mechanical legs. Multitudes of arms whipped and spun, some sporting blades, some spouting flames and some spitting bolts of electricity. Long tubes protruded from the body of the thing, coughing out mortar rounds in puffs of gray smoke. Large searchlight eyes shifted back and forth beneath a small, spinning antenna.

"Looks bad," Sparkle said. "I think it's going to get harder from here on out."

Timmy Gallahad had joined them by this time. "What looks bad?"

"Let's load her up," Little Elvis said, swinging down the ladder. The others needed little encouragement. Five minutes later, the caravan moved southeast towards Cheyenne at breakneck speed.

Two bikers broke ranks and chased them down easily. They passed the pickup and pulled up to driver's side of the Roadwarrior, motioning for Sparkle Jones to roll down his window.

"Pull over, ma'am," one of the bikers yelled. He rode one handed and waved to the side of the road. The other one waved a submachine gun in the air. "That's an order."

Sparkle turned to look at them. "On whose authority?"

"The United States Army!"

"The army?" Sparkle glanced at Little Elvis in the passenger seat and then looked back at the bikers. "The Hell's Angels are errand boys for the Man now?"

The biker looked uncomfortable holding debate at sixty three miles per hour. He spat out a bug. "It's a short term arrangement. Fate of the world and all that. Just pull over."

"It's too dangerous," Sparkle Jones shouted back. "Why don't we catch up when we're all a bit less busy?"

The spackle of warning shots fired across the front of the Roadwarrior's grill changed his mind.

As they climbed from the Roadwarrior, Little Elvis shushed Timmy Gallahad, waving him back into the shadows of the loft with its stacks of rifles, ammunition and canned meat products.

"What is the meaning of this?" The Reverend stepped forward, his dark-lined eyes flashing.

The bikers suddenly noticed his gender and both blushed. "Sorry, sir. We can't let you pass."

"Not sir," Sparkle Jones intoned. "Reverend." He held up his hands, fingers making the sign of a cross. "You do not merely impede me, gentlemen, you impede the Work of the Most High God."

The Last Mime LeFoie jumped up and down and waved his hands.

By now, Sister Mika and Aunty Ann had joined them. The bikers ignored the rather plump jam and jelly entrepreneur but took note of the lithe nun. "Shame on you both," she said. Then she smiled and blushed.

The Last Mime's jumping had become even more frantic now. He kept pointing to the horizon.

They turned and saw it: The monstrous legged and tentacled building-thing turned away from the army and bore down on the Winnebago Roadwarrior instead. And on its heels, the hobgoblin hordes and their incessant ululating followed.

"We have to go," Sparkle said.

"The Colonel will want to talk to you first. We're under strict orders —"

Little Elvis pointed at the alien thing approaching. "Can your Colonel take care of *that?*"

"We're not sure," one biker said. "He hasn't been around much lately."

"Well if *you're* not sure, *we're* not waiting."

And suddenly, the wind whipped up. Something blocked out the sun. A rushing, whistling, whining from the east. A blur of red, white and blue dropped from the sky, streaked across the ground and with a solid clang the mechanical thing lifted off the ground, victim of an unseen uppercut. On the ground, the troops cheered and rallied. Hobgoblins started dying. The metal thing and the streak of red white and blue tossed each other back and forth, bits of metal flying up into the air and landing helter-skelter on charred forests and smoking ruins.

The two bikers grinned. "I think the Colonel's back."

Little Elvis looked at Sparkle Jones who in turn looked at Aunty Ann. Sister Mika kept staring at the bikers.

Even the Last Mime opened his mouth to speak but remembered to close it.

"What is *that?*" Timmy Gallahad asked. He'd snuck out in the confusion, his Red Rider BB rifle ready.

"Not what, kid," the Reverend Sparkle Jones said. "Who."

Little Elvis Sanchez swept off his hat and put his right hand over his heart. "Exactly."

The battle lasted eight minutes. Afterwards, they had breakfast with the red, white and blue streak that had so completely pummeled the alien octo-battle-tank and sent the hobgoblins into

retreat: The myth, the man, the legend . . .
Colonel Patriot himself.

"Well," the Colonel said between bites of Colonel Patriot's
Frosted Choco-Balls, "I think you're insane."

"I told you it was a stupid plan," Timmy Gallahad said. He stayed
close to Colonel Patriot, his mouth slack-jawed most of the time.
He'd heard of superheroes but had never met one.

"No, Timmy," Colonel Patriot said, patting his shoulder. "The
plan is brilliant. The insanity is not letting me join your quest. Heck,
I could get to this . . . Shangrilla, is it? I could get there and back in
ten minutes tops, grail in hand."

"It doesn't work that way, Colonel. Though I wish to God it
did." The Reverend Sparkle Jones put down his spoon, dabbed his
lips carefully to not smear his fresh lipstick. "I know we could use
your help. But I also know what we were told."

"What *you* were told," Sister Mika said.

"What I was told," he agreed. "We are the chosen. And time is
short."

Colonel Patriot nodded. "It's a losing battle. There's no central
government left to speak of. Electronic transmissions are jammed.
Hell —" he blushed, looking at the women and Timmy, " — I mean
heck, I spend most of my time on the big bots or running messages
to scattered pockets of resistance. And they just keep coming back."

"Have you tried peeing on them?" Little Elvis asked.

Colonel Patriot nearly spit out his cereal. "What?"

"Never mind him," Aunty Ann said. "Isn't there anyone who
can help you?"

"Yeah," Timmy Gallahad said. "What about the others?"

Colonel Patriot shook his head. "Gone, as far as I can tell." He
held up his wrist, showing them the unblinking Super-Powered Friendship Bracelet. He looked around to make sure no soldiers were
watching and buried his head in his hands, massive shoulders heaving with his sobs. "I watched Kid Sling Shot and the Night Marauder burned to ashes myself during the first wave."

"Didn't they retire years ago?" Little Elvis asked.

Colonel Patriot sniffed and pulled himself together. "Oh, someone always picks up the capes and masks we drop."

In the uncomfortable silence, Sparkle Jones stood up. "Well,

Colonel, we really must get going. We've got a lot of ground to cover."

The rest stood. Colonel Patriot extended his hand to the Reverend. "I'll try to keep them busy."

Sparkle shook his hand. "We'll find the grail and then we'll show these third-rate invaders some good old fashioned Wrath of God."

"God bless you, Reverend Sparkle Jones. God bless you all."

Colonel Patriot blasted into the sky without another word.

Timmy Gallahad spat out the dust from his lift-off. "Wow. Now *that's* a real hero."

Sparkle Jones walked towards the waiting Winnebago Roadwarrior. "You ain't seen nothing yet," he said over his shoulder as he went.

No one knows exactly how or why it happened.

Scholars speculate that, far above the earth in the unseen spinning saucers, unimaginable and unearthly masters upgraded their invasion technology.

In short, the hobgoblins became smarter. And more of those nasty multi-legged machines showed up.

They were ambushed outside Denver.

The Winnebago Roadwarrior hit a sand-covered plank of nails and squealed to a stop with four flat tires. The pickup slammed into them from behind. The hobgoblins, now armed with garden tools, golf clubs and table lamps, poured out of nowhere.

The Reverend pulled his pistols. Little Elvis worked the pump of a sawed-off Remington. They both made for the door and Reverend Sparkle Jones broke a heel when he kicked it open. The Last Mime LeFoie broke out the small kitchen window and fired off a few bursts from an M-16 he'd found in Cheyenne before following the others out the door. Timmy Gallahad ignored being told to stay put and not touch anything. He grabbed the Winchester and shimmied out the driver-side window and onto the roof, wondering if the scope would improve his poor aim under pressure.

Hobgoblins, popping and sparking, were dragging the women from their pickup when Little Elvis roared and charged them. Sister

Mika struggled for her Magnum. It went off, kicking out her hand and throwing back one of her captors. Aunty Ann banshee-screamed and set about with a machete she always kept nearby.

"Let my people go!" Reverend Sparkle Jones yelled, firing off the pistols into the horde.

Little Elvis waded in, swinging the shotgun like a club until he stood over Sister Mika. Then he scooped her up and tossed her easily into the back of the pickup. He climbed up behind her and pumped buckshot into the hobgoblin horde, cutting them to shreds.

The Last Mime LeFoie rolled beneath the Roadwarrior and started firing careful rounds into kneecaps, his face a mask of pure glee.

Timmy Gallahad puzzled out the lever-action rifle, sighted in on a hobgoblin nostril suddenly the size of a manhole. He started to throw up at what happened next but then thought better of it, worked the lever again, and found another nostril.

Fifteen minutes later, the women turned their backs while the men limped around finishing the job. Afterwards, they zipped up (except for the Good Reverend of course) and took stock of their situation.

Little Elvis held a field dressing to his cheek, soaking up blood from a laceration. "One spare," he said. "Four flats."

Sparkle Jones straightened his wig. "We could run on the rims until we find a tire shop."

Sister Mika crouched by the plank and its upturned nails. "They're getting smarter," she said.

Aunty Ann side-stepped a puddle to kick a golf club out of a clawed hand. "They are."

"Sounds like we need to get smarter, too," Little Elvis said. Everyone looked at him. "Maybe we should get off the roads."

"We need bikes," Timmy Gallahad said.

Now everyone looked at the kid. Reverend Sparkle nodded. "Good thinking."

They had moved most of their essentials from the Roadwarrior to the bed of the pick-up when the Last Mime LeFoie started jumping up and down, pointing at something behind them.

They saw the cloud of dust moving over the rise of highway. They heard the thud thud thud of machinery. Something shrieked through the air and a Volkswagen erupted into flame. A building-sized box with waving tentacles crested the hill.

Sparkle Jones looked worried. "That didn't take long."

"What do we do now?" Sister Mika asked.

"We run for it," Aunty Ann said.

LeFoie pantomimed his agreement.

"We'll never make it," Timmy Gallahad said.

Sparkle Jones looked at the truck and then at the oncoming octo-battle-tank. "We might."

"No," Little Elvis said, a strange look washing his face. "No, you won't. This is it, gang." Without another word and without looking back, he climbed into the Winnebago. They heard the door lock behind him.

The strange look migrated to the Reverend's face. "What are you doing?" he shouted.

The engine roared alive.

He yelled again. "Little Elvis, what are you doing?"

The Winnebago rolled off towards Denver, away from the invaders, flat tires slapping the pavement. It picked up speed. Now whooping hobgoblin sounds became background noise for the approaching machine.

The Winnebago made a wide turn in a grocery store parking lot, still building speed, now coming back.

When the Roadwarrior flew past them, wheel-rims sparking, they saw Little Elvis's idiot grin and dark flashing eyes.

Mortar rounds whistled and exploded, tearing up chunks of asphalt and dropping trees. The Winnebago barreled on, faster and faster.

Hobgoblins bounced over and under the Roadwarrior as it raced forward. Little Elvis made minor course-corrections as the octo-battle-tank tried to sidestep at the last possible moment.

The Winnebago slammed into first one and then another of the long metal legs, and he threw the RV into a wide skid and rolled it. It went down, raising dust and smoke when it struck the ground. They heard Little Elvis's shouts above the noise of the thrashing arms and hobgoblin howls. Then, as the dust settled, they saw him scrambling over the fallen thing with a tire iron. It lurched to its feet, fell, lurched again. In a fit of final desperation, it turned its blades and flames onto itself in an effort to dislodge its unwanted Mexican.

"For God and Grail," Little Elvis shouted, bringing the tire iron down on one searchlight eye and another. Burned and bloody, he swung on the spinning antenna like an angry T-ball player.

And then Little Elvis — first of the grail-seekers to fall — fell.

The Reverend Sparkle Jones worked the actions on his twin Colts. He pulled himself up to full height and the wind caught his dress. He stared at the troupe, the band, the company, the grail-seekers. Then, without a word, he turned and raced after Little Elvis.

The Last Mime followed first, fixing a bayonet to his M-16.

Sister Mika shoved her Magnum into the pocket of her habit and hefted Little Elvis's discarded Remington. She set off at a brisk walk.

Aunty Ann, a machete in one hand and a 9mm Berretta in the other, caught up to her.

Timmy Gallahad stayed put. He dropped to the ground, reloaded the Winchester, and took careful aim.

The battle that followed was the bloodiest yet. They fought the battle without speaking. They fought it with tears coursing down their cheeks and teeth clenched with determined rage.

They fought it and prevailed.

And when they were finished: They buried Little Elvis Sanchez in a burned out Volkswagen just outside the smoldering remains of Denver.

The next morning they found a Harley shop on the other side of the burning city.

"Can you all ride?" Timmy Gallahad asked group.

"Of course," said Aunty Ann.

"A bit," said Sister Mika.

The Last Mime Le Foie snorted in a disparagingly French sort of way and rolled his eyes as if to say "Mais oui."

Sparkle Jones bit his lip.

"Reverend?"

"A little." The Reverend looked uncomfortable. "Some." He paused and looked down, embarrassed. "Not at all," he said in a quiet voice. "Not even a bicycle."

And so they found one with a sidecar and Timmy Gallahad, still a year away from his driver's license when the world fell apart, became designated driver.

Everything had changed at Denver. The death of Little Elvis punctuated the devastation of their world. Some maintain that the

shock of losing friends, families, neighbors, pets and everything else
finally wore off. By now the smoky haze smudging the sky had
taken on a burnt-pork and wood-smoke smell as the invaders burnt
the bodies in pyres by the millions in the still warm ashes of the
fallen cities.

The troupe loaded up saddlebags and compartments with ammunition, food, clean socks, and sleeping bags. They left the highway and avoided cities, stopping only to siphon gas out of abandoned cars when they needed it. Occasionally they saw ragged
bands of survivors moving under cover. Twice, they saw tall build-
ing-like shapes moving on the horizon. At night, huddled underneath
the stars without a fire, they saw searchlights sweeping the ground
and the glow of large, distant fires.

They talked a bit about their losses. They talked a bit about
their hopes. They curled into sleeping bags, taking turns with the
watch, and slept fitfully because of their dreams.

Aunty Ann was back in the desert wearing her veil, riding her
camel and thinking about her second wish — a dark-eyed man
accessorized with a large palace in a desert oasis.

Sister Mika relived that five-minute fumbling with Jimmy Lance
trying to figure out Peg A, Slot B and what those Latin words in that
song meant.

The Last Mime LeFoie dreamed of deep water and killing.

Timmy Gallahad drank coconut milk, ate fresh crab and played
every version of doctor, spin-the-bottle, post office and truth or dare
imaginable to man with a cadre of eager young women beneath a
tropically brilliant sun.

The Good Reverend dreamed about the grail. How it would
glitter as it tossed back the light. How it would thrum and tingle with
holy power. How it would look with a pair of sensible pumps, a
white leather purse and a conservative dress. And how he himself
would never get the chance to see it.

But then again, he'd known that all along.

They crossed Kansas and Missouri without incident, and finding the Mighty Mississippi's bridges blown or barricaded, they
crossed on an antique ferry somewhere between St. Louis and
Memphis. The Last Mime LeFoie fired it up with practiced confidence and piloted them across while doing a drunken sailor

imitation. Reverend Sparkle Jones kept his eyes closed the entire time, white knuckling the railing. No one asked and he said nothing.

They re-stocked canned food, women's shoes and ammunition at a Buy-Mart Big Box Everything Store on the outskirts of Paducah. The Klan Survivalists opened fire on them as they tried to leave the store. They abandoned their shopping carts and ducked back into the gloom, hiding behind empty cashier stations, racks of candy bars and end-caps full of products that had recently become irrelevant.

"We're a-watchin' the back, too," the recently appointed Grand Wizard shouted. "So why don't you make it easy on yourselves and send out them three women you got?"

"And what happens if we do?" Reverend Sparkle shouted, yelping as Sister Mika kicked him in the ankle.

"Why . . . we'll let y'all go, naturally. The world's suddenly found itself in a shortage of White Power."

"No. What happens to us women if we come out?" Reverend Sparkle asked.

Low voices discussed this. "Uh, *mister* —"

Sparkle Jones interrupted. "Not Mister . . . Reverend."

"Reverend."

More discussion.

"We don't play that way, Reverend. You'll be free to go as well." Yet more discussion as the conservative elements of the movement expressed dissenting views. "As to your women-folk, we'll take good care of them. They'll live like royalty in our New Jerusalem. They'll do their part to rebuild our pure race on this Earth once my brethren and I have eradicated these Unholy Extraterrestrial Hostiles." The Grand Wizard paused, giving his words time to set in. "So what do you think, Reverend? The easy way or the hard way?"

"I am afraid," Reverend Sparkle said, "that *we women-folk*, as you so quaintly put it, have both a previous engagement and a higher calling." He loaded a fresh clip into his pistol. "So we will decline your kind invitation." He punctuated his sentence with three rapid shots that shattered glass, spanged off asphalt and thudded into a Sparky the Vibrating Turtle ride positioned near the door.

"Get 'em boys," the Grand Wizard said.

The Last Mime LeFoie dropped the first Survivalist to cross the threshold. Aunty Ann took out the second (as well as a gum and rubber snake dispenser near the turtle.) Everything paused for nearly a full minute.

They heard the sound of boxes falling and metal clanging from the back of the store. The Reverend and Sister Mika repositioned themselves, pistols drawn, and watched the shadows.

Timmy Gallahad loaded a .38 revolver he'd recently liberated from the store's glass display case. Sparkle had told him to start small, work his way up. Apart from everyone dying, he found the New World Order simultaneously liberating and invigorating in ways no video game could ever touch.

A rack of deeply discounted women's plus-size clothing jumped and fell, accompanied by the sound of cursing. The cursing turned to screams as Sparkle put a few rounds in the bumbling redneck.

Sister Mika, her eyes adjusting to the darkness, took care of his skulking partner where he crouched in the lingerie.

"I don't have time for this," the Grand Wizard yelled.

"Then don't do it," Sparkle Jones shouted back. "It'll go easier for you if you don't. We're on a job for the Lord Most High."

History at this point becomes a bit murky. We know that the Grand Wizard Toby and his Klan Pure Whitehood Survivalist Confederacy had the stated intent of taking the grail-seeker women for their own. Because of this, speculation abounds as to why what happened next happened at all. Most believe that more conservative elements within the short-lived movement, taking issue with the notion of an ordained cross-dressing minister consorting with mimes and nuns, exercised their democratic right to dissent. Others believe it was simply a sad, stupid mistake perpetrated (as per usual) by sad, stupid white men between the ages of sixteen and sixty.

Regardless, at that moment, something small, egg-shaped and metal landed inside the store and rolled under a candy display.

And the Last Mime LeFoie surprised them all by uttering his first words of the journey . . . yay, his first words of the past twenty seven years. "Grenade!"

They scrambled.

Hot metal, smoke, melted chocolate, fire, a deafening boom followed by a crystalline ringing.

They looked around at each other, waiting for their hearing to return, trying to figure out what had happened and what seemed out of place.

Sister Mika noticed first that Aunty Ann was missing.

The Last Mime also noticed and duck walked back to the cashier stations, rifle raised. Sparkle Jones followed. Outside, they heard arguing.

" — the hell you say, Jim Bob. They elected me, fair and square, and if you don't like it you get the fuck out."

"I'm not going in. Billy Joe and Ike and Larry and Paul went in and they ain't come back out."

"You threw it and I say you're going in."

When Jim Bob did poke his head around the corner of the doorway, face outlined by light from a hot Kentucky sun, it made the Last Mime's work that much easier. He didn't stop there. As if, somehow, speaking had opened up some blocked red river between his ears, he continued his duck walk to the door and poured around the corner with vengeful grace.

The others gathered around Aunty Ann, holding her hand, wiping the blood out of her eyes and off her mouth, while she whimpered and cried and asked where her legs were.

Pop. A scream, the thud of something heavy falling. Pop. Another scream. Boom — a high caliber rifle going off. Pop.

Aunty Ann's lips quivered. "Come here," she said to Timmy Gallahad.

Timmy Gallahad wept. He stepped forward, knelt, and let her clutch his hand.

"Listen." She coughed, spraying blood. "Do not despair on that Dread Day in your Hour of Need." She licked her lips, fighting for breath.

Timmy waited. She said nothing. "Yes?" he finally asked.

Aunty Ann fixed her eyes on his. "If you rub it," she said in a hoarse whisper, "he will come."

Then, as the double entendre took root in her fading mind, she blushed furiously and died.

And after the Last Mime LeFoie returned, they buried Aunty Ann of Aunty Ann's Jams and Jellies in a frozen food cabinet of the Paducah Buy-Mart Big Box Everything Store, marking the place with stuffed animals and jars of raspberry preserves that bore her smiling likeness on the labels.

When they finished, they went outside and Reverend Sparkle Jones hiked up his dress.

"These ones don't come back," Timmy Gallahad told him.

Sparkle Jones nodded. "I know that. But I'm willing to make an exception."

This time, even Sister Mika joined in.

Hobgoblins howled to the north of them when they fired up their bikes and turned towards Atlanta.

They holed up in a farmhouse, having grief, spam and canned peaches for supper.

"I'm not doing this anymore," Timmy Gallahad said, wiping his bloodshot eyes and drinking the syrup out of the can.

"Spam's better fried but I don't think a fire is a good idea," Sparkle Jones said. His eyes were red, too.

Timmy tossed his empty can over the back of the couch. "Not the food. The quest. I'm not doing it anymore." He stood up, hefting the rifle. "Tomorrow morning, I go my own way."

"Son," the Reverend said, "I know it's hard. But it's a calling. It's *your* calling. And callings are neither easy nor easy to cast aside."

Timmy Gallahad looked at the troupe, the company, the band of grail-seekers. He opened his mouth to speak, then closed it and shook his head more to himself than anyone else. Sniffing, he wiped his nose with his sleeve and walked out of the house.

Sister Mika stood up. "I'll talk to him."

Sparkle Jones nodded. He pulled the lever on the lounge and the foot rest popped up. He lay back, watching the Last Mime wipe off his makeup for the night.

Jones took off his wig and scratched his scalp. "I know about you," he said with a quiet voice.

LeFoie looked up, a blank look on his face.

"I had my suspicions, of course." He nodded to the M-16. "You're awfully handy with that."

LeFoie shrugged and went back to scrubbing his face.

"You're not even really French, I'll bet," the Reverend said, more to himself. He yawned and stretched. "Special forces, I'd say."

Now the Last Mime looked up, eyes narrow. Slowly, he rolled up the sleeve of his black and white shirt, exposing his bicep and his tattoo of a cartoon frog wearing a sailor's cap and sporting an M-16. Over the top and underneath were the words *The Quick . . . or the Dead.*

Sparkle Jones saluted half-heartedly. "I was Army, myself. Severely hydrophobic. But all that wool in the summer was just sinful. And I found the skirts rather unflattering."

LeFoie nodded, spreading out his sleeping bag.

"I reckon," the Reverend continued, "that you know where all of this is going?"

Again, the Last Mime nodded.

"Good," Sparkle Jones said. "That boy is the world's last hope." He chuckled and then repeated something he'd told the group not so long . . . and yet forever . . . ago. "The name's a dead giveaway. So you keep him safe."

For the third time, LeFoie nodded.

"And I'm glad you're not French. It pleases me."

That said, Sparkle Jones slipped into sleep.

"Just until Atlanta," Timmy Gallahad said in the morning. "Then I'll head north and see what I can find."

No one argued with him.

They pressed on.

Meanwhile, far above them in metal compartments filled with foul-smelling yellow clouds, otherworldly minds ran upgrades on their invasion program and the hobgoblins below twitched and jerked with sudden know-how pumped into their skullcaps from on high.

Outside Atlanta, when they ventured onto a highway in search of another Buy-Mart, a Crack Commando Hobgoblin Assault Force opened up on them with weapons looted from the local National Guard Armory and pillaged from fallen U.S. soldiers.

Fortunately, they were terrible shots due to a lagging satellite signal.

Still, what they lacked in quality they made up for in quantity. Bullets thudded into the ground, clipped LeFoie's little French cap, shattered the headlight on Sister Mika's bike and popped the left front tire of an abandoned SUV.

They swerved away and opened their throttles, putting distance between them and the invaders. They skirted the city, stopping in the suburbs to the southeast.

"Now they've got guns," Sister Mika said.

"No shit," Timmy Gallahad said.

"We're running out of time," Sparkle Jones added. "They'll be driving soon."

Timmy Gallahad kicked a rock. "Makes no sense to me. First, they come at us with nothing. Then tools, sticks, golf-clubs and those walking things. Now they're shooting guns."

"It's simply economic," the Reverend said.

"Huh? We've killed dozens of them. That can't be cheap."

"Not economic like money. Economic like the thrifty management of resources. And I don't think we've killed any of them, really. I don't think the hobgoblins are our invaders. I think they're just puppets on electronic strings." Sparkle Jones paused, then continued. "They're only putting forth the effort they *need* to put forth. They're using our own weapons against us. They're upgrading their technology when they need to. And I'll bet those giant walking things are recycled out of salvaged wreckage."

"Pretty weird strategy after traversing vast reaches of space," Timmy Gallahad said.

The Reverend offered a grim smile. "That's why we call them alien."

"So what now?" Sister Mika asked.

Reverend Sparkle Jones climbed into the sidecar of the Harley. "We turn south. We're not far now."

Sister Mika and the Last Mime LeFoie climbed onto their bikes as well.

Timmy Gallahad stood alone. He kicked the ground again, watching the rocks and dust move. Then, he looked up and stared into Sparkle Jones's eyes. "I meant it. What I said yesterday."

"Fine," Sparkle said. "We'll talk about it at dinner."

Timmy Gallahad kicked more dirt. "No. I'm leaving. Now."

For a moment, no one spoke. Sister Mika bit her lip, looked at the Reverend and then back at Timmy. "I know it's been a lot to handle, Timmy."

Timmy snorted. "A lot to handle? *Tenth grade* algebra is a lot to handle. This is . . . This is . . ." He started to cry.

Just as he did, another Crack Commando Hobgoblin Assault squad broke cover and opened fire.

"Get down!" Sister Mika shouted, throwing herself at Timmy. The two of them went down hard and lay still.

The Last Mime LeFoie dropped prone, his M-16 popping.

The Reverend climbed from the sidecar, tugging at his pistols. A ricochet clipped his arm, tearing the sleeve of his dress and leaving a long red gash. Blowing blond hair from his face, he raised both Colts and starting squeezing rounds.

Sister Mika kept Timmy pinned. "Just stay put," she whispered. He struggled against her, wanting into the fight, but she was strong and nearly dead weight. Finally, he gave in. He felt something warm and wet on his stomach.

"Sister?" he asked.

Her eyes were closed. They fluttered open. "Timmy?"

"Are you shot?"

She smiled a sweet smile. "Just a little."

The Last Mime ran silently after the last of the hobgoblins. The Reverend ran screaming beside him. Timmy lay still. "How much is just a little?"

"I'll be fine."

"Really?"

She kissed his cheek. "No. But listen to me."

"Yes?"

"Be a good boy and find that grail for me."

He opened his mouth to say no, to say fuck this, I've watched my friends and family and planet die and I'm done now. I'm going away. I'm going someplace where I can be a kid again. But instead, he said: "Okay. I will."

She said something he couldn't quite understand. "Remember those words."

"What?"

"The song that was playing when I lost my . . . *you* know."

He didn't know.

"Virginity," she said, chuckling.

Timmy Gallahad blushed. "Your . . . ? I thought —"

"It wasn't that great. That's the night I decided to become a nun. Just don't forget, down the road that you must travel."

"Forget what?"

"Kyrie eleison," she said. "It means Lord have mercy."

Then Sister Mika the Singing Nun died.

Hobgoblins in Humvees chased them into Ft. Lauderdale. Octo-battle-tanks closed in from the north and south in an attempt to cut them off. In the last day, their aim had improved exponentially. Bullets zipped and zinged past the speeding motorcycles as they raced towards the canal and the burned-out houses that lined the strip of waterfront.

"What are we looking for?" Timmy Gallahad yelled above the gunfire and roaring engines.

"You'll know it when you see it."

And they did. It loomed above them, a massive crystalline cathedral stretched high above the ruins, casting back bright sunlight. The bombs had spared none of its neighbors but somehow, it still stood.

"Is that it?"

Reverend Sparkle Jones twisted in his seat, fired a few rounds behind them. "Yes. She's waiting for us there."

"Who's waiting?"

Sparkle Jones reloaded. The driveway, blinding white cobblestones beneath a gold archway, was coming up quickly to the left. "Turn here."

Timmy took the corner, the bike tipping as he did. The driveway forked, one path leading to the cathedral and an another to the burned-out remains of an equally massive parsonage.

"I saw her on TV once," the Reverend said. "She's a beauty." He pointed to the right fork, towards the remains of the parsonage. "There. That way."

The Last Mime rooted through his satchel, pulling out one of the hand grenades he'd looted from the Kentucky Klan Survivalists. He pulled the pin with his teeth and tossed it back over his shoulder. It landed beneath the Humvee and pitched the vehicle into the air with a whomp. It exploded a second time as the gas tank caught fire.

"Down there," Sparkle Jones shouted. He pointed at the boathouse.

Timmy cut the bike left and braked hard. It careened to a stop, burning rubber.

The Reverend Sparkle Jones leaped out of the sidecar and blasted the deadbolt out of the boathouse door. "Get our gear onboard, Timmy, and get the main doors open."

LeFoie put his Harley into a low slide, the metal sparking on the cobblestones as he drew Sister Mika's Magnum and shattered the windshield of another oncoming Humvee with three well-placed shots. It tore past them, plowed into a flimsy wood railing, and flipped over and into the canal, wheels spinning. The thud-thud-thud of machinery grew closer as the octo-battle-tanks drew near.

"We've got maybe two minutes," the Reverend told the Last Mime.

LeFoie nodded, holstered his pistol, and ducked into the boathouse. Reverend Sparkle Jones stood watch while Timmy loaded the boat and LeFoie fired her up.

Timmy looked at the big bright words painted on the stern and bow. *God's Deliverance*, it read.

Sparkle Jones grabbed Timmy as he rushed past with a satchel of canned food. "Take this." He pushed the map into his hands.

"But —"

"This is how it goes, kid," the Reverend Sparkle Jones said, pulling up his pantyhose. "I saw it in a dream. Get on board." He drew his Colts. They gleamed in the sun like twin Excaliburs.

Reinforcements showed up. Hobgoblins spilled out of trucks, taking up positions. Large metal legs crashed into concrete down the street as mortars thumped to life. A fire-blackened palm tree exploded to their left.

The Reverend Sparkle Jones looked at LeFoie. "Remember what I told you."

LeFoie nodded.

"But —" Timmy said again.

Sparkle Jones gripped his shoulders and pushed him forcibly towards the waiting yacht. "Go save the world, Timmy Gallahad. I have work to do."

Timmy scrambled onto the bow. The Reverend unhooked the rope and tossed it to him. LeFoie started backing the boat out into the sunlight.

The last time they saw Reverend Sparkle Jones, he was charging the hobgoblin horde, pistols blazing, belting out show-tunes at the top of his lungs, his back to the water. When the sunlight caught the highlights of his wig, he looked like an avenging angel in a conservative dress and sensible shoes.

They looted a dive shop before entering the Atlantic.

Timmy stood watch on the dock while the Last Mime LeFoie grabbed gear and topped off the fuel.

With the sun setting behind them, they turned south towards the grail.

Timmy Gallahad stretched and yawned. "Already?"

LeFoie nodded.

Timmy Gallahad sat up in the bed. It was his first bed in a while, and though the rock and pitch of the yacht had been hard to get used to, he'd slept through the night.

He grabbed a can of Coke from the refrigerator on his way upstairs.

The Last Mime pointed at a small island.

"You're sure?"

He nodded. LeFoie motioned Timmy over to a chart spread out over the small table, then unfolded the Reverend's map. Using a grease pencil, he triangulated their position.

He tapped the position with the pencil as if to punctuate it.

"Okay," Timmy said. "What now?"

The Last Mime climbed down from the pilothouse and stripped down. His pale skin, scarred and pocked, was nearly the color of his grease-painted face. He strapped on a knife and sat down on the gunwale to slide into the air tank and wriggle into his fins. He pulled down the mask, fitted his regulator, and gave Timmy a thumb's up.

"What do I do?" Timmy asked.

The Last Mime shrugged, then tipped over backwards.

When Timmy looked over the side all he saw were bubbles.

Ted's Lady of the Lake lay on her side at a hundred feet. The Last Mime kicked down to her, gave the shipwreck a cursory inspection, and carefully entered her main cabin.

Fortunately, Mrs. Sandowsky — wife of oil tycoon Theodore Sandowsky, who had actually wrecked the yacht intentionally upon hearing of her husband's indiscretions with their pretty young Cuban dog-walker — had it engraved, making it easier to find. *Ted's Holy Grail*, an oversized coffee mug really, lay beneath a pile of broken porcelain plates in a cupboard next to the sink. LeFoie grabbed it and returned to the surface with the hope of mankind clenched tightly in one fist.

*

The Last Mime LeFoie handed the grail to Timmy and climbed into the boat.

Above them, the sky twisted and bent. Large spinning disks descended, graying the morning light.

"I don't know what to do with it," Timmy said.

LeFoie watched the saucers come down. Rays shot down from their bellies, hissing into the waters. One of them meandered in their direction, boiling the ocean as it came.

And Timmy remembered.

Rubbing the grail furiously he chanted Sister Mika's song. "Kyrie Eleison, Kyrie Eleison, Kyrie Eleison."

The grail changed. The pewter peeled away in light. A massive, bright being took form before them.

It looked around, scratching itself and stretching. "What's up boys?" the being asked.

"Are you a genie?" Timmy Gallahad asked.

It laughed. "Nope. My name's Bubba. I'm an Angel of the Lord."

"Bubba?"

Bubba nodded. "I guard that there grail now. Used to guard me a garden but I lost my job on account of some meddling kids." He leaned in, his eyebrows catching fire from the fierceness of his eyes. "You a meddling kid?"

Timmy Gallahad took a step back. "Uh . . . no sir."

The Last Mime LeFoie shook his head as well.

"Then you might should toss that grail over the side and let me get back to sleep. Took me two thousand years to find this job and I don't mean to mess to it up."

"Well," Timmy said, "actually we need your help."

"I'm not a helping angel. I'm a guarding angel." Bubba put his hands on his hips. "There's a difference you know."

Timmy Gallahad frowned. "But the world's in a bad way —"

Bubba waved him off. "I don't guard the world. I guard the grail."

The bow of the yacht caught fire.

"What about now?" Timmy Gallahad asked.

Bubba shook his head. "Boat sinks, grail sinks. I don't see a problem."

The Last Mime LeFoie grabbed up a fire extinguisher and put out the flames.

And suddenly, the heat ray cut out and a booming voice from Heaven filled the air. "GIVE US THE GRAIL," the voice said. Everyone looked up.

"GIVE US THE GRAIL, TIMMY GALLAHAD." Above them, a saucer hovered. A small gray man with an oversized head materialized in the pilothouse. He held something like an egg-beater with a pistol grip in his hand.

LeFoie reached for his M-16 and the egg-beaters whirred to life, evaporating the World's Last Mime in a puff of yellow smoke.

"What do you want with it?" Timmy asked. A wind whipped up on the water, pitching the boat.

"SPECIES ARCHIVE SEVEN THREE OH OH FOUR TWO DATA RETRIEVAL SECTOR SIX SIX FIVE INDICATES ARTIFACT IS UNACCEPTABLE THREAT LEVEL TO OVERKEEPER MANAGEMENT PROGRAM." Static hissed. Then Reverend Sparkle Jones's voice filled the sky as well. "Go ahead, you alien bastards, do your worst to me. But once Timmy Gallahad has the grail, you'll have the Holy Combat Boot of the Lord in your extraterrestrial ass." Then a scream. Then silence. Then the booming voice. "GIVE US THE GRAIL, TIMMY GALLAHAD."

Bubba looked pissed and impatient. "Ask them what they're going to do with it."

The voice did not wait for Timmy to repeat the angel's question. "THE GRAIL MUST BE DESTROYED."

Bubba looked at Timmy Gallahad, looked back at the saucers and popped his knuckles. "Now that fella done went and said the wrong thing," he said. "Let's get 'em boys."

The little gray man flew into pieces as Bubba shot through him.

Flashes of light like meteors blazed across the sky as angels took form around the globe, blasting through the saucers like lawn darts through kleenex. It rained metal. Around the world, hobgoblins twitched, jerked and fell over.

Part of a flying saucer landing strut hit Timmy Gallahad in the head and he fell over, too, dropping the grail back into the Atlantic Ocean where presumably it still lays.

Their work finished, Bubba and the Heavenly Host went back to sleep.

*

Timmy Gallahad looked around.

A double-wide trailer sat in a clearing full of unkempt grass, yard gnomes, miniature windmills, and old tires. Outbuildings and wrecked cars in various states of rust and repair surrounded the trailer. Pine trees surrounded the clearing.

Above, a hot sun blazed in a perfect sky.

Timmy climbed the creaking wooden steps onto the deck. A hand-painted toilet seat hung near the doorbell, the words *God's on His Throne . . . All's Right With the World* stood out on it in gold glitter.

The door opened and Little Elvis smiled out at him, waving for him to come in.

Timmy went inside.

The living room was a hodge-podge of mismatched couches surrounding an empty recliner. The Reverend Sparkle Jones, Sister Mika the Singing Nun, Aunty Ann of Aunty Ann's Jellies and Jams, and the World's Last Mime LeFoie stood up as Timmy entered. All of them were dressed to the nines in clean dresses, habits, mime-gear and western wear.

Little Elvis Sanchez pushed a bottle of ice-cold Yoohoo into Timmy's hands.

For a long time, no one spoke. They just grinned at him.

Finally, Timmy Gallahad broke the silence. "So *this* is how it ends?" He looked around at the troupe, the company, the band, taking them in one at a time. "I told you it was a stupid plan."

Somewhere in the back of the trailer a toilet flushed.

An old man with an enormous beard shuffled out. He wore purple velour track pants and a black t-shirt that rode high above his beer gut. The shirt bore a faded psychedelic butterfly and the words *Lorenz Rules!* in flaking letters.

"Sit down, sit down," the old man said, waving to the couches as he plopped down into the recliner. He looked at Timmy Gallahad. "You were saying?"

Everyone sat. Timmy Gallahad looked at the old man, then shook his head slowly.

The Reverend Sparkle Jones cleared his voice. "I guess you'd like an explanation?"

Timmy shrugged. "Is there one?"

The Reverend glanced at the old man. The old man smiled and raised his eyebrows. Sparkle Jones looked at the rest of the grail-seekers. They nodded for him to go on.

"You see, Timmy," he started, "life is full strange events, unexplainable situations, quirky people, nonsensical problems and ridiculous solutions that, on the surface, seem meaningless and random and perhaps even silly."

Timmy's face went red. "You mean like traveling across the country battling vicious alien invaders with a mime, a nun and a cross-dressing minister in order to find a Goddamn coffee mug?"

"Well," the old man said, "it seemed clever at the time."

Timmy glared.

Reverend Sparkle went on. "And beneath the surface of it all, if you look carefully for it, you'll find meaning and —"

Timmy interrupted with a snort. "And all this time," he said, "I thought it was a tale told by an idiot, full of sound and fury, signifying nothing."

The Reverend's eyebrows shot up. "You know Shakespeare?"

Timmy Gallahad's brow furrowed. "Shakespeare? No . . . *Macbeth 5: Deathmatch in Dunsinane*. Sheesh."

Everyone rolled their eyes except the old man. He chuckled.

"So," Reverend Sparkle Jones continued, "what I'm trying to say is that how a thing ends is not nearly as important as what it means." He shrugged. "Life's a journey and all that." He looked over at the old man. "How'd I do?"

The old man gave Timmy Gallahad a long look. Then he took a long drink of his Yoohoo. "Hell if I know," the Lord God Almighty His Own Self said, "I've been writing this damn thing forever and I still don't know what it means."

"You don't?" Timmy Gallahad asked.

The Lord shook his head. "Nope." He leaned forward. "But I *do* know how it ends," he said.

"How does it end?" Timmy Gallahad asked.

It ends like this:

First, he heard lapping water and the grind of wood on stone. Second, he heard voices. Timmy Gallahad opened his eyes and stared up at a blue sky so bright it hurt. His head throbbed in time with the beating sun. Voices?

"Of course it's a Goddamned sign, Mary Lou," one of the voices said.

"It must be," another said.

"You think so, Sue Ellen?"

"Look, Amy Jo, what did Sister Margaret tell us?"

A pause. "Um. 'Don't worry, girls, you'll win next year if you practice really, really hard?'"

"No, you idiot. When she and Father McMurphy left us here," Sue Ellen said.

Timmy Gallahad shifted, not sure what to do.

"Um. She said 'Wait for God's Deliverance?'"

"Exactly! And what does that say right there?"

"God's Deliverance," Amy Jo said.

"It's a sign," Sue Ellen said.

More voices echoed agreement.

"Of what?" Amy Jo asked in a meek voice.

Sue Ellen sighed. "Think about it, Amy Jo. We may be the *last* girls on earth. The Lord sent us this boat so that we can get off this Goddamned island, find us some boys, and repopulate the world."

Timmy heard nervous giggles. He sat up and went to the gunwale. The yacht had drifted into a lagoon and caught on some rocks. A dozen cheerleaders, their St. Catherine's cheer uniforms ripped and torn, exposing lots of suntanned curving skin, stood on the shore near the bow of *God's Deliverance*. Slowly, first one and then the others looked up at him.

Their cheer-captain, Sue Ellen, stepped forward, her big blue eyes growing wide with wonder beneath her sun-bleached hair. "Are you the last boy on earth?" she asked, biting her lip.

The rest of the cheer-squad blushed and looked down at the sand, then looked back up at him. He took a moment to meet all of their eyes with his own and smiled reassuringly at them.

Finally, he smiled at Sue Ellen. "You know," he said, "I just might be."

And he lived happily ever after.

AFTERWORD:
A RETURN TO THE IMAGINATION FOREST

Welcome back. I'm a little surprised to see you so soon. It seems like just the other day, we were wandering through the last batch of stories and here we are back with another collection.

A lot has changed since *Long Walks, Last Flights and Other Strange Journeys*. I'm a dad now to two beautiful twin girls, and I'm learning the tricky balance of writing with babies. I'm also a novelist now. *Lamentation* debuted nicely, picked up an award and a lot of nice reviews, and *Canticle* followed on its heels to even more nice reviews. I'm working on the fourth book of a five book series and I rarely get to play in short fiction anymore. So it was a lot of fun to dig into my inventory and come up with this latest offering. It will likely be my last collection for a while, until the well fills up again with short work in the midst of all the longer stories I'm telling these days.

This particular corner of the Imagination Forest collects some pieces that were published early and some that were published since *Long Walks, Last Flights and Other Strange Journeys* came together.

I know I always enjoyed knowing a bit about where a writer's stories came from so I thought I'd do the same thing here that I did with the last collection and talk a bit about my paper children. If it doesn't interest you, I'll meet you on the other side. If does, sit back and relax.

Close your eyes.

Can you hear the sound of old growth creaking?

A WEEPING CZAR BEHOLDS THE FALLEN MOON

Writing is a powerful processing tool for me. Most of the time, it's subconscious and the work my psyche is up to is revealed after the fact. Sometimes, I know going in that I'm working on something.

I started "A Weeping Czar Beholds the Fallen Moon" just weeks before Tor made their offer. I was working on *Canticle* and wanted to tell a story set in that world but further back in its history. My mother's health took a turn for the worst and she died just after the book deal when I was in the midst of writing this novelette. For the longest stretch, I could not write at all. I pushed and pushed and finally was able to come back to this love story about the last Weeping Czar and his impossible love for Amal Y'Zir. But now, fueled by grief, I bent it into a story about my own bereavement dressed up as something else. In many ways, my relationship with my mom was impossible due to her mental illness, and there was a vast distance between us with no way to meet in the middle. A lot of that showed up here, though I intentionally couched it in the terms of a love story since that's what I'd started to write in the first place. When I started, I didn't know how it would end. And it's safe to say it might've ended differently if my mother had not died. But here it is. And as such, it became a pretty significant tie-in to the Psalms of Isaak.

When I was in New York for the World Fantasy Convention, I was just at the point where I needed to name the young woman in the story. And when I met the talented and charming Amal el Mohtar I suddenly knew I had my name and the near spitting-image of the girl I was writing about. Later, I told her I'd stolen her name, and when she read the resulting novelette, she asked "Did you know that I played the harp?"

I surely didn't. Nice how things work out sometimes.

I like this one. It's a tale I hope to expand someday into a series of its own. Frederico's Bargain becomes important later in the Psalms of Isaak and I'm eager to tell that story once I wrap up the story of what happened to his descendants as a result of the Moon Wizard Who Fell.

Tor.com picked it up and ran with it the week that *Lamentation* came out in February 2009.

THE NIGHT THE STARS SANG OUT MY NAME

I wrote this for John Pitts. About him, actually. He mentions it in the introduction.

I needed something short — probably for *Talebones Live!* — and he'd just come back from a writing workshop. He was all fired up and had a crazed look in his eye that I now recognize as confident excitement. Still, we got into a bit of a verbal duel over writing and what I could or couldn't, should or shouldn't do. I don't even remember the specifics but I remember thinking that John just didn't seem like himself and it got me wondering what I'd do without that big oaf if anything happened that he suddenly weren't around. He's been one of the most important friends I've had — seen me through some tough times and had an eye on my stories for a dozen years. He was my best man when Jen and I married.

So I tossed that in with a bit of military SF and some experimental writing and came up with this little story about a man and his jiminy escaping from a POW camp on a hostile world. It came out in *Abyss and Apex* and in their best-of anthology. I was surprised that so many people liked it. When I wrote it, like so many other stories, I thought it was a writing exercise.

I'll be doing more in this world, I'm certain. I've got other pieces I've started around the Chib War, and one short story I've wanted to write for over a decade called "Reilly Chose Home" about the veterans at the end of that war.

THE GOD-VOICES OF SETTLER'S REST

This short story was the first I wrote after finishing *Lamentation*. I wrote it in a few sittings early in 2007. It was also me bellying up to the bar and deciding to write more female characters after a long stretch of writing only what I knew. But somewhere along the way, I decided I'd only learn how to do it well if I practiced. There are a few stories in here that are a part of that practice.

Religion has also been an important topic for me. And in this instance, I imagined looped voices that one could mistake as gods — voices that are the ghosts of former inhabitants of an ancient civilization preserved somehow and only heard by the female colonists. The voices are compassionate and compelling at first, and even give them hints as to where to find valuable archaeological information, but over the course of their cycle, they become angry and despondent. From this, I extrapolated how people might react to it, learn to live with it, as these "god-voices" showed up in recurring cycles.

In this one, I also explore Abigail's sacrifice of the life she thought she'd have for the one she comes to feel chosen for. It gave me a place to explore my own past as a minister, dressed up in a speculative setting.

I think if it were to have a thesis, it is that we are not alone as long as we have one another and that we're often blinded by the simplicity of this, trying to create Someone to help us feel less lonely about our place in the universe.

Intergalactic Medicine Show published it in 2008.

THE MUSIC OF THE SPHERES

I was in Reno, Nevada, for the Rural Economic Development Conference in spring of 2003. I picked up a nasty virus my last two days and found myself stuck in the room with my laptop. I went to find something on the radio and I kid you not: Every station I stopped at was playing country music. It's the only type of music I actively dislike.

So when I sat down to write, the line about shit-kickers ruling the airwaves came to mind and I ran with it, not knowing where I'd end up. I wrote the story over the course of a few hours and found myself tapping into my love of music, the joy I feel when I'm performing and the notion of an intergalactic war where song is what holds evil at bay.

It's one of the older pieces in the collection and it was eventually picked up by the folks at Subatomic Books for their anthology *One Step Beyond*.

FOUR CLOWNS OF THE APOCALYPSE AND THE MECCA OF MIRTH

Some of my stories are Jay Lake's fault. I think I said that quite a bit in the last collection. Here's another of those. And one of the few stories in this collection that hasn't yet been published.

Back in 2005 or 2006, Jay was co-editing an anthology called *44 Clowns*. And the theme was simple: Eleven tales about the Four Clowns of the Apocalypse, with the authors free to interpret as they saw fit. Jay asked me for a story and I imagined a post-apocalyptic landscape with an order of clowns — Giggles, Cuddles, Bunko and Stan — acting as super-heroes in the midst of a blighted world.

The story was accepted but the project never got off the ground. It may still at some point but I decided after checking in with Jay that it was time to let this story see the light of day. I'm actually working with my friends Spencer and Chrissy Ellsworth on a comic book adaptation for this one, though we've been working on it in fits and starts for years in the midst of of babies all around. Still, someday, I expect this story will spawn more stories about these characters and this imagined future. That's been the plan.

In this one, I was trying to explore a cinematic viewpoint that never got into the head of the characters. It seemed to work just fine. And of course, there's more homage (tongue in cheek) to my former life. I actually met a few gospel clowns. They were a bit scarier in my estimation than the normal variety, truth be told.

THE BOY WHO COULD BEND AND FALL

One day I was chatting with my friend Rachel Dryden and we were both feeling like we needed a bit of a kick in the pants to get us writing. So we gave each other story prompts. I gave her "grapes."

My prompt was the word "slinky." And voila. Another paper child.

This one was a bit of literary exploration, born around the same time as "Soon We Shall All Be Saunders" and "Grief-Stepping to the Widower's Waltz." I just let my hair down and wrote it out in one sitting. When I finished, I passed it over to John and he said it still needed something, so I added the scene with the therapist and that seemed to do the trick.

I think the gist of it is that our hero Focus learns to bend and fall to survive, and later, when the world comes down around him, this survival skill comes in pretty handy. But there's a loneliness in the story that re-minds me a bit of how I felt as the geeky misfit boy in high school, and when Focus does manage to save himself in the end, he can *only* save himself.

It came out in *Electric Velocipede* in 2009.

THE SECOND GIFT GIVEN

I started this piece in 2002 hoping to sell it to a distant future anthol-ogy about the sun going red dwarf. But life got in the way and it languished in the Home for Unfinished Short Stories until 2004 or 2005.

I'd been reading a lot of Cordwainer Smith and also Waldrop's story "The Dynasters" when I started it. And what I didn't know at the time was that even then, I was creating a continuity of my own. This and a few other stories are quietly connected to The Psalms of Isaak.

The title initially stumped me. And those of you who know me understand that I rarely have trouble with finding a title. Originally, it was called "Long Travelers Into Night," and then for a while became "Young From The Fire" before I came around to "The Second Gift Given." I even ended up doing a contest with an online writing group to finally settle on the right one.

I think my friend Dave Goldman was the winner.

I wanted to tell a story here about humans who had long left earth and evolved coming back to meet with their devolved cousins, seeking to restore that lost branch of a scattered tribe through a child. And at the same time, I wanted to tell a story about what love does. Because I believe strongly love is demonstrated by action.

Sometimes I wonder what became of Tal's daughter and I suspect someday I'll need to go tell that story, too.

"The Second Gift Given" came out in *Clarkesworld Magazine* in 2009.

INVISIBLE EMPIRE OF ASCENDING LIGHT

I wrote this story on Memorial Day of 2005. I think.

We'd just come home from John's place up in Bellevue the night before and this landed in my head. I think it was right around the time that we were talking a lot about whether I was writing stories or exercises. John was right on that one. And I remember when I sent this over by email after cranking it out in one sitting that he wrote back something to the effect of "Where the hell did *this* come from?"

I'm still not sure. But it was buried in my head. And now, I can see pretty clearly that this wants to be a much longer work — a trilogy, I think. And it's definitely another foray into my religious background. While I consider myself wholly secular these days, I still find the concept of gods intriguing and the speculative curiosity in me likes to imagine just what a world with gods in it might look like. "Invisible Empire" is about the death of a god and the re-invention of the concept in a way that better meets humanity's needs. I think fleshing it out as a longer work will be a lot of meaningful fun.

Jonathan Strahan picked this one up for his anthology, *Eclipse 2*, and it came out in 2009.

THERE ONCE WAS A GIRL FROM NANTUCKET (A FORTEAN LOVE STORY)

This was my first collaboration.

John and I were at Norwescon in 2005 and met Jeremy Tolbert, who was editing *Fortean Bureau* at the time. He told us there was going to be a special, guest-edited, poetry edition of the webzine and since I'd appeared there twice before, I thought it would be fun to take a stab at it.

I think John and I instantly agreed to tackle it together and started it within a month or so of that meeting.

We both learned a lot in that process and as he mentioned in the introduction, it stretched our writing and our friendship a bit. But we came out of it with a Fortean love story that I am very fond of.

I'm curious to know if anyone can see which parts are John's and which are mine. Any guesses? Okay, I'll tell you. John wrote the opening scene and I wrote the following scenes, then we both edited one another's words.

I like how it turned out and Jeremy did, too. It came out in *Fortean Bureau*'s last issue in 2005.

THE TAKING NIGHT

This is how Patrick Swenson became my literary Dad.

I was taking his class in Seattle and had written several stories for it. When I came to this one, he told me he really enjoyed it and that if I couldn't find a home for it in the pro-markets, I should submit it to *Talebones*. But he was most insistent that I try the better paying markets first because he felt it was pro-level writing.

I sent it around to them and after it was soundly rejected in all quarters, I came back to Patrick. He bought it and it became my first sale, published in Winter 2000.

I left it out of the first collection because I wanted to clean it up — it had some date references that were, um, outdated.

There's a lot about this story that's drawn from life. I based the character of Vic on my grandfather, who lost all but one of his four children before he himself died. And the scene where the men in blue arrive is drawn from my memory of the day I learned of my brother's death when I was four.

I actually outlined this story with a sentence about each scene before I wrote it. And it wrote itself fairly quickly.

ON THE SETTLING OF ANCIENT SCORES

This is my "God and the Devil walk into a bar" story. It's an earlier piece. I wrote it back in 2002. At this point, I was still moving through a loose Christianity and into an even looser Agnosticism, and my subconscious was toying with the notion of what if humanity (through Everyman, a popular character in Christian morality tales) grew tired of the war between Heaven and Hell and took matters into their own hands. And what if, when reason could not prevail, we placed the universe under own management through an act of violence?

It should be noted that this particular redheaded devil showed up in my fiction about a year before Jen showed up in my life. Coincidence? I think not.

For God, I based his character upon the brilliant and kind Bruce Taylor, aka Mr. Magic Realism, with his white suit and tophat.

It came out in *Son and Foe* in November 2005. I think it was a quiet story that slipped under the radar.

IN TIME OF DESPAIR AND GREAT DARKNESS

In 2008 I attended an anthology workshop at the Oregon Coast taught by Denise Little, Dean Wesley Smith and Kristine Kathryn Rusch. In it, we wrote stories for imaginary themed anthologies that ended up both becoming real. The first was called *Swordplay* and I wrote this piece for it. It should be noted that John Pitts also wrote towards this anthology, creating the short story that has become the opening round in his urban fantasy series.

I wanted to tell an Excalibur tale. But I also wanted to throw in Nazis and Baptists and young lovers facing separation, and the dustbowl. So at the end of it all, "In Time of Despair" emerged.

It didn't make the cut for the anthology but *Realms of Fantasy* picked it up and published it in Winter 2009.

OF MISSING KINGS AND BACKWARD DREAMS AND THE HONORING OF LIES

This story changed my life. Sorta.

When I saw the art for "Of Metal Men and Scarlet Thread and Dancing with the Sunrise," I knew suddenly, jarringly, that there was much more to write about Isaak and Rudolfo and the others. Initially, I was convinced — absolutely convinced — that what I was writing was a series of four short stories. I thought maybe, if I could pull it off, I might be able to bridge them into one novella called *The Androfrancine Cycle*.

Boy was I wrong.

I wrote this as the follow up to the first story and Shawna McCarthy at *Realms of Fantasy* — with some heavy, heavy lifting by Jen and Jay — ultimately convinced me that I needed to write a novel by rejecting this story with a note on it that said "Go write a novel in this world with these characters."

This happened just before the infamous tater-tot taunting that Jay and Jen subjected me to, which resulted in me taking the dare and cranking out *Lamentation* in a six and a half week blur.

Of course, with *Realms of Fantasy* not picking up the second story, I had to put my notion of four short stories aside.

But there's a lot in this one that made it into the novel. When I wrote the novel, I bookended it with the first story at the beginning and the second story at the end. I changed the color of those words to red so I'd know which parts were from the short story and required shoring up. "Of Metal Men" was largely unchanged, but by the time I reached the end of the book, much had happened, so Sethbert's trial, the revelation of Jin Li Tam's pregnancy, and the arrival of the missing king Petronus are pretty different here. Still, the end of the novel and the end of the story are pretty much the same.

So I threw this in the collection, never before published, for those fans of the series that might come checking out my short fiction in between novels.

Sometimes I wonder what would've happened if I'd stayed stubbornly resolved to write the Psalms of Isaak as four short stories.

I'm glad I listened.

GRIEF-STEPPING TO THE WIDOWERS WALTZ

I wrote this one in October 2005. I was giving a lot of thought to the five stages of grief and thinking I'd like to tackle a magic realism story. This was right around the time I wrote "Soon We Shall All Be Saunders," and like that story, this one came together quickly and said just what I wanted it to.

Each scene is focused on one of the stages as our protagonist wades through the loss of his wife. Only, she keeps showing up throughout.

It was picked up by the *Polyphony* series and Deb Layne was kind enough to consent to its inclusion in the collection since its publication there has been delayed a bit.

It will hopefully be the last of my stories to end on an implied act of necrophilia.

LOVE IN THE TIME OF CAR ALARMS

Remember that anthology workshop? There was also a call for stories for *The Trouble With Heroes*. My first story, "Behind Every Greek Man," (a rousing romp about Jason and his Argonauts told from Medea's point of view) wasn't picked up, but Denise told us we could write something else and sling it her way. So the morning after I got home, I sat down and tried this one on for size.

This love story takes us back to the universe of Night Marauder and Kid Slingshot, first viewed in "Action Team Ups Number Thirty Seven," and we get an inside view of the dating life of another superhero mentioned in that story, Colonel Patriot. I'd wanted something light and fun here and seem to have landed it just right. Denise picked it up and it came out in 2009 alongside stories from a lot of friends of mine also attending the workshop. It's the newest story in this collection.

WHAT CHILD IS THIS I ASK THE MIDNIGHT CLEAR

Why yes, I do believe in Santa.

Only the Santa I believe in can be pretty bad ass. There are reasons I go back to that iconic character in my fiction that are deeply personal mingled in with just the fascination of an eternal character whose purpose is to give.

I wanted to tell a story about the universe giving back to its greatest giver. And I wanted to explore the psyche of someone who lived apart from us enough to see our graces and flaws clearly.

I also wanted to explore some of my fears around becoming a parent — this was a few years before Lizzy and Rae showed up on the scene.

And of course, there had to be some apocalypse thrown in for good measure. I do seem drawn to desolation in my fiction.

This story came about in 2007, just before my mom's death shut down my writing for a bit. Beth Wodzinski and Mary Robinette Kowal over at *Shimmer* had asked me if I'd write a Christmas story that they could give out as a gift to subscribers. I love that magazine and those people, so it wasn't hard to say "yes." I sat down and ended up writing out what's now become one of my favorite paper children.

I find something tragically beautiful about a cynical St. Nick out delivering shotgun shells and aspirin, sometimes delivering assassinations and rescues, continuing to serve a species he's grown disillusioned with. And when I'm reading this one publically, and I reach the part about the girl raised up among the reindeer and elves, I usually choke a little. It resonates with something deep and nameless inside of me.

Funny, I got twice what I wanted just a few years later in my two red-headed daughters. And I understand just a little better now what a great gift the universe has given me.

GRAIL-DIVING IN SHANGRILLA WITH THE WORLD'S LAST MIME

This is my "everything but the kitchen sink" story. I crammed a lot into it and it was tricky finding a home for this one until Bill at *Subterranean* gave it a home in 2008. I remember one editor telling me outright that it was just too over the top. Which of course, was my intention.

I wanted to speak to the random and absurd nature of life, following a cross-dressing Baptist minister and his ragged group of survivors as they race across an apocalyptic continent in search of the holy grail that might stem the tide of an alien invasion. I threw in characters from "Action Team-Ups Number Thirty-Seven," "Love in the Time of Car Alarms," and "East of Eden and Just a Bit South." And of course, Catholic schoolgirl cheerleaders, a mime named Liver, and white supremacists in the Deep South. Why not?

As mad romps in a paean to chaos go, this one did what I wanted it to.

*

And that brings us to the end.

I hope you enjoyed your time. It's been a fun trip down memory lane, looking over these stories spanning the length of my writing career.

Many hands brought this second collection into *your* hands and I'd like to thank some of them.

Patrick, thanks for your faith in my words. I remember hoping someday that you'd be publishing my collections and here we are with a new one for the shelf. Thanks for that class, and for buying that first story. And most of all, thanks for being not only a great editor but a great friend.

John, you read all of these stories when they were first written. As always, your eye has been sharp and you're a fine brother. Thanks for introducing this one. And big thanks, as always, to the rest of the J-Team for ongoing support and cheerleading.

I'm also grateful to Lynne Waite for her skillful eye in the copyediting process.

As always, I couldn't do any of this very well without the support of my amazing partner and wonder-wife, Jen. Thanks, darling, for keeping me moving forward in the midst of books and babies.

And last, I'm thankful for you, Dear Reader, for taking time out of your life to visit me here in my imagination forest once again. I hope you've enjoyed your time and that you'll join me again soon.

— Ken Scholes
Saint Helens, OR
April 17, 2010

ABOUT THE AUTHOR

Ken Scholes is a Pacific Northwest original whose quirky, off-beat short stories have been showing up in magazines and anthologies for a decade.

His award winning series *The Psalms of Isaak* is available from Tor books. His first collection *Long Walks, Last Flights and Other Strange Journeys* is also available from Fairwood Press.

Ken lives in Saint Helens, Oregon, with his wife and twin daughters. He invites readers to look him up at www.kenscholes.com

LaVergne, TN USA
15 October 2010
200961LV00003B/2/P